*Praise for Jasinda*

"Poetic and sinfully provocative . . . Highly innovative and addictive! *Madame X* not only seduced me, it invited me into a sensual world where I was one of the wicked participants. This isn't just a sizzling hot read, it's an exhilarating, unforgettable experience."

—Katy Evans, *New York Times* bestselling author

"Jasinda Wilder like you've never seen her before. *Madame X* draws you in from the first page and doesn't let go until long after the last."

—K. Bromberg, *New York Times* bestselling author of the Driven series

"Jasinda outdid herself! Every word, every line in this book was a treat and I savored every bite. Sensual, intelligent, and well-paced, I am on the edge of my seat and needing more!"

—Alessandra Torre, *New York Times* bestselling author

"Wilder . . . pulls out all the stops for this spellbinding novel of identity, passion, and fear . . . The intense, violent, erotic story is told in the first-person voice of X herself, with impressively well-handled second-person passages directed at her often odious clients . . . Once readers fall into X's story, they'll be desperate for the next installments."

—*Publishers Weekly* (starred review)

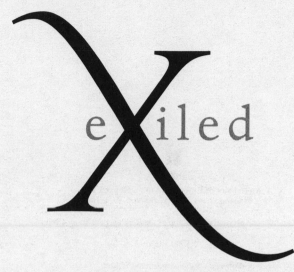

# eXiled

## A MADAME X NOVEL

# JASINDA WILDER

BERKLEY BOOKS, NEW YORK

## BERKLEY

An imprint of Penguin Random House LLC
375 Hudson Street, New York, New York 10014

This book is an original publication of the Berkley Publishing Group.

EXILED

An application to register this book for cataloging has been submitted to the Library of Congress.

ISBN: 9781101986912

PUBLISHING HISTORY
Berkley trade paperback edition / August 2016

PRINTED IN THE UNITED STATES OF AMERICA

10  9  8  7  6  5  4  3  2  1

Cover photos: Woman © yurok/Shutterstock; Skyline © Songquan Deng/Shutterstock.
Cover design by Sarah Hansen.
Interior text design by Laura K. Corless.

Penguin
Random
House

# ONE

Once upon a time, in a faraway land, there was a boy. His name was Jakob." Your voice is a murmur I must strain to hear. The cadence of your speech, the length of your vowels, and the hardness of your consonants . . . they shift and cross continents. "Jakob? He was a spoiled little brat. Anything he wanted, he had. And more. If he wanted it, he had but to point, and it was his. Never was he told 'no.' His father, you see, was a wealthy merchant who had the good fortune to marry an even wealthier Jewish woman. So this boy, he grew up believing in his very heart of hearts that he owned all of Prague. This little brat, this spoiled princeling, he would march about the city, trailed by his doting father and adoring mother and watchful nanny, shouting and demanding and pouting and scheming. He was not forced to attend anything so pedestrian as *school*, this Jakob. Oh no, he was educated by a private tutor. History, maths, science, the classical languages, Jakob was given a world-class education in his very own library. He was taught to play the piano, which he detested. Also the violin, at which he was a virtuoso. He learned fencing, horsemanship, politics, economics. Jakob, as spoiled as he was, possessed an exceedingly keen mind and an even keener hunger for knowledge.

"His world was small, and perfect. Until one day, mere weeks after his sixteenth birthday, young Jakob returned home from a riding lesson to find his home empty. His father and mother were both gone. And the housekeeper, she was incoherent, babbling in her native Greek so fast no one could understand a word, except 'sick.' Sick, she said. Over and over and over, sick, so sick. 'Who is sick?' she was asked, but the poor woman could only shake her head and weep.

"And for the first time in Jakob's charmed life, he felt the touch of a truly unpleasant emotion, heretofore unknown: fear. Just a seedling. A germinating sprout of fear. So Jakob went with his nanny to the hospital. He was received by a kindly and sympathetic nurse, and guided down hushed corridors to a darkened room. The curtains were drawn, bathing the room in shadows. It smelled. Like sickness, like death. Jakob didn't know that, then. Just that it smelled horrible. He approached the bed with trepidation, tiptoeing ever so carefully, as if by walking too loudly he might accidentally make his worst fears come true."

You pause, a long, fraught silence. Unblinking, unmoving. A stone statue.

"Jakob's father, he was a strong man. You must understand this. So strong. Tall, quiet, and stern. He was not a man given to outbursts of emotion. He loved his wife very much, however. Very, very much. Too much, perhaps. To him, she hung the moon, and scattered the stars in the sky, and even set the very sun to blazing. It was obvious to all, though Jakob's father never said as much. It was merely a fact, as true and undeniable as gravity. But he was *strong*. So when Jakob, with trembling knees, moved through the

shadows and stench of that hospital room, and saw his father weeping . . . it was as if the sun had failed to rise. A shocking blow, the
kind that leaves an indelible impression upon a young mind.

"'What is wrong?' Jakob asked his father. Jakob refused to look
at the still form in the bed. He was too petulant, you see. As if by
refusing to see, the truth could be denied. But Jakob's father would
not speak. He could only weep, his shoulders shaking like dead
leaves on a tree branch in autumn. Jakob grew angry. It was his way.
When faced with anything untoward or unpleasant, spoiled little
Jakob would grow angry. Stomp his feet, scream and shout and
curse and throw things. Even at sixteen, nearly a man, he would
throw these tantrums if he didn't get his way instantly. So Jakob
grew angry. He hit his father. Beat him about the face and shoulders
with his fists and demanded to be told what was going on. But his
father was not moved. Could not be roused from his tears. So Jakob
finally was forced to see his mother. He was forced to look at the bed,
and see his mother there."

Another long, long, pause. A silence that feels . . . deep. Chasmic.
I cannot speak, do not dare move for fear of breaking the spell.

"She was so still. So pale. Like a sculpture carved from porcelain.
There were tubes in her nose, and in her mouth. To young Jakob
they looked like . . . like translucent serpents, sneaking their vile
way into her body so they could steal her life away. Jakob was a
child, you see. He had never been forced to grow up. So when he
saw her lying there, his reaction was that of a child. No, he said. No.
No. He screamed, and stomped his feet, and cursed. He even tried
to wake her up. He grabbed her shoulders, and shook her. Not hard,
not violently. Just . . . to wake her up. But this . . . this finally roused
his father. He leaped up out of his chair, rushed at his son, at Jakob,
and threw him to the floor.

"'Leave her alone!' Jakob's father shouted. He never shouted. He never raised his voice. He rarely even spoke at all, really. So a shout? It was . . . Jakob could not fathom it. He lay on the ground, disbelieving, truly afraid for the first time in his life. His nanny drew him away. Led him from the room. Sat the boy in the waiting room and brought him tea and promised him it would all be okay. But it wouldn't be okay. Jakob knew this, in his heart of hearts, he knew it. The way he'd once known he was the master of all of Prague, he now knew nothing would ever be all right ever again. A day, he sat in that waiting room. Two days. He was dragged away finally by his tutor and his nanny, forced to eat. Forced to sleep. But he returned as soon as he could. He tried to gain entrance to his mother's room, but his father refused him. Shoved him away. Without words, but with sudden and frightening violence, his father threw him out of the room. He was blind with grief, you see. Unreasoning.

"And then, after nearly a week of waiting, Jakob's father emerged from the room. He was . . . stooped. Thin. Frail. It was as if that week in the hospital room had sapped him of all life. As if a vampire had drained the blood from him, leaving only a half-alive shell. He did not look at his son. He merely shuffled out of the hospital. Alone. Jakob threw off the attentive and worried hands of his nanny and tutor, and went after his father. He followed him home. Into his office. Jakob's father locked the door, and remained there for many hours. Young, terrified Jakob sat on the floor outside his father's office and waited. There was a very long period of utter silence.

"And then there was a single gunshot. Jakob did not go in. He was a child in a young man's body, and a coward. So he remained sitting on the floor as the police arrived. Jakob was carried away, eventually. He allowed this, because he knew what had happened. He knew where his father was. But Jakob was pretending not to know. So Jakob allowed himself to be dressed in his finest clothes. He gripped the handle of the suitcase that was placed in his hand. He boarded the large, intercontinental airliner and took his seat in the first-class section. He sat there as the airplane flew him to America. He was brought to a distant cousin's house, a cousin of his father's. But his father's cousin was not a good man. He was selfish, and mean-spirited, and cruel. So Jakob lived in a tiny room in a place called Harlem, with a distant cousin who spoke no German, no Czech, no Yiddish, not even French and certainly not Greek or Latin. He only spoke English, which, Jakob had always been taught, was a barbaric language. Jakob did speak English, of course, but poorly.

"Jakob endured this for one month. And then his father's cousin received a large sum of money. It was Jakob's inheritance, the estate of his parents wired to him from Prague, sent to the care of Jakob's cousin. It was a really extraordinary sum of money. And this cousin? He lured Jakob out of the little flat in a place called Harlem, and led him onto a subway car. After a very long ride on the train, he led Jakob up out of the subway and out onto a street in a much different part of the city, and just . . . left him there. Jakob's father's cousin vanished into the crowd, and for the first time in his life, Jakob was utterly alone. He didn't know the address where his cousin lived. He didn't know where he was. He had no money. Only the clothes on his back, and a rather remarkable education in a wide array of completely useless subjects. What good did it do Jakob to be able to read and write Latin and Greek, to play Bach concertos on a violin, or to perform advanced mathematics with ease? No good at all. Not if Jakob couldn't even feed himself. And so Jakob starved, there on the streets of a place called New York.

"Or . . . he would have."

You pause once more. You let out a breath. A rough, pained breath.

And then you resume.

"Instead, Jakob was taken in by a woman named Amy. Miss

Amy. She was beautiful, worldly, intelligent. She dressed provocatively, which excited young Jakob. She fed him. Gave him a room in which to sleep. At first, he thought she did this out of the kindness of her heart. But, it turned out, this was not the case. Jakob was young, but he was tall for his age, and strong from fencing and horse riding. He was rather good-looking . . . and naïve. And desperate. Well, one day Miss Amy brought over a friend. This friend was well dressed, with fancy hair and fancy fingernails and fancy shoes and a fancy purse. Miss Amy told young Jakob that if he wanted to keep being fed, if he wanted to continue to have a roof under which to sleep, he would accommodate her friend's every request. Miss Amy then left Jakob alone with her friend.

"That was a rather eye-opening experience for Jakob. Miss Amy's friend had a lot of requests, all of which were . . . new . . . to Jakob. As I said, he was naïve, and sheltered. That was the beginning of a whole new kind of education for Jakob. It began that day, with that one friend. But, it turned out, Miss Amy had a rather lot of friends. They all came to Miss Amy's condominium in a wealthy part of the city, one at a time. Friends, coming over for lunch dates, brunch, coffee, aperitifs, dessert, drinks. And if they happened to catch a glimpse of Jakob, and happened to want to spend a little time with him . . . well, who would be the wiser? It began slowly. One friend a week. And then twice a week. And then three times a week. And then every day. And then twice a day. And if Jakob asked too many questions, Miss Amy would show him the door. Lead him outside, and tell him to go. Make his own way, if he wished. He'd spent several weeks alone on the streets. He'd been near death when Miss Amy found him, huddled alone in an alley, shivering, gaunt, too resigned to death to even cry. He did not want to do that again. He had no money. He still spoke very limited conversational English. So he continued to entertain Miss Amy's friends.

"And then, when Jakob began having bad dreams, Miss Amy gave him a pill to help him sleep. That was another beginning, that little pill. Another education, this time in things that could take away the bad dreams, things that could calm the boil inside him. He was still angry, you see. So Miss Amy gave him pills. And then one day, she tied a piece of rubber around Jakob's arm, and slid a needle into his vein, and pressed the plunger down. After that, Jakob couldn't go a day without that injection. He needed it, and Miss Amy had it. So the arrangement continued."

I cannot move. I can barely breathe. I want you to be lying, to be weaving a fiction for my benefit. But your eyes, they see only the past, your voice holds the weight of old pain, and I know you are telling the truth. Or part of it, at least.

"Eventually, Miss Amy put Jakob into his own apartment. But she paid the rent. And she provided him with the medicine that would keep the shivers and itches and aches at bay. The stream of friends was constant. They all adored Jakob. They couldn't get enough time with him. They came back for more, and more, and more. Some of her friends were not women, but they wanted the same thing. And other things. And Jakob let them do them, did what they wanted, because he remembered starving, and now he needed the medicine. He knew it was drugs, in the deepest part of his soul. He knew what he was, in the dark places of his mind. But he didn't dwell on it. He entertained Miss Amy's friends, and he injected the medicine into his veins, and he refused to think about it.

"And then . . . one day . . . Miss Amy died. An accident. She was crossing the street, and a cabdriver wasn't paying attention. She died instantly. And once again, Jakob was alone. But now he had an addiction. And without Miss Amy, no way to get the medicine to feed the addiction. He found her condo, and tore it apart looking for the medicine. But she wasn't stupid, so he didn't find any drugs.

"Instead, he found something better: a Rolodex. It was well hidden, in the false bottom of a jewelry box, hidden deep in the back of a closet. He knew the names of many of the people in the files, so he knew what it was. And he knew what he could do with it. He'd lived with Miss Amy's arrangement for several years by this point, and didn't know anything else. So he set himself up in Miss Amy's apartment, and when friends came calling, he made it clear business would continue as usual, but he would be receiving the payment.

"It should have been simple, but it wasn't. He went through withdrawal. The apartment got taken away because he wasn't on the lease and didn't know how to pay the rent. But now he had a little money, and he was out from under the grip of the medicine. So he improvised. Found somewhere else to live. Invited his friends over. That would have been the end of Jakob's story. It should have been, honestly. But it's not. Once you have a taste of money, it's more addictive a drug than heroin, or meth, or cocaine. Jakob had a taste, and he wanted more.

"So when he stumbled across a teenaged girl, huddled alone in an alley, starving, he knew what to do. He fed her. Clothed her. Gave her somewhere to live. And, after a while, Jakob introduced the girl to a certain lonely acquaintance who was willing to part with a sum of money in exchange for an hour alone with her. And then Jakob found another girl, in similar straits. And another. This being New York, there was no shortage of lonely men with money to spare, nor desperate, starving girls to entertain them."

I'm sick now. I see the shape of things.

But you aren't done.

"But Jakob remembered how it felt to be like those girls. So once his income was stable, he learned to diversify. He saved his money and bought a business, a legitimate business. And then another. And for every successful business venture he started, Jakob freed a girl.

Got her a job and an apartment. He'd never allowed any of his girls to become hooked on drugs, because he remembered how that felt as well. Eventually, his legitimate business ventures were all that remained."

Your eyes finally go to me. See me.

"And then, one day, Jakob walked out of his condo, sold all his businesses, boarded a plane bound for Prague, and never returned. No one ever saw Jakob again."

# TWO

You seem to think that's the end of it. You stand up, cross the room with quick, angry strides, pour a measure of scotch from the decanter. Down it in a single swallow. Pour; swallow. You repeat this twice more, until you must lean on the table, glass under your palm, breathing hard. A third of the contents of the decanter are now in your belly.

"And that's the story of Jakob Kasparek." The storyteller's cadence is gone. The distant, vacant expression is gone. The mask is back in place. "Anything else you wish to know?"

"Where is Logan?"

You do not even bother to glance at me. "The morgue, I would presume."

"I don't believe you."

You shrug. "No matter to me whether you believe it or not. He's dead and you're mine."

"I am not yours."

You gesture at the door. "Then leave."

I am at the door in three strides. The knob is in my hand, twisted. The door opens. But I cannot leave. Not because I am yours, but because there are still so many questions.

"If Jakob Kasparek vanished, then how is it he signed me out of the hospital, rather than Caleb Indigo?"

A silence greets that question.

Something else you said has been percolating.

"You said I have been yours since I was sixteen, Caleb. What did that mean?"

More silence.

"How old am I? Why did you tell me I was mugged, when I was really in a car accident? Why did you tell me I was eighteen when I went into the coma? How long was I in the coma?" I'm stalking closer to you with each question. My voice rises with each question. "What is the truth? What is the truth about me, Caleb? Or Jakob, should I say?"

You fly across the intervening space in the blink of an eye. Your huge powerful hand grips my chin, my throat. Tips my head backward. Your other hand curls around the base of my spine and jerks me flush against your body.

"Jakob Kasparek is no more. He is no one. He does not exist. My *name* . . . is *Caleb*." Your voice is ice, sharp as razors and deadly as a viper's venom.

Your fingers crush my jaw, pinch my windpipe. I am pinioned against you. Helpless. And then your lips crash against mine. Roughly, at first. Angrily. Violently. With shocking, lip-bruising force . . .

You *kiss* me.

With mesmerizing, hypnotic passion, you kiss me. Rough becomes gentle. This, perhaps more than the kiss itself, stuns me. The tenderness, it is exquisite. You kiss me delicately. Skillfully. You kiss me, and you kiss me, and I am breathless. Your tongue whispers against my lips, slips graceful between my teeth and tangles with my tongue. Your palms play against my back. Fingertips dimple my flesh, and slide lower.

What is happening?

Your sorcery, it is not this affection. This is some new magic. Some new witchcraft.

The kiss, your kiss, Caleb, it is like nothing I have ever felt in my life. You kiss me as if you've been waiting for all of eternity to kiss me thus, as if you are starved for my lips, thirsting for my mouth. You clutch my back and hold me to you as if you are terrified to lose me. And your hand, clutching and crushing my jaw, loosens. Gentles. Glides up, over my cheek, past my ear, and into my hair. You lean into me, until I am bent backward over your palm, and I am held up by your strength alone.

There is no breath, with this kiss. No thought. Nothing. Just this kiss.

"God, Isabel. Isabel." You whisper this against my lower lip. It is a breath only, so low I might have imagined it.

It is a plea, that whisper. A broken, pain-barbed plea.

What does it mean? I cannot begin to understand.

You break the kiss. Stagger backward as if wounded. Your eyes are shadows. Haunted. As if for the first time in all the years I've known you, a curtain has been pulled aside, and I am suddenly truly seeing the contents of your soul.

For a moment then, you are Jakob. A young boy abandoned to fate, abandoned to the cruel streets of New York. I see the truth in the tale you told. You wipe your mouth with your wrist, brow wrinkled in confusion. Eyes coruscating with agony. You are sixteen-year-old Jakob, the whore-boy. The drug addict. The plaything.

And it is Jakob who kisses me once more. Who with hesitancy

and tenderness unzips my dress. Plucks open my bra. Slides off my
panties. It is Jakob who divests himself of his clothes. Who presses
his skin against mine.

I am wrapped up, woven into a spell, tangled in the fabric of a
lie engineered out of truth. It is Jakob who lifts me off my feet, carries me to my bed. Lays me down.

Who kisses me,

and kisses me,

and kisses me . . .

It is Jakob.

And God, Jakob is something I cannot resist. Caleb's power, skill,
and relentless hunger, but with a tenderness and vulnerability only
Jakob could possess. Confusion and hatred and loathing and disgust
boil in some secret cauldron within my soul, but Jakob's fiery touch
sears it away. I know this touch. It knows me. Knows my body, knows
how to bring me to writhing need with but a whisper of a fingertip
against me, just so.

Jakob, Caleb, the names tangle. The vulnerability in your eyes
is at war with shadows. Violence is an oil slick across the gentility
in your features.

Fuck, I am lost. I am drowning.

You stare down at me, and you let me see something in you.
Some hint of a soul. And it is a soul at war. A soul in pain. You kiss
me with that pain, and it is jagged. Your breath is rough and ragged
as you lave kisses over my breasts. As you finger my opening and
drive me to moans as only you can. You drag a thick finger through
my wetness and caress me to orgasm, and you kiss me as I whimper.
While you are kissing me, while I am whimpering and clenching
and writhing and shaking, you thrust your hips, and you enter me.
And when your hip bones clash against mine, you break the kiss and
you fix your embattled, pain-racked eyes on mine. Your eyes do not

leave me as you push into me. Do not leave mine as you withdraw. Your face takes on the expression of a man in utter agony. As if you are ripping away a mask surgically implanted in your skin. As if you are ripping open your soul and letting me see the gaping wounds life has left in you.

You make love to me as if it hurts to do so. As if the pleasure of being inside me is too much, and thus is pain. Exquisite torment. An agony of ecstasy. That term is much bandied about, but when it really occurs—a true agony of ecstasy—the reality of it is hellish to witness. Such overpowering bliss it is an overload. A too-long hit of pure oxygen to dying lungs. A feast of rich food on an empty, starving stomach.

Your hips piston against mine. You are levered over me, staring down at me as you drive in and out of me like a madman, like a man possessed. I hold on to you and try to pierce the wildness in your eyes, try to see into you, try to catch some glimpse of who you are and why you're doing this, what it means.

You moan, brokenly. Tortured groans. Your manic, fucking thrusts falter with intensity, and you release inside me. You are not blinking, not even breathing now, thrust deep, spasming. Hips fluttering.

A groan escapes you. The sound of a shredded soul.

Your forehead lowers to mine.

You are gasping, each outbreath a grunt, a moan, a groan.

"Isabel." That whisper again.

As if my name is an incantation. A prayer to an unknown god.

A time without measure, seconds, minutes. I do not know.

And then you lift your head, seek my eyes. Looking for something.

"Caleb?"

You flinch as if struck. Shudder.

And then

you

kiss

me.

Slow. Deep. Sweetly, even.

You touch my face. My cheek. Fingertips fluttering over my eyelids, tracing the contour of my nose. Memorizing.

You pull away, and look at me once more.

And then I watch as the mask clicks into place. I can almost hear the *clink-snick* of the armor plates touching and fusing.

And I wonder . . .

Did I speak the wrong name?

# THREE

You roll off me, slide off the bed with slow, languid, lithe movements. Stand up, move to the doorway. You are silhouetted. Thick thighs. Taut calves. Round, iron-hard buttocks. Back a rippling field of muscle. Broad shoulders, brawny biceps cut from living marble as if by Michelangelo's very hand. You clutch the doorpost, sagging for a moment as if weak. Turn your head slightly, almost but not quite looking at me. Face in profile.

I think you are about to speak. You even open your mouth, but then . . . you straighten. Iron turns your spine rigid. Shoulders go back. Head up.

And you turn away from me. Vanish.

I hear my door open, close. Hear the elevator.

And I am left to wonder: What just happened?

Who was that in my bed, making love to me? That was not Caleb. But it wasn't Jakob, either. It was some chimera of the two. And now he is gone. That was a man I would have . . . the thought pierces me . . . a man I could have fallen in love with. I wanted to know the source of his pain. I wanted to heal him. Protect him. Comfort him. Hold him close and know his secrets so I can tell him I love him for them, in spite of them, beyond them.

But he is gone.

Shoved back down into the depths of your unfathomable soul. Locked away behind the iron mask you wear.

A thought occurs to me:

I just had sex with Caleb. Again.

I fell under his sorcery. Again.

But it was *different*, a part of me argues—

*He faced you; he did it naked; he held your eyes the whole time; it* meant *something*—

Everything inside me crumples, and collapses.

Suddenly, I am sobbing.

Who am I?

What kind of woman am I that I could make love to the man who has so continually lied to me about who I am?

That man. God, that man.

You.

You hide me from me. You lie to me. You obfuscate. You refuse to answer. You run away rather than just tell me the truth. Why? *Why?* What horrible secret lies in our shared past that you are so afraid of me knowing?

And how can I allow you to take my body and use it at your desire? How can I allow you to *fuck* me again and again and again, knowing nothing will ever change?

You killed Logan.

Logan.

God, Logan. How could I face him now? Even if he were alive, how could I face him? How could I go to him and tell him that I allowed you to *fuck me* yet again, after what Logan and I shared?

Was that fucking, between you and me, Caleb?

No; it was something else. I don't know what. Something raw and ragged and desperate.

Wrong.

Yet . . . it was more real and honest than any other moment I've ever spent in your presence.

But Logan. Logan. I fall into renewed sobs at the thought of him—

*I don't fall easy, Isabel. But when I do, I fall hard and fast.*

*There's no going back for me now—*

I can hear his voice, almost. I can see the light in his indigo eyes as he gazes at me. The brilliance of his easy smile.

And I hear my own words, my promise to him—*You are my path, Logan.*

I am a horrible, weak, despicable person.

I have no path. Only a road paved with sins and scars and pain and mistakes.

But yet, I do not give in.

I cannot.

Will not.

Some internal compulsion has me leaving the bed. Washing you from my body. Tying my damp hair into a knot at my nape, and dressing in the clothes I began the day with, an expensive dress, the sleeves ripped off, neckline torn open to reveal a little too much cleavage.

Slip my feet into a pair of heels.

I do not know what is driving me.

But I am leaving the building. Ignoring the eyes as I push through the revolving door and out onto the street. The voices wash over me, the rush of cars, the horns, the groan of engines. But I am not brought to my knees by panic.

I see a car idling at the curb a few dozen yards away, window open. A white car with lights on top; NYPD. I lean into the open passenger window.

"Excuse me, sir. Can you tell me where the nearest hospital is?"

The man within, the police officer, is older, portly, graying. "St. Vincent. Eighth and Thirty-fourth." Gruffly, impolite.

"Thank you, officer." I turn away, start walking.

"Hey!" The officer's voice calls out. I glance back, and he's pointing from the window in the opposite direction. "You're goin' the wrong way, sweetheart."

I find my way to St. Vincent. The woman behind the reception counter is young, Hispanic, in scrubs.

"I'm looking for someone who might be a patient here. Logan Ryder."

The woman says nothing, just taps at a keyboard, eyes flicking across the screen. "Nope. Sorry."

"Anyone with a gunshot wound admitted last night?"

*Tap-tap-tap-tap* . . . "Nope. Sorry."

I think back, and realize he wouldn't be here. This is the closest hospital to me, not to where we were when Logan was shot.

When YOU shot Logan.

We were . . . where did Logan say he was taking me? I wasn't paying attention to the streets while he drove.

Brooklyn.

"What is the name of the hospital in Brooklyn?" I ask.

The woman frowns at me. "There's, like, a dozen. Mount Sinai Brooklyn. New York Methodist. SUNY Downstate. A bunch."

"How do I get there?"

She shrugs. "Go to Brooklyn?"

"But if I'm looking for someone, but don't know which hospital—"

"Then you'll have to ask at each one till you find him. NEXT!"

I wander out of the hospital, feeling hope bleeding away. How do I get to Brooklyn? How do I find out which hospital he's in? How do I even know he's still alive?

He is.

I can just . . . feel it. He is. He has to be.

I ask someone which way to Brooklyn, and get a response in a language I don't understand. Ask again, get a thumb jerk in what I hope is the correct direction.

I walk that direction until my feet ache. I don't know how long. Until I see water in the distance.

And then a black SUV glides to a halt beside me. A tinted window rolls down. Thomas.

Impassive black face, dark eyes staring. A slow blink. "Get in."

I hesitate.

"He is alive. I will take you. Get in." A voice like thunder in the distance. Like rich, thick syrup. Like the bottom of a well. Thickly accented English.

"Thomas, why would you—"

"You want to see him?"

I breathe my answer. "Yes."

"Then get in."

I get in. Miles in silence, and then I have to know.

"This isn't the first time you've helped me when I know you shouldn't be. Why?"

A shrug of a heavy shoulder. "I do not know. Sometimes, there are things a man must do. He knows. And he does them. Perhaps I have known your soul, in another time."

I have no idea what that means. It doesn't matter. Thomas is an utter enigma. Frightening. The largest man I have ever seen in my life, skin so black it is shadow made flesh. A mountain of silence and darkness. Eyes that see everything and give away nothing. A sense of tightly coiled violence. But yet again Thomas has helped me, in what seems to be direct violation of what you would want.

Thomas drives me unerringly to a hospital far, far from your world, from the enclave of wealthy Manhattan. Slides to a stop under the portico. Glances at me. "He is here."

"Thank you, Thomas."

A shrug. "Go. And Indigo . . . he will come to you again. You know this. Yes?"

I nod. I do know it. I feel it. "Yes. I know."

"Good. Do not forget it."

I exit the SUV, close the door behind me. Watch as Thomas drives away, slow, careful, unobtrusive. For the second time now, Thomas has been my deus ex machina. I do not know what to make of it, of the man. Why Thomas, so utterly unlike Len, your other henchman, continues to help me. Len is a known quantity; vicious, violent, and utterly loyal to you. Unapologetically a killer. Thomas, however, is different.

I push aside thoughts of Thomas and Len, and of you. The receptionist at this hospital—I do not know which, have once again failed to pay attention to where I have been taken—is an elderly white woman with tired, apathetic eyes.

"May I help you?"

"I'm looking for a man whom I believe is a patient here. Logan Ryder?"

*Tap-tap-tap-tap . . . taptaptap . . . tap.* "Yes. Room five thirteen." Slides a large green sticker toward me, tosses a ballpoint pen on top. "Print your name on the visitor's badge and stick it somewhere visible."

I write my name: *Isabel de la Vega.* Affix the sticker to my chest near my shoulder. Take the elevators up to the fifth floor. The hallways are wide and harshly lit with fluorescent bulbs. My heels click loudly on the floor. The smell of disinfectant and illness assaults my nostrils. Count the rooms, 503 on my left, 504 on my right . . . turn a corner, 511 . . . 512 . . . 513. The door is closed. The ward is hushed. An orderly or nurse pushes a cart past me, one caster wobbling and squealing. A doctor, then. Tall, male, Indian, slender, stethoscope thumping at his chest, flipping through a chart and barely paying attention to where he is going.

I do not want to go in. I do not want to see Logan wounded. Perhaps dying. Unconscious. Unable to remember me. Fading away, thin and frail and pale. Wrapped up in bandages like a mummy.

Panic flutters in my throat, in my belly. I blink, and choke back a ragged panting gasp. Blink again, and I feel dizzy. Disoriented. I have to lean against the door frame, rest my head against the wood of the door. Close my eyes.

*D*arkness.
    *Warmth.*
*Pain.*

*A steady beeping. Snoring. My eyes open, flutter. Haze, blurriness. Disorientation. Open my eyes again. They will not quite open all the way. Won't focus properly. My skull feels thick, stuffed with cotton. I can see enough to know I am in a hospital. But where? Why? What happened? I hear the snoring again. Scan the room as best as I am able. There. In the corner. A chair reclined into a makeshift bed, thin white blanket pulled over a large, muscular body. A glimpse of black hair.*

*A snort, squeaking plasticky leather, and the form shifts, twists. I can see the face now.*

*Jakob?*

*What is Jakob doing here?*

*My throat is clogged. Something is lodged down my throat. Taped to my nose. I can't speak. I try to moan.*

*Jakob starts, sits up immediately.*

*"Isabel?" His voice is scratchy, muzzy with sleep.*


M iss?" A concerned male voice, lilting, accented. The doctor. A
hand cool on my cheek. "Are you okay?"

I straighten. Nudge his hand away. "Yes. Yes. Thank you. I
just . . . I got dizzy."

"Are you visiting a patient on this floor, miss?" A penlight, shin-
ing in my eyes. Tracking their motion. "Look down, please. Up . . .
left . . . and to the right." I do as instructed. "Very good. When was
the last time you have eaten, please?"

"Recently. An hour or two ago."

"Do you feel ill to your stomach? Queasy, at all?" Cool thin long
fingers check my pulse at my neck, kind brown eyes watching an
analog watch.

I shrug off his concern. "I'm fine. Just . . . a long day." I breathe
and compose myself. "I'm visiting someone. Logan Ryder. He's in
here." I reach for the door lever.

"Ah. I am Dr. Kalawat. Mr. Ryder is very, very fortunate indeed
to be alive. Some would even call it miraculous. He is also very
tough, I think. Extremely determined."

I hesitate to ask, but must. "How is he? I mean . . . I haven't seen
him yet, since—since . . ." I am reluctant to speak the words.

"Since someone tried to murder him, you mean?" A hardness
laces the doctor's eyes. "As I have said, he is lucky to be alive. The
bullet entered his eye socket on an angle oblique enough to pass
through without damaging his brain. He lost the eye, of course, and
needed rather extensive reconstructive surgery. If the angle had
been even a few millimeters different, he would be dead right now,

or at best, would have suffered rather more severe brain damage. It's too soon to be totally sure, of course, but we think he will make a full recovery without any lasting brain damage."

Lost the eye? God, Logan.

"Can I see him?"

"If he is resting, please allow him to remain asleep. He needs his rest so that he may heal more swiftly."

"All right. Thank you, Doctor."

A nod. "Of course. And if you feel dizzy again, please, page the nurse. You are in a hospital, after all." A gentle smile in farewell.

When he is gone, I softly open Logan's door. Tiptoe in.

*Beep—beep—beep.* I know that sound. It echoes in my skull, in my gut. In my memory. I feel disoriented once more, but shake it off.

Logan is sleeping on his back, the bed inclined upward slightly. Pressure bandages are wrapped around his head, covering his left eye and cheekbone. His mouth is slack. Arms on top of the thin white blanket.

I want to cry.

He has been through so much, and now, again, he is near death. For me. Because of me.

My eyes water. Sight blurs. Hot salt burns my vision. I am weak in the knees, unable to support my weight. Sick to my stomach. I wasn't queasy when Dr. Kalawat asked, but I am now. Queasy. Unsettled. Dizzy. My mouth waters, saliva running, pooling against my teeth. My stomach tightens. My gorge rises. I barely make it to the adjoining bathroom. My gut rebels, convulses, and I forcefully empty the contents of my stomach into the toilet. Again. Again. Until there is nothing left but bile and saliva. When it seems as if my stomach has quieted, I rinse my mouth at the sink, wash my hands.

Logan is awake when I return to his room.

"Isabel?" His voice is rough, scratchy.

I pull the visitor's chair close to his bed. Take his hand. "I'm here, Logan."

"You got . . . away?" God, he sounds so weak.

I try to smile. Squeeze his hand. "Sort of, yes. Don't worry about that."

He smiles back. Gestures toward his bandaged eye socket. "Arrggh. I'm a pirate."

I can't help but laugh at that. "God, Logan." I lean closer. Shudder. "I'm so—I'm so sorry. I'm so sorry."

His hand squeezes mine. His other flutters like a sparrow and finds my shoulder. "Ssshhhh. Don't be. I'm here. I'm alive."

"You almost weren't. Because of me."

"But I am." His gaze flicks to the bathroom. "You're sick?"

I lift a shoulder. "I don't know. It hit rather suddenly. I'm fine now."

"If you're sick, you shouldn't be in a hospital."

I frown at him. "That doesn't make any sense."

"You'll just get more sick. Lots of germs in these places."

"I'm not sick, Logan. I just . . . felt queasy. I don't know what it was, but I'm fine now. I'm not leaving your side. Not until you leave the hospital."

Logan tugs at me. Shifts to one side, making room on the bed. I lie beside him, on my side, wedged onto the very edge of the bed. His arm curls around my waist. For a moment, at least, I can pretend to feel at peace. In Logan's arms again. Listening to his heartbeat. Except for the monitor beeping, I could almost pretend we're in his bed, at his house. Tangled up together. No worries. No lies. No mistakes. No missing eyes.

He sighs. "About Caleb—"

"I don't want to talk about Caleb. Don't worry about him."

"Always worry about Caleb. He doesn't let go. Doesn't forget."

"I know. But I'm here now. With you."

"For how long?"

I don't know. Until I tell him what I did.

"You need to rest." I whisper it. Pleading.

"Can't avoid it forever, Is." He sounds sleepy, groggy. Fading, but fighting it.

"I know, Logan. I know." I twist against him, gently, so very gently kiss his jaw. "Rest. Please."

He breathes out, long and slow and resigned. "Stubborn girl."

"You were shot. You need to rest so you can heal."

"You sound like Dr. Kalawat."

"I suppose. I met him outside, just before I came in."

"Good doctor. Nice guy."

"Yes." I pat his chest. "Logan?"

"Hmm?"

"Shut up and rest."

"Stubborn girl."

I smile. He's still unequivocally, quintessentially Logan.


I wake up some time later. The room is darkened, but afternoon light peeks through a crack in the curtains.

He's staring at the ceiling, lost in thought. He sees me, and the pensive expression is replaced by a brighter, happier one. He's putting on a brave face for me, I think.

"Hey, you," he says.

I stretch. "Hi."

"Dr. Kalawat was here. He wants to do some follow-up scans, make doubly sure there's no damage to my brain. Assuming those come back clear, they'll keep me a few more days for observation, and then I can go home. I'll be limited for a while, though. Lots of rest, no exercise, no driving. He wanted to be sure I'd have someone with me."

"I'll be there with you, if that's what you want."

He seems a little confused by my statement. "Of course I do. Why wouldn't I?"

"I don't know. I guess you would."

"Isabel?"

"He's still out there. Nothing has really changed. But now you're injured. You lost an eye." I have to pause for breath, for courage. "All this is because of me. He wouldn't care about you if I weren't in the picture. I'm dangerous to you."

"Does he know you're here?"

I shrug. "I don't know."

"How did you get away?"

To explain that, I'd have to tell him. How do I tell him?

I hesitated too long.

"Isabel?" His voice is unsure. "Talk to me."

A shaky sigh escapes me. "Nothing makes any sense anymore."

"What do you mean?"

I can't do this lying in his arms. I get up, poke the curtains open a little wider; nothing to see beyond but a wall opposite, windows, a square of roof below, white pebbles and spinning air-conditioning units. I speak to the window.

"He drugged me. I saw Thomas a split second before it all happened. Thomas hit you. Len injected me with some kind of drug to knock me out. Maybe that's why I threw up, the drug? I don't know. I saw Thomas hit you. I heard the gunshot. I knew he'd shot you. And then . . . I woke up. Back in my apartment. Everything like it used to be . . . before you. He was calling me X again. Acting like nothing had happened. But I had a dream. Or a memory? I don't know. It felt like . . . like he knows more than he's saying."

"That's what I've been telling you all along, Is."

"I know. And I'm realizing you're right. But it just feels like . . . like *what* he knows is . . . much different from what he's been telling me. Nothing makes sense. Nothing adds up. And he won't answer me. He won't tell me the truth. I've asked him over and over to just tell me the fucking truth, but he doesn't. He won't. He ignores me, or gives a non-answer, or just . . . distracts me. And I just . . . I want to *know*, Logan. I want to know who I am. I want to know what happened to me."

I cannot bring myself to say it: *I slept with Caleb again. I FUCKED Caleb again.*

And I surely cannot even begin to verbalize what it was like. How different it was.

I turn around, and Logan is facing me, but his eye isn't on me. It's downcast. At the sheet over his lap. "Isabel, I—"

"I have to tell you something, Logan."

"I lied to you." He says this over me.

"I—what? You did? About what?"

"Caleb . . . Jakob Kasparek. I said—I told you I couldn't find anything on that name. That was a lie. I just—I was worried it would all be too much for you. I figured I'd fill you in later, when I had a chance to look into it more."

"So you do know something about . . . Jakob?"

He nods. "Yeah. There really isn't much." He pauses. Deep breath in, and lets it out. "Jakob Kasparek was born in 1976 to Tomás and Marta Kasparek. Tomás was a businessman from an extremely wealthy Czech family, and Marta was an Ashkenazi Jew from Vienna, from an even wealthier family. Which means Jakob was born into extreme wealth, in Prague, what was then Czechoslova-kia. His mother died suddenly, and his father committed suicide not long after. The particulars are sparse, but it seems Marta's family disowned her after she married Tomás, since he was a gentile. So she had family, but they were in Vienna and refused to have any-thing to do with the kid after his parents passed. Tomás only had one distant cousin, living here in the States, in New York. After Tomás shot himself, Jakob was sent here to live with the cousin, but from what I could find, that didn't last long. Jakob vanished then, around about the same time when his cousin rather suddenly came into a lot of money. Theory is the cousin took Jakob's inheritance from his parents' estate and tossed the kid out on the street." He glances at me, but I keep my expression neutral. Nothing new, so far, and it matches what you told me. I turn away, look out the window as I listen. "This is where I really had to pull out my ama-teur detective skills. In the early nineties there was a prostitution ring working in several of the New York boroughs, operated by a woman named Amy Llewellyn. She was a pretty slick figure, I've been told. No one could ever pin anything down on her, even though the operation wasn't precisely secret. Amy primarily catered to the extremely wealthy socialites, the upper-crust businessmen with a taste for a little something illicit on the side. She didn't run escorts, didn't run a brothel or women working the streets. Every-thing I'm telling you right now I learned from a retired detective who worked the case back in the nineties. He could never get enough evidence to nail her or take her down, despite that fact that Miss Amy, as she was called, was a known madam. Jakob, I think, got pulled into her ring somehow. There were interviews with some of Miss Amy's former call girls who heard talk of a young man who worked for Amy, but not as part of the central ring. Privately, on the side, so to speak. This is hearsay, mind you. No one I spoke to ever actually met him. No one could find anyone who would admit to being a client of his. It was all very mysterious. So, basically, I'm just guessing. But it all fits.

"See, Miss Amy was killed in 1998, hit by a distracted cabbie. Should have been the end of the ring. And, when it comes to her ring of call girls, it was. They all scattered after her death, either were able to find legitimate work or were snapped up by someone else. But then the antiprostitution task force started getting evidence of a *new* ring. All young girls, all former runaways and homeless girls. Their pimp was, once again, hard to pin down, impossible to find. They wouldn't talk about him, on the rare occasion his girls were picked up. And I say rare, because they didn't operate like typical escorts or call girls, and certainly not like your average whore. Much more discreet, and, if you can apply such a word to prostitution— elegant. The girls were paid on commission, sort of. They were paid a flat base salary, and earned commission and bonuses based on repeat clients, extra time requests, that sort of thing. The setup allowed them to get ahead, in a way most prostitutes can't, usually, unless they're high-end escorts, who are usually only in the business temporarily anyway. The other unusual thing is the girls were always totally clean, no drugs, no diseases."

He pauses, scratches carefully over the bandage near his eye, and then winces.

"This is where things get tricky. Jakob Kasparek suddenly reap- peared, legally speaking. Meaning, there was evidence of his exis- tence. He suddenly had money, and was spending it. He bought a restaurant. A shipping company a few months later. An import-export business a year after that. A big corporate accounting firm next. A hotel. One after another, bam-bam-bam. Big dollars. And one by one, the prostitutes I suspect he formerly employed were living legit lives, in nice apartments, working jobs that didn't involve being on their backs or knees. They gave plenty of interviews to the task force my guy was part of, but they couldn't give anything concrete. They didn't know his last name, didn't know where he lived, didn't know anything about him. Jakob, that's all they knew. Tall, dark, and good-looking. Possibly from Europe, somewhere.

"And then, abruptly, Jakob disappeared. No reason, no explanation. Sold all of his businesses and properties for a massive profit, and just . . . poof. Vanished. Gone. No one ever heard from him or spoke his name again."

Another pause, this one for effect, I think. I turn to face Logan.

A glance at me. "Not long after, the first rumors of a man named Caleb Indigo started percolating around the New York business world. A property here, a business there."

I breathe out. "None of this seems to have anything to do with me."

He tips his head to one side. "Gotta go back to Jakob. The prostitutes. The girls the task force spoke to all told very similar stories. They weren't kidnapped and forced into prostitution. It wasn't accidental, like 'I'm starving, can I give you a blow job for ten bucks?' They were all homeless, runaways, orphans, addicts. Young girls with no one who cared, with nowhere to go. They talked about how Jakob took care of them. Took them in. Fed them, clothed them. Got them off drugs. The prostitution was added gradually, and the girls were always given a choice. They weren't tossed into a locked room with horny criminals. They were introduced to 'friends of Jakob's.' They had no money of their own, nowhere to go, and were usually desperate to avoid being back on the street. Hunger is a powerful motivator. It's . . . manipulative, shitty, shady, and disgusting. But incredibly effective. They essentially *chose* it. Wasn't much of a choice, whore yourself out or starve, but . . . still." A glance at me again. "Sounding familiar, yet?"

"What are you implying?"

"Well, number one, it's obvious Jakob became Caleb Indigo." A breath, a pause. "Jakob preyed on lonely, desperate young women. Some of them were only sixteen or seventeen when they met Caleb. He never personally touched them, they were always very clear on that. After the car accident, what were you? A sixteen-year-old girl, beautiful, orphaned, and without a memory. No past, no future. A blank slate. A piece of clay he could manipulate into being whatever he wanted you to be. A pet. A project."

"Stop." I shake my head. "What are you saying, Logan?"

"The accident that killed your parents, nearly killed you and stole your memory. I looked at the reports again. Compared them to other similar reports I was able to get my hands on. The reports are . . . vague at best. Inconsistent. Basic info on your parents, the VIN of your parents' car. But there's nothing on the other driver. No witnesses, no VIN, no tickets, nothing. The report says it was a crash, but not into what. Another car? A building? It doesn't say. It's all vague. So much so as to be useless."

"Make your claim, Logan."

"What if it wasn't an accident? What if he wanted you, because he had a predilection for young girls, so he did what he had to do to make you his?"

"Logan—"

"It fits, Is. All the girls, every single one, they were all sixteen, seventeen, eighteen. Young, beautiful, and desperate. And what could be more desperate than a girl with not only no parents, but no identity?"

"Why would he need to fake an accident?"

"The accident wasn't faked, Isabel. It was real. Your parents died."

"Arranged, then. But how could he be sure I wouldn't die?

Memory loss . . . is not well understood, Logan. It is impossible for
him to have been able to arrange a car accident in such a way that
he could be sure I'd lose my memory. That's crazy, Logan. And just
impossible."

"True. But . . . there's something there, Is. *Something* he's not telling you, or lying about."

Crazy. Impossible.

But . . . the flashes of memory I've had . . . they seem to be hint-
ing that I knew Jakob *before* my memory loss. But then, he told me
I lost my memory suddenly, after surgery.

The lies you've told don't match with the accidental truths you've
spilled. 2006? 2009? Sixteen? Eighteen? Car accident? Mugging?

*Isabel* . . .

The whisper on your lips as you come.

Your forehead against mine.

——*Y*ou *were so frail, so slight. So young. Only sixteen, I think. Or
thereabouts. Sixteen, seventeen. A girl, still. But so beautiful
already. Dying, terrified, lost, and your eyes, when I set you down on the
stretcher when we got to the ER, you looked up at me with those great big
black eyes of yours and I just . . . I couldn't walk away—*

|sabel?" Logan's voice. Far away. Warm, concerned. Loving.

Far away. Faint.

I'm dizzy.

Something sparks, in my skull. Deep in my chest. A vision. A
thought.

Life, relived:

―――――――

*I* am alone. I should be in school, but I'm not. It is warm, a beautiful, sunny day. I am in my favorite dress. I've curled my hair, stolen Mama's makeup and a pair of earrings. I feel beautiful. Excited, but scared. Down the stairs to the subway, onto the train. Only a few stops, and then I get off. Ascend to the street, cross the intersection. There, the café. OUR café. He's here every morning, so I know he'll be here now.

I hurry, because I am excited.

There, I see him. God, so handsome. So tall, such broad shoulders. He's sitting at a table, sipping espresso. At ease, powerful, in command of his surroundings. He looks up . . . he sees me! My heart pitter-patters. I blush, trip a step. He stands as I approach, and I breeze past the hostess, through the doors and out onto the patio. Into his arms.

He grabs my shoulders and touches his chin to the top of my head. I have an instant, a glorious instant, where I'm pressed up to him, engulfed by him. But only briefly, and then he lets go, steps back.

"Caleb!" I breathe his name.

"Hey, gorgeous. How are you?" Oh, his English is so flawless. I am jealous. You can barely hear his accent.

"I am well, Caleb. How are you?" Ugh. I sound so SPANISH. Not American at all.

"You should be in school, shouldn't you?" He says it with a teasing grin.

"I had to see you." I say this in Spanish. I can't help it; if I don't consciously think about it, Spanish comes out.

"English, Isabel."

I think it through. Make sure it is correct. "I am very well, Caleb. How are you?"

"That wasn't the question, Isabel." Another teasing grin, as we sit down.

"Brute. Don't be mean to me." More Spanish.

"Isabel. ENGLISH." This is a scold, very serious.

I sigh again. "I wanted to very badly see you. School is dull. It is for children, and I am not a children."

"Not a CHILD," he corrects.

"Yes, that. Whatever."

"If you want to sound American, you have to get it right." He flags the waitress, indicates another espresso.

"I know. But it is hard." I sound petulant, like a child. I am irritated with myself. "What are we going to do today, Caleb?"

He sips his espresso, eyeing me over the rim of the little cup. "You are going back to school. I have work."

"Caleb. Please. I came all this way to see you. Spend time with me." This is in Spanish.

He doesn't correct me, responds in his perfect American English. "We've talked about this, Isabel. That's not possible. You shouldn't be here. We can only be friends."

"But WHY?" Again, I sound so childish.

"Because you are only sixteen. Too young."

This makes me so angry. "I am not a CHILD!" I say it in English, for emphasis. "I know what I want."

"There's more to it than that." But his eyes, oh, those eyes.

They WANT me. I know what desire looks like. The boys at school, those little sniveling brats, they look at me the same way. But they wouldn't know what to do with me if they had me. Caleb would know.

"Isabel. I'm not going anywhere." He leans forward, takes my hands in his. Smiles beautifully at me. "When you graduate and turn eighteen, we can talk about this. But not until then."

"I hate you." I stand up, yanking my hands away.

"Isabel, don't be—"

"Childish? I can't help it, can I? Since I'm just a child." I storm away, stomping my feet.

*Feeling rejected. Feeling stupid. I put on makeup for him. I put on ear-rings for him. I wore my favorite blue dress for him. I looked in the mirror before I came, and I know I look much older than sixteen. Eighteen, at least. With my hair done right and a little makeup, everyone thinks I'm far older than I am. But not Caleb.*

*I can't help but steal a backward glance at Caleb. He's reading a news-paper now. Sipping espresso. Not a care in the world, as if he didn't just break my heart.*

*I wait for him to look up at me, but he doesn't.*

*I walk back home with tears blurring my vision. I scrub off my makeup, change into blue jeans, tie my hair back. Catch a train to school, and pre-tend nothing is wrong. As if I were just late for school, overslept, perhaps. Not heartbroken.*

feel myself falling. Hit the floor, but I don't feel the pain.

Only the memory. Clear as crystal. Each emotion, what I was thinking. The way he looked. The openness of his expression, not the mask.

The dress, the blue dress.

I wore the blue dress for him.

For Caleb.

# FOUR

*B*eep—*beep*—*beep* . . .

For a few moments, time is distorted. Time folds back on itself.

For a moment, I am a nameless young woman lying in a hospital bed with no recollection of myself, my past, anything. I am nothing. No one.

But then I open my eyes, and everything floods through me. Caleb . . . Jakob. Logan.

The memory. My first full, clear, complete memory from before the accident.

You *knew* me, Caleb. You've known me this whole time. You let me believe I was nameless. But you knew? You KNEW?

I think I pass out again, because I feel myself waking up once more. And this time, I am not alone.

"Miss de la Vega." Dr. Kalawat. "How are you feeling?"

I twist my head, see him standing beside my bed, reading a chart. "What happened?"

"You fainted, Miss de la Vega. You took a pretty nasty tumble, I'm afraid. Bumped your head rather badly, but nothing to worry about. Not even a concussion."

Casters rattle, and Dr. Kalawat is pressing a hand to my head, my cheek, feeling my pulse. Checking the dilation and focus of my eyes. I notice a round Band-Aid on my left arm, near my elbow.

"What's this?" I ask, pointing to it.

Dr. Kalawat glances. "Oh. We did a blood test."

I frown. "Why?"

Dr. Kalawat sets down the chart, crosses one knee over the other. "Mr. Ryder tells me you vomited, not long after we spoke."

"Yes. I was feeling queasy, after I saw you. It hit suddenly, and then passed. Why?"

"Might I ask you a rather personal question, Miss de la Vega?" This is rhetorical, as Dr. Kalawat continues without pausing to allow me an answer. "When was your last cycle, can you please tell me?"

I frown. "Um. My life has been rather chaotic lately, so—" Something cold and sharp hits me, flows through me. "Dr. Kalawat . . . what are you saying?"

A smile at me, kind, gentle. "I had thought you might be pregnant, but the test came back negative. Better to be sure, I think. Yes?"

"So I'm not?"

Dr. Kalawat tips his head side to side. "Well, I am not ruling it out. It may simply be too early to tell. If you are late to get your next cycle, or it doesn't come at all, then I would recommend taking a test, either at home or in an office." With sure, deft fingers, the doctor removes the monitor leads. "You may go. So far as I am able to determine at this time, you are perfectly healthy."

I get out of the bed. "Thank you, Doctor."

Another of those smiles. "It is my pleasure."

The door shuts with a soft click, and I am alone.

Pregnant? Please, no. No. There is no way.

But . . . my last cycle . . . I have to think hard. Before Logan gave me my name. Middle of the month, as it has always been, since my first period at twelve years old.

And today . . . what day is today? What is the date? I cannot remember. Am I late?

I stumble out of the room, to the nearest nurses' station. "Excuse me. What is the date?"

The nurse doesn't look up. "Thursday, August eleventh."

Not late, then. It usually comes middle of the second week of the month.

The relief is not as all-pervading as I would wish. Not as complete.

I find Logan's room. He is typing in his phone once again when I walk in. "Isabel! Are you okay?"

"I'm fine," I say. "Just bumped my head, that's all."

"You scared the shit out of me, Is. You just . . . fainted."

I perch on the edge of his bed. "There is a lot going on."

"Isabel." He touches my chin. "Don't hold out on me."

I sigh. "I remembered something. From before."

He lights up. "You did? What?"

"I knew Jakob. Or . . . Caleb. Whatever. I knew him. Before. I was in love with him, I think. I don't know how we met, just that I skipped school to go see him at a café somewhere. I wanted us to be together, but he—he turned me down, because I was only sixteen."

A long silence. "Holy shit."

"Yes. The implications are worrisome."

"I can see why you passed out." He tangles our fingers together. "He's been lying to you all this time, then."

"Yes. For a very long time, it would seem. He . . . he let me believe—he let me—" I can't finish it. I shake my head. "I can't. I can't. I can't think about it. I'll have a panic attack."

He pulls me against his chest. His heart thumps reassuringly under my ear. "Don't. We can talk it through later. Dr. Kalawat said I can go home tomorrow. Just give it some time, okay? It'll be okay. You'll be okay. I'll be okay. Everything's going to be fine."

Will it, though?

You are still out there. You haven't let me go. I don't think you *can*. And until you tell me the truth, I do not know if I can let you go either. If I am capable of just walking away without knowing the truth.

But will you ever tell me the truth? Can you? Are you capable of the truth?

I remember the look you gave me, when I said your name—when I said "Caleb" instead of "Jakob." If I had said the other name, what might have happened? What would you have said? Would you have stayed? Held me? Kissed me? Made love to me again?

Would I have wanted that? Would it have . . . changed things, somehow? I don't know. I don't know.

I feel sick all over again, because I know I have to tell Logan what happened. Or some of it, at least.

But not yet.

Not while he's still healing.

I cannot drive. Logan calls a car service when he is discharged, five days after the surgery. Walk beside his wheelchair as the nurse wheels him out. Hold his hand as he stands up. Lean into him, duck under his arm and press my cheek to his chest. Walk with him to the black sedan. He reaches for the roof, for balance. Misses.

"My depth perception is completely fucked," he grumbles under his breath. "Gonna take some adjusting." I slide my hand underneath his, guide his palm to the roof of the car, but he jerks his hand away. "Don't need fucking help."

I drop my hand and step back, stung by his outburst. "I'm sorry, Logan. I didn't mean—"

He leans against the door frame of the car, scrubs his hands through his hair, groaning. "No, Isabel, I'm sorry. That was uncalled for. I'm just—" He shakes his head, shrugs. "It's a lot to deal with."

"I get it," I say. "It's fine."

He shakes his head. "It's not fine. It's not fair for me to lash out at you. I'm just not used to needing help."

"And I'll be here to help you. Whatever you need." I offer him a smile, lean into him, wrap my arms around him.

He palms my back, plants a brief kiss to my lips, and then swings himself into the car gingerly, slowly. Slides across so I can get in. It is hard to look at him. Hard to see him thus, the pressure bandage wrapped around his head. Wounded. Vulnerable. Unsteady on his feet. Reaching for something and missing. Logan has always been so capable, so unflappable. But now he needs me, and I'll be there for him, as he has for me.

The drive to his brownstone is long and quiet. Serene. He holds my hand, stares out the window.

The driver turns onto Logan's street, and that's when Logan looks at me, a soft smile on his face. "I don't blame you," he says. "I hope you understand that."

"Well, I do. There's no one else to blame, Logan. Aside from Caleb, that is."

"Don't."

"But Logan, if it weren't for me—"

"Stop." It's an order. Quiet but sharp. "I knew going in that Caleb—Jakob, whatever the fuck his name is—I knew going in that he's dangerous. I knew you were tangled up with him. I knew I was taking a risk letting myself get close to you. I took that risk eyes open, so this is on me. He's not a man who forgives, nor does he forget, and he certainly doesn't let go of what he considers his. So, this is on me. Okay?"

"You cannot just order me to not feel guilty and expect me to just . . . *obey*, Logan. I don't work that way." I shake my head. "And no, this isn't on you, or me, really. It's on Caleb. He *shot* you, intending to kill you. There's no excuse for that." I feel bile in my throat at the thought of what I did with Caleb, knowing all the while what he'd done.

"I know that. I just mean I understood the risk I was running dealing with Caleb. I'm not blaming myself, just saying, I can't say I didn't know."

"That's a meaningless distinction, Logan."

"Is it, though?" Logan questions. "I lost my eye. I want to be—I *am*—angry. I want fucking revenge, Isabel. I want to hunt that bastard down and gouge his goddamned eyes out. Now he's not only cost me five years in prison, but my eye, and nearly my life."

"That's totally understandable, Logan—" I start.

But he interrupts me. "I had five years in prison to think about revenge. I had almost a week on my back in the hospital to think about it again. Where is revenge going to get me? I hunt him down and kill him, or whatever. What does that make me? I've seen enough death in my life. Don't forget, I'm a combat veteran. I've killed people. I know what that shit feels like, and I have no desire whatsoever to feel that again. Not even a piece of shit like Caleb, not even after everything he's done to me. Do I forgive him? No. He better hope I never lay eyes on him again."

It strikes me that Logan's outburst is only tangentially connected to what we were talking about. It seems like there's a lot going on under the surface, when it comes to Logan.

The driver halts precisely in front of Logan's address, puts the vehicle into park, gets out, opens Logan's door. He's stubborn, so he's out before I can hop out and run around. He doesn't want to need my help. But he does. He has a hard time getting the key into the lock, but I let him do it. He won't adjust if he doesn't try, right? I hate watching him fumble, though.

We're in, hitting lights, and Logan is working on the alarm. I move past him, to let out Cocoa, his bear-sized chocolate lab. I notice something, though. Tufts of cotton, drifting across the hardwood floor. A scrap of gray fabric, lying partway out of the hallway.

"Logan?"

"Yeah, babe."

"Is there anyone who would have checked on Cocoa?"

"I e-mailed Beth and asked her to check in. Why?" He moves to stand beside me. Another ball of wadded cotton bounces across the floor like a tumbleweed. "Oh. Shit. She must've gotten out."

Another step farther into the house. More damage. A leather loafer lies on its side in the hallway leading to the bedroom, chewed to bits. Another few steps—a hooded sweatshirt, torn to pieces, chewed, wet with doggy saliva. The other loafer, similarly destroyed.

"Goddamn it." Logan sighs, but doesn't seem angry. "Cocoa? C'mere, girl! Daddy's home!"

*Daddy's home.* That hurts my heart in an odd, terrifying place. I stuff that hurt down, stuff the simmering thoughts and fears down. It's not true. Not possible. It's just not. Just no.

I follow Logan into the hallway. More clothes are strewn across the floor in the hallway, all of them chewed, slobbered on, utterly shredded. No sign of Cocoa, though. A thudding sound is audible, however: *thumpthumpthumpthumpthump*. A tail hitting a mattress, possibly?

Logan kicks at the piles of destroyed clothing. Shirts, slacks, shoes, boots, a leather jacket. A towel.

We arrive at the doorway of the spare room where Logan keeps Cocoa while he's gone. The doorway is . . . just gone. Splintered. There's a bit of door attached at the hinges, the shredded, splintered frame, the knob on the floor. But the door itself? No more. Splinters coat the carpet in the spare room, lie scattered across the hardwood floor of the hallway in a blast radius that extends into the bathroom and Logan's room. It looks like explosive charges were leveled at the door.

My heart in my throat, I follow Logan into his bedroom, peering over his shoulder.

The room is wrecked. The TV has been knocked over, shattered. The bedside lamp, same. The headboard has been chewed to splinters, same with the footboard. The blankets and sheets are twisted into a pile on the bed, chewed, slobbered, clawed. And in the middle of the bed, under the pile of sheets and blankets? Cocoa.

Tail thumping steadily. Chin on her paws, ears drooping. Eyes wide. The perfect picture of canine innocence.

"Holy fucking shit, Cocoa!"

I'm not sure what to expect from him. Anger? Frustration, at least. Instead, he kneels on the floor, pats his thigh.

"Cocoa. Come." His voice is low, but firm. Not angry, not threatening.

She shimmies like liquid, inches toward the edge of the bed, but doesn't get down.

"Cocoa, come *here*. Now, girl."

That gets her. She hops off the bed but immediately goes down to her belly, tail tucked under, head to the floor. Her eyes never leave Logan. She shimmies closer and closer until she's at Logan's feet.

"What did you *do*, Cocoa?" He seems close to laughter. Holding it in, but barely.

"She looks so sorry, Logan!" I say.

"She missed me. I've never been gone this long. She was afraid." He goes to his butt on the floor, grabs the dog around her middle, and hauls her onto his lap. She rolls to her back, tail beginning to thud once more, and then leans up and licks his chin. Hesitantly, at first, but then with increasing happiness. "I know, girl. I know. I missed you too. It's okay, I'm here."

I have to hold back tears. Something about the sight of Logan with his beloved puppy on his lap—a giant, eighty-pound puppy—reunited, happy, it makes me emotional.

Damn it—*no*.

I blink it all away, kneel beside man and dog, and scratch Cocoa on her head, behind her ears. She gives me a quick wet doggy kiss, and then goes back to Logan. She scrambles to her feet, backs up, and then seems to notice the bandage. She gives a long, high-pitched whine from the back of her throat and sniffs the bandage covering his eye. Glances at me, as if for answers, and then at Logan. Puts her front paws on his legs and sniffs, sniffs, sniffs. Whines again.

God, that's so sweet. She's worried about him. She sees he's hurt, and wants to know what's going on.

I'm fighting tears again, damn it.

"I'm fine, girl. I promise." He palms her ears and rubs vigorously, until she pulls away and shakes her head so her ears flop wildly.

I'm okay. I'm fine. I'm just . . . emotional. Nearly a week spent at Logan's side in the hospital, sleeping poorly in the visitor's chair. They let me stay through the night in contravention of visitors' hours, because I have nowhere else to go, and because I think Logan somehow bribed or otherwise convinced/coerced them into letting me. I'm just emotional. There's a lot going on, a lot to be worried and emotional again.

Logan hands me his phone. "Can you call Beth? Let her know what's going and that we need help cleaning up. I don't really do PAs, but she's the closest thing I've got. The code is seven-nine-one-five." He stands up, pats his thigh. "Go outside, Cocoa?"

He's gone, the dog's claws scrabbling on wood, doing her happy *yes-I-want-to-go-outside* yipping bark.

I stare at the phone for a moment. 7-9-1-5; type it in, and the phone unlocks. The picture in the background behind the rows of icons is me. Asleep, in Logan's bed. Before I got my haircut, when it was still long. It's splayed around my head on Logan's white pillow, like spilled ink. My face is twisted to the side, and my hand is curled in front of my face. I look serene, beautiful, at peace.

7-9-1-5.

07-09-15.

The date we met. The date of the stupid auction party I went to with Jonathan.

That sends a spasm of emotion through me too, that the date we met is his unlock code for his phone.

I crush the emotion, ruthlessly, and find Beth's name in the contacts. Dial.

"Hey, boss. How are you feeling? We're all worried about you." The voice is high and sweet, a little too much of both.

"Beth? It's—this isn't Logan. Obviously. It's Isabel."

"Isabel?" A silence, which somehow feels confused. "*Ohhhhhh. Isabel. The Isabel?"

"I guess? Unless he knows another one."

"No, no. Just you." Another silence. "So, what—um . . . how can I help you?"

"Did you come to his house and check on Cocoa at all?"

Beth responds immediately, a little defensively. "Yes! I went over the moment he e-mailed me. I fed her, let her out, made sure she had some water. I even threw the ball for her a bit. She's such a sweet dog."

"She really is. It's just—"

"I went back the next day, too. Not yesterday, because I got swamped with work. I meant to, but I just—" Beth cuts herself off. "Did something happen? Is she okay?" Beth sounds worried.

"She's fine, yes. But she got out."

"Got out? How? I shut the door, I'm sure I did. I even checked to make sure it latched all the way."

"She kind of clawed *through* the door. Like, destroyed it completely. Along with a lot of Logan's clothes and his TV. It's a mess. He asked me to call you and see if you would come and help clean up."

"Through the door? Geez. Okay, well sure, I'll be right there. But—why are you calling? Is Logan okay?"

"He's with Cocoa. They're reuniting, I guess." I'm not sure what he told her about how badly he's hurt. Best to let him handle that.

"Okay, well, I'll be there in a little bit." Another silence. This one feels bated. "All he would tell me is that there was an accident. Is he—is Logan okay? He's never been gone this long."

"I—I'm not sure what I should say, honestly. That's something he should tell you, not me."

"It's bad. You would tell me if it was nothing important."

"So we'll see you soon?" I really don't know how to answer, so I avoid the question.

A sigh. "Yeah. Half hour, forty-five minutes or so."

"Okay. Thank you."

The line goes dead, and I lock the phone, set it on the bedside table. Stare around me at the mess, let out a haggard breath. I feel so tired, suddenly. But the bed is torn up, and the floor is buried under shredded clothes. The closet door is open, yanked off the track, hanging askew. Clothes dangle partially ripped off hangers, and more hangers are strewn on the floor. More clothes are piled on the floor at the bottom of the closet, but those don't seem destroyed.

I right the TV, set it with great difficulty onto the stand. It is massive, heavy, but I manage it. Strip the bedclothes from the mattress, toss them aside. Begin tossing destroyed clothing onto that pile, handfuls at a time, until there's nothing left but the pile on the floor of the closet.

"Isabel, what are you doing?" Logan, from behind me.

I shrug, gesture at the bed. "I wanted to lie down, but the bed is a mess, and so is the floor. Anyway, Beth will be here soon."

"You should have left it. That's why I pay Beth."

"I thought she wasn't your personal assistant?"

"She's not. But she's always eager for any excuse to get out of the office, so I send her on errands." He rights the lamp. Stares at me from across the bed. "Isabel, I didn't mean to sound like I was handing out orders, earlier."

"Facts are facts, Logan. If you hadn't gotten involved with me, you wouldn't have been shot. That's a fact. The only reason you're alive is because either Caleb is a poor shot, or you got really lucky. You could be dead right now."

"And like I said, I knew there was a risk Caleb would lash out at me at some point. I took the risk to get involved with you understanding that was a possibility. That absolves you of any guilt. If you'd lied about him or something, that'd be different. But I knew."

"That doesn't make it any easier to deal with. You were shot. You lost an eye. Because of me."

Logan rounds the end of the bed, grabs me by the arms, holds me at arm's length. "Stop. Please. I'm okay. I'm alive. Yeah, I'm short an eyeball. But now I get to wear an eyepatch and act like a pirate, and no one can say shit about it."

I can't help but laugh. "God, Logan. You are ridiculous. You would do that, wouldn't you?"

He crooks an index finger into a hook. "Arrrgh, matey. You bet your doubloons I would!"

"That's a terrible pirate voice."

"Oh yeah? Let's hear you do better."

I shake my head and stifle another laugh. "I don't think so."

"Well, then you can't knock mine if you won't try it."

"I can criticize without emulating, Logan."

"Those who can't do, teach. And those who can't teach become critics."

"I'm not saying I'm a professional pirate voice critic—"

Logan bursts out laughing, drowning me out and cutting me off. "Professional pirate voice critic? And *I'm* ridiculous?"

"Yes." I sound petulant.

"Come on, Is. Just give me one little 'arrrgghhh, matey!'"

"No."

He ducks so his face is in front of mine and makes a pathetic moue. "You wouldn't say no to a one-eyed man, would you?"

"Oh my God. You're guilting me?"

He shrugs. "If it'll get you to loosen up, sure. Might as well get some mileage out of my . . . *life-altering injury*."

"Logan."

"Too soon?"

"Yes. *Way* too soon." I glance at him. "And . . . loosen up? What does that mean?"

"Just that you're a little uptight. Wound tight, you know? You take everything so seriously." A shrug. His voice is matter-of-fact, as if everyone should know this.

"I am not uptight."

He laughs, a sharp bark. "You are too! I think I've heard you say, like, three jokes in the entire time I've known you. That, my sexy little Spanish beauty, is the epitome of uptight. If you don't tell jokes, shit will make you crazy. Lighten up."

"And to, as you say, lighten up, I should speak in a dreadfully historically inaccurate pirate voice?"

"It's a broad caricature, Isabel. It's socially understood to be humorous rather than accurate. If you want to be all *uptight* about it."

I glare at him. But then, because he has a way of pulling things out of me, I curl my lip and make my voice rough. "Arrrrggghhh."

"She has a sense of humor!" Logan waves his hands in the air. "Gods be praised!"

"I have a sense of humor."

"Then tell a joke."

"A joke?"

He crosses his arms over his chest. "Yes. A joke. Tell me a joke."

"Why did the—"

"That's not a joke. Try again."

I think hard but come up blank. "I don't know any jokes. But that doesn't mean I don't have a sense of humor."

"Did you hear about the pirate movie?"

"What pirate movie?"

"It was rated *arrrgghhhh*."

"Oh my God. That's terrible."

"What did the first mate see when he looked in the toilet?"

"Logan—"

"The captain's log."

"That's disgusting."

"Why couldn't the pirate play cards?"

I stare at him. "Logan."

"Guess."

"I don't know."

A beat of silence. For emphasis, probably. "Because he was sitting on the deck."

"That's not even funny."

"Funnier than the joke you told."

"But I didn't tell one."

"Exactly!" He stabs a finger at me. "Now try the *arrrgghhh* again. This time with feeling!"

I hesitate. It's stupid. So, so stupid. But it's for Logan. "Arrrgghh."

"That was pathetic. You aren't even trying." He clears his throat. "*AAARRRGGGHHH!*"

"I'm not doing that." But I'm fighting a grin.

"Sissy." He sticks his tongue out at me. "Stick-in-the-mud."

"Name calling, Logan? Really?"

"You won't even *arrgghh* like a pirate. What are you afraid of?"

"*AAARRRGGGHHH!*" I do it loud and deep.

And Logan's face lights up. "There you go! That wasn't so hard, was it?"

"Was it funny?"

He nods. "Hysterical." Pulls me close. Kisses me. "Knock knock."

"Um."

"Jesus, Isabel, it's a knock-knock joke. You say, 'Who's there?'"

"Who's there?"

"Boo." He leans in and whispers in my ear. "Now you say, 'Boo who?'"

"Boo who?"

"Hey, whatcha cryin' for?" Another kiss, this one to my throat.

I laugh, because I can't help it. "How can you make jokes at a time like this?"

He shrugs. "How can I not? I don't know how to deal with this shit, Isabel. It'd be all too easy to feel sorry for myself, to let myself get all depressed and mope around like a sad sack of shit. But I refuse to let myself do that. Am I suppressing some of my more negative emotions? Probably. Am I overcompensating with humor? Again, probably. But how else am I supposed to cope, Isabel?" He shoots me a glance. "Have you ever heard the phrase 'laugh or go crazy'?"

"No, but there's an in-between, isn't there?"

"Not really. I'm not making light of this. I just . . . I have to cope somehow, babe. Humor is how I'm doing it." He sighs. "If I don't, I'll mope and be depressed and get all ragey. It'll be terrible. So just . . . humor my inappropriate humor. Okay?"

I nuzzle against him. "Okay. Just . . . try to let me help you. Please?"

"I'll do my best. That's all I can promise." He taps my nose with his forefinger. "Now, let me hear the *arrgghh* again. Even louder this time, and with feeling."

I sigh, a dramatic, long-suffering sound. "Fine." Like he did, I clear my throat. *"AAARRRGGGHHH!"* Loud as I can.

And that's when we hear a throat clear behind us. "Um . . . hey, Logan. Did I miss the pirate convention?"

He turns. "There ya *aarrgghh*! Right on time."

Beth is silent for a very long time. "Logan? What—what happened?"

Unlike many people, Beth's voice and physical appearance match perfectly. High, sweet voice, like a slightly overeager schoolteacher, perhaps; short, slender, not exactly beautiful, but attractive. Bobbed blond hair. Unassuming. It's easy to skip right over Beth in a crowd.

He waves in dismissal. "Nothing to worry about. I'm fine."

"That looks pretty serious." Beth seems close to tears.

"I'm fine."

"What happened?"

He hesitates. "I—got mugged. The gun went off. Missed my

brain via my eyeball. And now I'm a pirate. Gonna get a patch and everything."

"How can you be telling jokes at a time like this, Logan?" Beth hasn't moved from the entryway, a box of contractor garbage bags in hand.

"This is starting to feel like déjà vu." He groans. "When things are at their hardest and most painful is the best time to tell jokes, Beth."

Beth is just blinking. Staring. "You lost your eye?"

Logan shrugs. "Well, I haven't seen underneath the bandage, but that's what they told me at the hospital, yes." He grabs the box of garbage bags from Beth. "So. We'll just bag up and toss all the ruined clothing and clean up the remnants of my door. Also have to order a new TV and have the broken one removed. I will also need an eyepatch supplier. I don't even know where to get them. Is there, like, an eyepatch store? I'll want cool ones, not just plain boring black ones. You can probably get them online, I'm guessing."

"See, I'm not sure if you're joking or not." A pause. "About the eyepatches, I mean."

"Not at all. I knew a guy in Blackwater who was missing an eye. He was support staff. Super cool guy. A real tough motherfucker. Like, the real deal. Scary as hell. So, if he was in the office, doing everyday sort of work, he left his eye socket empty, didn't cover it, no prosthetic. It was . . . creepy, I don't mind admitting. Just disconcerting. You couldn't help but stare, you know? That was just how Eric was, though. Didn't give one single shit what anyone thought. If he had to dress up at all, he'd wear a patch. He just had this one. He had a guy in our unit that was a pretty fantastic artist draw an amazingly lifelike eye on the patch, so it was even *more* disconcerting than without it, in a way. And I always thought, if I were to ever lose an eye, I'd get all sorts of cool shit to cover it. Like, steampunk, or Goth, funny designs, holiday patches, all that. A collection, as it were. And now that I've actually gone and lost my eye, that's what's happening. So, yeah, totally serious. Get me options."

"Sure thing, boss." She seems to be at a loss for words, so she takes the box of bags back and moves into Logan's room.

Plastic crinkles as clothes are stuffed into the bags, out of sight. Logan takes my hand and leads me into the living room. Collapses backward onto the couch, taking me with him. I squeal with laughter as he falls, his arms wrapped around me, taking me down to the couch. Twists with me, so I'm between the back of the couch and his big hard body, my cheek on his chest, his hands possessively cupping my backside.

I can take it for a few moments, and then I get antsy. "Logan. Let go. We should help Beth. Or, I should, at least."

"Nope."

"Logan—"

"I'm paying her time and a half for this. And she works best alone. Time to rest."

He's got me pinned. And it's warm here. Comfy. I'm content, drifting. It's impossible not to let myself float away, to pretend, once more, that Logan is all that exists. That this time with him is all there is.

I drowse, doze.

Sink under the warm buzzing swell of sleep, in Logan's arms.

I wake up, and Logan is gone.

Evening light streams through the sliding glass door, deep golden, bathing me in warmth. I roll, and my hand flops over the side of the couch; something wet touches my fingers, and I make a startled noise in my throat. A brown nose appears, followed by whiskers, liquid brown eyes, floppy ears. Cocoa. Before I can even register her presence, she's licking me.

"Yes, oh my God, Cocoa, yes. Hi. Yes, girl, I love you too." I stop her from licking me but don't push her away.

She rests her chin on the edge of the couch and just looks at me. As if she sees into my soul and does not find me wanting. The innocent, complete love of a dog is such a wonderful thing.

I nuzzle against her, rub her ears, her soft fine fur.

"What do I do, Cocoa? Huh? It's all so impossible," I murmur against her neck. "There's no end. There's no way out. But he needs me, you know? And I need him. But then, there will always be Caleb. And now Jakob? How do I reconcile the two? There's no way. And I might never get another glimpse at Jakob. Because, really, I feel like they're two different people, Caleb and Jakob. But Jakob, he's a part of Caleb that he keeps buried way down deep. So deep I don't think that part of him will ever come out again. Which is sad, because that's a part of Caleb that I could have maybe—no. No. I can't go there. Can't think that way."

Cocoa whines, yips gently, head tilted to one side. As if to say, *Yes, I'm listening.*

I lower my voice to a whisper so quiet it is nearly inaudible even to me, nearly subvocalization. "I love Logan, Cocoa. So much. I really, really do. So . . . how did I let that happen, again, with Caleb? How can I be that weak? I hate myself for it." *Yip, ruff, yip,* Cocoa talking back to me. "Will he forgive me? I don't know. I want to believe he will, but . . . I don't know. Do I even deserve it?"

A doorknob twists somewhere, and I sit up. Logan, a towel wrapped around his waist, emerges from the bathroom. Bandaged, but otherwise incredible. Lean, sharp, gorgeous. "Talking to the dog?"

I smile and nuzzle Cocoa, who pants a couple of times and then licks me once before trotting over to Logan. "Yes. She's an excellent listener."

"Isn't she? Never argues, never gives shitty advice."

"Exactly."

I glance at him, frowning. "You're not supposed to take showers, Logan. You can't get your dressing wet."

He waves a hand in dismissal. "I didn't shower; I took a bath. Didn't get my dressing wet. My hair is gonna be greasy until I can take a normal shower, but I needed to feel clean. Don't worry about it."

"Of course I'm going to worry about it."

He seems about to argue but then takes a deep breath, lets it out slowly, and smiles at me. "I know you are, and I'm grateful that you care enough to worry."

"I care so much it scares me sometimes, Logan." I gesture at his hair. "See, if you'd let me help you, I could have washed your hair without getting the bandage wet."

"Next time, then. I'm just . . . I'm not used to asking for help in anything. It'll take time, that's all." There's a moment of silence, and then he reaches down and rubs Cocoa's ears. "I didn't hear what you were saying to her, by the way." He's telepathic, apparently. "I just heard Cocoa making that noise she makes when she's talking back to someone. I swear she understands what we're saying, you know?"

"I do. It did seem that way."

I want to run my hands over his body. Taste his skin. Feel his muscles under my palms. Take his hardness into my hands, feel him love me the way only he can. I don't move, though. I can't do that to him. I don't deserve that with him. Not anymore. Not until I've come clean, admitted my sins and begged him to forgive me, if he can, for betraying him, cheating on him. That's what it was, betrayal, infidelity. I love Logan. *Only* Logan.

But I am an addict. Weak, hooked, unable to control myself.

Logan must see or sense my inner turmoil. He grips the towel and moves to kneel beside me. "Hey. What's up?"

I shrug. "It's just a lot."

"What is?"

I laugh, a bitter, humorless sound. "Everything, Logan. My life. Just . . . everything."

He sweeps a palm across my cheek. "Talk to me, Isabel."

I shake my head. "Why? The last thing you need right now is to take on my stick-in-the-mud angst. You need to rest. To heal. Not to worry about me. I should be worrying about *you*."

He blows out a breath. "Isabel, why don't you get this? I am *going* to worry about you. I am *going* to care about your problems. They're my problems, because I want them to be. It's what you do when you're in a relationship."

*In a relationship.* My gut lurches. "I don't know how to do that. How to be . . . that."

"Who does? You make it up as you go, babe."

"You make it sound easy."

"Not easy, but simple. You trust me, I trust you. We confide in each other. Depend on each other. Give freely so we're both getting what we need."

"That sounds . . . lovely."

He's close. One knee on the couch, near my hip. Staring down at me. Indigo eyes warm, inviting, fiery with desire. God, those eyes. That look. The expression that says he wants me, all of me, only me. Needs me. Can't go another minute without me, without tasting me, feeling me.

I take a breath to unburden myself of the guilt, but he steals it with a kiss. Buries his palm in my hair, cupping the back of my head. Lifting me up into the kiss. Grabbing a handful of hair at the roots and tugging my head gently but firmly backward so he can plunder my mouth. Leaning farther over me.

I can't not touch him, when he kisses me like this. Smooth my hands over his sides. Roam the curves of his shoulders, the broad plain of his back. Somehow, the towel comes loose. I find myself brushing it away, cupping, gripping, clutching, scratching his backside. Pulling him closer. Feeling him harden between us.

He's propping himself up with one hand, searching for the hem of my dress with the other. Tugging it up, out of the way. Probing with a finger, sliding it under the gusset of my panties. Finding me wet. Hot. Ready. Touching and touching and touching, until I'm gasping against his kiss and stroking his hardness. Lifting my hips, needing him. Ready for him. Eager. Hungry.

He's ripping at my panties, and I've got him gripped in my fist. I can feel by the tension in his belly and the way he's breathing that he's ready. Beyond ready.

"Is . . . God, Isabel." He murmurs in my ear. His voice is low and rough, but it blasts me with remembrance.

"Logan, wait."

He touches his forehead to my chest for a brief moment, but then he's leaning back, upright. Cock jutting hard and ready, eyes tortured with need. "What do you need, babe?" He stares down at me. "If you're worried about me, don't. I'm perfectly healthy enough for this, I promise."

"It's not that, Logan." I close my eyes tight, summon courage.

"Then what?"

I can't look at him, or I'll forget it all. The desire to obliterate everything with the heat of his kiss and the hardness of his body and the glory of feeling him orgasm in and on and all over me is too strong. If I look at him thus, naked, hard, ready, I'll forget what I need to do.

"Isabel?" Logan's voice, prompting me.

I suck in a breath. "We can't do this, yet. I want to, need to, but I can't."

He shifts, plops to the cushion beside me. Drapes the towel over his lap. It tents, somewhat comically, over his massive erection. I force my eyes to focus on his face.

He sees now. This . . . isn't good.

"Shit." A breath, a palm passed over his face. "Spill."

"I don't even . . . I don't know where to start."

He eyes me. There's an anger and a hardness in his gaze. "Well, then let me venture a guess: Caleb mind-fucked you again. Got you all mixed up and feeling sorry for yourself or for him, or something. Worked whatever magic hold he has on you, got you to sleep with him again. Is that it? That's it, isn't it? You let Caleb fuck you again."

"Logan, I—"

"*Yes*—or—*no*, Isabel?"

A tear slides down my cheek. Another. A whole host. "Yes." A broken sound, a shattered word, a shredded syllable.

"Fuck." He rises, paces away, towel dropping to the floor, forgotten. Stomps angrily to his room. Pauses, head hanging, glances back at me. And then slams his fist into his bedroom door, a furious smashing blow that splinters the door. "Now I need two goddamn doors."

"Logan, wait."

"Just give me a few minutes, okay? I need to calm down, and I need to process this." He's not looking at me. Just standing naked in the doorway, blood on his knuckles, bandages diagonal across his head. "Don't leave. Don't drink. Just . . . wait."

"All right."

I try to push down the panic. The sobs. The self-loathing. But it's bubbling up and threatening to spill over. It's a very long time before Logan emerges. He's dressed, in loose track pants and a tight T-shirt, barefoot. Band-Aids on his knuckles.

Takes a seat on the couch beside me. Breathes deeply, lets it out, and finally looks at me. I keep my eyes downcast. I don't deserve to look at him.

"Is. Look at me."

I shake my head. I can't. Don't. Won't.

He touches my chin, but I resist. Pull away. Feel his fingers slide across my cheek, brushing away tears. "Isabel de la Vega. Look at me now, please."

I have to, the way he says it. The whip and crack of command in his voice is inexorable. "What, Logan?"

"I hate the hooks he has in you. The way he's brainwashed you."

"It's addiction, Logan. Pure and simple."

"Addiction can be broken."

"He's not a substance I can merely stop buying. I can't just suffer the withdrawals, or go to rehab, or a clinic. I can't just quit him. It's not that simple. He holds my past. He *is* my past. I hate it, too, the way he affects me. The way I can't seem to . . . *not*. No matter how badly I want to, no matter how hard I try."

"What was it this time?"

"Jakob."

"So what I told you, you already knew?"

"Some of it. I confronted him about the name on my discharge papers. And he told me about Jakob. But he told it as if it were someone else. Not him. The last thing he said to me was that Jakob Kasparek does not exist anymore. That his name was Caleb. But then . . . he . . . he showed me that Jakob *does* exist. Almost as a separate person within him, but there, nonetheless."

"Excuse me if that doesn't move me."

"I'm not expecting it to." I wipe at my face. "I don't expect . . . anything from you. Except a good-bye, perhaps."

"No, Isabel. No. Not that. Never that."

"Why? How?"

"Love is not so weak as that, Isabel. At least mine isn't."

"But mine is, apparently."

"I didn't say so," Logan says.

"You didn't have to." I finally look at him of my own volition. It is so hard, nearly impossible, and painful. To see the anger and the pain directed at me . . . it is nearly too much to bear. "I hate myself for it, Logan. Truly, I do. The moment he left, I—I wanted to undo it."

What I don't tell him, what I don't even allow myself to fully think, is that there is a seed of doubt buried deep within me. Now that I've seen such a secret, vulnerable, *human* side of you, I cannot help but wonder what else there is within you, that no one else has ever seen. I wonder. I doubt myself. I doubt everything.

And that doubt is murderous. Treacherous.

But I do not doubt Logan. I do not doubt my feelings for him.

I twist to face him. Take his hands in mine. Meet his eyes. "Logan, please . . . forgive me. If you can. I don't know what this means for us, for the future, but . . . I do love you. I hope you don't doubt that."

"It's hard not to. I want to believe that if you loved me enough, you wouldn't let anything come between us. But then I tell myself that I'm not in your shoes. I can't understand or fathom what you've been through. But what I keep coming back to is . . . this isn't the first time you've gone back to him after promising you were done. It's not even the second. And—he's still out there. He still considers you his property, and he'll come for you. And I—I can't help being afraid, especially now, that you might just choose him over me if it came down to it." He touches his lips to my knuckles, all ten, one at a time, slowly. "So, yes. I forgive you. Of course I do. But it will take time. I just . . . I need time. Stay here with me. Just be with me. And give me time to process it all."

"I swear I—"

"Don't. No promises, Isabel. You can't make any promises to me, not about Caleb."

He's right, and I know it. I know it, and I hate it.

I cry, and he doesn't shush me. Doesn't tell me to stop. Doesn't tell me it's okay. It's not, and we both know it. But he does hold me. He wraps his arms around me, pulls me against his chest, and lets me cry.

Sometimes it's all there is, to cry and know it's not okay.

# FIVE

We spend a week in an odd domestic stasis. Eating. Sleeping—together, but not *sleeping together*. He doesn't touch me with sexual intent and I do not attempt to instigate it either. We both know we need time between you and me and Logan and me. We go grocery shopping. We pick out a new TV and new bedside table lamps. I accompany Logan to work and act as a sort of personal assistant, out of boredom and a desire to be useful. We go to dinner at restaurants, both fancy and plain.

He takes me shopping, and for the first time in my memory, I get to choose my own wardrobe. Bras, underwear, jeans, T-shirts, sweaters, skirts, simple cotton dresses, tennis shoes, sandals, flats, socks, tights, leggings, sweatshirts, shorts, workout gear. A whole new wardrobe of simple, attractive, comfortable clothes. He expresses his opinion on certain items, which ones he likes and which he doesn't, but leaves every decision up to me. Nothing is excessively expensive, nothing is formal or uncomfortable. They are clothes that reflect *me*, and it's a gift from Logan the value of which I don't think he or anyone can fathom. Just choosing my own wardrobe, it makes me feel like a real person, like a woman with her own identity. I have a *style*, and it is utterly and solely my own. And Logan expects nothing in return. That in itself is wonderful and amazing, to be given something freely. Always before, I felt like everything I did, everything I had came with a price, physical or emotional or psychological. Logan is content with a simple "thank you" and the happiness so evident in me.

He takes me to a movie at a theater—a wonderful first for me, an experience I want to repeat as often as possible. It is rapturous, transporting me into a world where I do not exist. A pleasing escape.

We take Cocoa for long meandering walks through Logan's neighborhood.

Logan writes up a business plan for me. *Comportment*, he calls the business. I'm not sold on the name, but it will do for now. He guides me in constructing a business vision and a mission statement. All businesses need those two things, he says. We scout for locations; he writes up the loan contract; we squabble about both.

We go to an outpatient doctor to have the pressure bandage removed and the area checked. It's healing nicely, we're told. Wash it gently with warm water, don't rub it too much. Leaking tears are normal, and so is a little blood in the tears. Logan refuses the prosthetics offered, both temporary and permanent. Not the way he wants to go. Not going to pretend to have an eye.

Beth has come by a few times over the last week with patches— leather, silk, combinations of materials, plain, ornate, and everything in between. Logan sorts through them, discarding some and keeping others.

He vanishes into the bathroom at the doctor's office and emerges wearing a patch that, to me, suits him perfectly. It is made from thick, aged brown leather, hand tooled with ornate swirling designs, the rim of the patch itself lined with brass rivets.

He grins at me expectantly. "So? What d'you think?"

I can't help but laugh at his eager expression. "It looks great."

"I'm glad you like it." He glances at me. "I didn't want anything boring, but I was worried it'd be too much."

"You make it look . . . cool."

He scrapes his hand through his hair, tosses it dramatically. "That's me. King of cool."

I snort. "Not anymore. Dork."

"If I didn't know any better, I'd say you were teasing me." He quirks an eyebrow at me. With the eyepatch, the effect is even more dramatic.

We're at his SUV now; yes, he drove, carefully and with prior approval. *Just leave extra stopping distance,* he was told, *until you get used to the change in depth perception.* He climbs up and in, starts the engine while I buckle. Out into traffic, music on low.

"You act as if I'm a stick-in-the-mud, Logan. I *do* have a sense of humor."

"Not a stick-in-the-mud, babe. Just . . . serious. As if it doesn't always occur to you to laugh or crack jokes."

I turn my gaze out the window, away from him. "Well, my life up until recently hasn't precisely lent itself to frequent jocularity."

"'Frequent jocularity.'" He laughs. "See? That's what I mean. Who says things like that?"

"Me?"

He reaches out and squeezes my knee, takes my hand. "Yes, you. And I love it. You speak with concision, with eloquence and elegance. It's amazing. It's almost like you have a script writer feeding you lines, but it's just the way you talk."

"My reeducation came from classic literature. I had to relearn how to speak, and for a long time, after I finished speech and physical therapy, the only person I spoke to was Caleb. And he is . . . formal. Always. And that is something I really never even truly understood until I met you. You're the opposite. Not in a bad way, just . . . different. You are the polar opposite to Caleb's upright, formal, precise manner. It's . . . refreshing. As if I can let loose. Let my hair down, metaphorically speaking."

"I get it. As much as I can, at least."

Home, then.

Home?

Home.

Yes, Logan is home. Logan is freedom. Logan is where I am learning to be me. Learning who I am. What I like, what I don't like. I exercise when I want to. And when I don't want to, I don't. I eat what I like, when I like. I have a taste for unhealthy food, I discover. Pizza, nachos, potato chips. Logan has to step in, remind me that I can't eat all that stuff all the time. So I find a balance, gradually. Revert to healthy food. Organic, locally produced. Lean meats, vegetables, very little bread, very little processed food. But I splurge once in a while on yummy unhealthy food, just because I can. I exercise, but my way, at my pace, my routines. I like to run, I discover. I could never do that, before. But now I run. With Cocoa and Logan, I run. Logan got me an iPod and earbuds, and we run miles and miles and miles, not talking to each other, just running, breathing, pounding pavement endlessly. I can tune out the world when I run, focus on the music and the rhythm of my soles on the concrete, and not think about you or Logan or my addiction to you or the fact that I should have gotten my period two days ago.

It's only two days late. I've been stressed out. Life has been chaotic and painful and impossible, and such things can throw off a woman's cycle.

It's only two days.

Nothing to worry about.

A week and a half late.

I'm refusing to panic. Refusing to worry. Burying my head in the sand. Not even thinking about it. Any of it.

If I let myself start thinking about it, I will lose all control over everything. I'm unbalanced. Tripping along the edge of a cliff, arms windmilling wildly.

But I know, deep down, that I am going to fall.

With my period now two weeks late, I find myself ill in the morning. Nauseous. Stomach roiling. Sometimes I barely make it to the toilet. Fortunately, Logan is an early riser and follows a regular routine: up at five, eat a quick breakfast and drink a cup of coffee, then upstairs to work out. In the shower by seven, out the door to work by eight, in the office by eight thirty, usually.

My illness—I know the term, but refuse to think it—usually happens around six thirty. While Logan is in the gym upstairs. Sometimes later, while he's in the shower. Or after he's gone. It hasn't happened while he's been around to see it. He'd know what it means—what it *might* mean. *Could* mean.

He has me stay at his house, working from home. Writing out lesson ideas for my business, creating materials, my own version of the informational pamphlet Indigo clients received.

The sickness usually passes once I've vomited, but I have to eat directly after. Light food. Fruit, an egg-white omelette, tea. No cheese; I tried, and my stomach rebelled, which is odd because I usually love cheese. I tried a sandwich for lunch one day and couldn't keep the lunch meat down. Or, no red meat. White meat was fine. But not red. No red meat, no cheese, nothing too salty or too sweet. Bland food, then. Unusual, once again, because I typically prefer rich, flavorful food.

My moods are unpredictable, too.

Weepy and sad one moment, for no reason. Irritable the next. Giddy and manic another.

I steadfastly refuse to consider what it all might mean.

Logan comes home early from work one day, when I'm nearing three weeks late. Lays a garment bag across the back of the couch and just grins at me.

I put on the dress. It's sexy, alluring, a little risqué for my usual taste, but I decide I like it. Black, low cut, edgy lines, a slit up the left thigh nearly to my hip, fabric gathered tight across my torso into a bunch over my left hip.

When I emerge wearing the gown, Logan's eyes go wide and rake over me. And, for the first time in nearly a month, there's lust in his gaze. Not that it's been absent all this while, but he hides it. Tamps it down, refuses to act on it.

This time, he slides close to me, wraps a palm around my back, low, just above my buttocks, and tugs me against his front. "Gorgeous, Isabel."

"Thank you," I say. Breathe a moment, feel his heart thumping, feel his fingers dimpling against my spine, edging lower to the swell of my bottom. "What's the occasion?"

"A business associate of mine had extra tickets to an opera performance at Lincoln Center tonight. I managed to wangle a table at a fancy dinner place near it, so we've got a fun night out."

"Opera sounds delightful. I've always wanted to attend a performance."

Logan shrugs, makes a face. "I dunno. Opera isn't really my thing, I don't think, but you don't turn down free seats to Lincoln Center, especially not when they're prime seats. So we'll go and be fancy."

I notice now that he's changed into a tuxedo, and has replaced his eyepatch with a black one that somehow adheres to his face without a strap. The tux is bespoke, with glinting sapphire and titanium cuff links, an expertly tied bow tie. Hair slicked back, bound low at his nape. He looks sleek, elegant, and powerful. Virile. Indigo eye matching the jewels in his cuff links. Indeed, his eye is brighter, more arresting and iridescent than the sapphire.

He reaches into the inside pocket of his tuxedo, pulls out a long thin box: a necklace, sapphire and titanium to match his cuff links, and his eye. He glides behind me, and I can suddenly feel him everywhere. His heat, his hard body looming behind me. His hands tickling across my breastbone, laying the gleaming blue pendant just above my cleavage, clasping it at my neck. Setting the box aside, reaching into his trouser pocket for another box, this one smaller, and square. Earrings, to complete the set. Gentle, sure, nimble fingers sliding the post through my earlobe, attaching the back.

And then his palms are carving down my hips. Pulling me back against him. Lips to my ear. Not whispering or speaking or kissing, just a momentary resting of his lips against my ear, a pause on their downward journey. Back of my ear, the knob of bone just there. And then to my neck. The curve where neck becomes shoulder. Feather-light kisses. Drifting touches of his lips.

Goose bumps pebble my skin.

My nipples ache.

Thoughts leave me.

He continues to press soft slow careful kisses onto my skin, neck, shoulder, my back where the cut of the dress leaves my flesh bare. And his fingers, at my hips, gathering the fabric of the dress. The hem rises. Rises. I gasp and focus on his kisses, and on the cool air on my bare flesh as the hem of the dress glides upward.

Breathing becomes difficult, then.

He hooks his thumbs into the waistband of my panties. They are simple, and new. Plain cotton briefs. Comfortable, and not at all attractive; I hadn't gotten around to changing into anything more fancy yet. This thought too is blasted away as he lowers the undergarment. I step out. And now I'm bare for him, the dress hiked up around my waist.

"Nothing underneath, tonight." His voice in my ear is low, a murmur, a growl.

"What?" I gasp.

"No panties tonight."

"Logan—"

He nips at my earlobe. "Hush."

I go silent on a breath, an outrush of surprise. His fingers are dancing over my hip bone. Over my belly, to my opposite hip. Teasing. Lower, lower. Tickling my thighs, outside to inside. Tracing across my pudendum.

I whimper.

I want his touch.

It's been so long. A month of celibacy, for us both.

I feel wild with need. Frantic. I've buried it under worry, brushed it aside in favor of ignoring everything, pretending this is life, running, exercising, eating with Logan, sleeping with Logan, working on material for Comportment.

But now, with his fingers easing closer to my core, feathering over my labia—I need him. *Need*.

"God, Logan."

"What, baby?"

I can't help gyrating my hips. "Please."

"Please what, Isabel?"

"Touch me."

He doesn't answer with words. His middle finger slides into me, slides deep into my wet, hot core. Curls, moves, withdraws. I ache now. Ache all over. I'm shaking. Lay my head back against his shoulder and widen my knees. He touches me again, this time applying a gentle pressure to my clitoris. I whimper, gasp, and my knees buckle as lightning sears through me.

It feels like an eternity since I've felt Logan thus, felt this touch, this bliss, this connection I feel only with him.

A rising, expanding violence within me. A detonation, impending. A susurrus in my ears, a roaring of blood in my veins. Heat in my belly. A rush of sensation.

He slides that one finger into me again, withdraws it. Smears my wetness over my clit. One hand is holding up my dress, keeping it out of the way, the other at my core, his thighs hard against the backs of mine. I'm leaning back against him, limp. Capable of nothing but the motion of my hips as he slides his finger in, and out. In, and out. Against my clit. In, and out. Two fingers, then, suddenly.

Climax burgeons.

I'm gasping, arching my spine, fully giving in to the bursting wildness.

And then he stops.

Lets my dress fall down around my ankles, and crouches behind me. He's fetched a pair of my shoes to match the dress, black Blahniks with a three-inch stiletto heel. He circles my ankle with his strong fingers, lifts my foot, slides the shoe on. I transfer my weight, let him ease the other shoe on, next. I'm out of breath, aching, a little angry that he stopped.

"Logan . . ." I start.

He stands up in front of me, brushes the pad of his thumb over my cheekbone. "Isabel?"

"You stopped."

There's a knock at the door. Logan leans in, kisses me. A brief, scorching scouring of his lips against mine. Too short, but intense. "Time to go."

"I haven't done my makeup."

"Don't need any. You're fucking sexy just like that. And I guarantee you'll be the most beautiful woman there, makeup or no."

"I can't go to the Met without makeup on, Logan. It isn't done."

"Dinner is in forty, and we'll be pushing it with traffic like it is."

"I can be quick."

Another knock.

"Grab some stuff and bring it with. Do it in the car."

"I'm not ready, Logan. I—a quiet dinner, maybe. But the opera? The Met? People will be watching. You can't just—just spring this on me."

He moves past me, into the bathroom. I hear makeup cases and tubes clattering, a zipper closing. And then he's hustling me out the door, a black leather case in his hands. I glance behind me as he's closing the door. The last thing I see are my panties on the floor of his living room, a pile of gray cotton, abandoned.

My core aches. I don't want to go. I don't want to sit through a dinner and an opera. I want Logan. I want him to finish what he started.

There's a long black limousine waiting, a driver at the open passenger door.

Logan waits while I lower myself in, and then he's beside me.

I lean close, whisper in his ear. "Logan. I'm not wearing any panties."

He nips at my earlobe. "I know."

"I don't like it."

"You will."

"I haven't done my hair."

"Don't need to."

"I don't have any makeup."

He hands me the case, unzips it. My makeup, all of it, including my compact mirror. "Gotcha covered. Anything else?"

I take a moment. Breathe. Focus on applying makeup, just a little. Lipstick, blush, mascara. Check it in the mirror, and then close the leather case, set it aside. Breathe in silence for—I don't know how long, trying to gather myself.

"You stopped," I say, at last.

He checks that the privacy glass is in place, and then turns to me. Faces me. Leans against me. Presses his face into my cleavage and inhales. Tugs the straps of the dress off my shoulder, pulls the bodice down to bare my breasts.

"Logan!"

"Keep quiet, Isabel."

His fingers slide into the slit of the dress at my thigh, steal inward.

God, here?

Oh God.

I slide lower in the seat, spread my legs. I want it. I don't care. I can't think of anything but the orgasm I almost had, of getting there.

There's no toying, no hesitation. He slides his finger into me, and I gasp.

"Hush, baby." His breath is warm on my nipple. "No sounds."

I bite down on my lip until it hurts.

He nibbles at my nipple with sharp teeth. Slides his lips over it. Tugs. Licks. It's already hard and standing tall, but every lick and touch of his teeth and tongue make my nipple harder, more erect. Until it aches. And then he moves to the other, and works it the same way. And all the while, his fingers are busy. Sliding in and out, pressing against my clit, circling, pinching, sliding in.

Lips, fingers, breath.

They are my world, Logan's lips, Logan's fingers, Logan's breath.

When I come, I bite down on my lip so hard I taste blood, and Logan kisses me, swallows my whimper and licks at my lip, soothing the hurt. But his fingers continue to circle my clit as I come, working me harder, faster, bringing my climax higher, pushing me to heights of wildness that leave me breathless, that leave me aching and limp.

And then he withdraws his fingers from my core, lifts them, dripping my essence, to his mouth. Licks them clean.

"Better?" he asks.

I can only gasp against his tuxedo coat, smelling his cologne and the faint acridity of cigarettes, the tang of cinnamon gum.

Logan scent.

But I am still afraid of this night. Being out, with Logan, in public. Not just to a movie or a little diner. Something . . . *public.*

On his arm. There will be pictures, probably.

I'm not wearing any underwear.

I've just had an orgasm, so I'm flushed and breathless and feeling on edge, wild, rife with lust.

I'm scared witless.

But I feel beautiful, because Logan's touch always does that. Makes me feel needed. Wanted. Beautiful. Even when he doesn't say a word.

He adjusts my dress so I'm covered.

There is silence, then, in which I attempt to quiet my nerves.

The limo pulls to a stop, and there is a moment of waiting as the driver exits and circles, opens the door. Logan rises up out of the limousine elegantly, easily. Extends a hand to me, lifts me out. A black awning, doormen in uniforms with brass buttons on their coats stand to either side of the doorway. I adjust the drape of my dress, feeling the soft swish of the fabric against my backside, against my bare, still-tingling core. I feel as if everyone who sees me will know I'm not wearing anything under the dress. I even glance down at myself, but . . . it isn't as obvious as it feels to me.

Logan threads his fingers through mine, pulls me closer to his body, so I'm flush against him. Held up by him. His arm goes around my waist, almost inappropriately low. Claiming me as his.

"You are exquisite, Isabel," he murmurs in my ear. "The loveliest woman in any room. And you're on *my* arm. Makes me the luckiest man in any room."

"Thank you, Logan."

"I love that you can take a compliment with grace," he remarks.

I'm unsure how I should respond, so I don't.

A maître d' greets Logan by name, guides us to a booth in a shadowed corner of the back of the restaurant. A single candle provides some illumination, but not much. All the other tables are similarly cloaked in shadow, providing privacy for each booth.

I am uneasy. Off balance. This feels right, but . . . something is off. Within me.

I ignore it.

Peruse the menu.

Logan does not suggest anything, and when the server appears to take our orders, Logan allows me to speak for myself. I like that. Deciding what I want, making my own decisions.

Dinner is long, broken into several courses. I refuse wine, which perplexes Logan, but he doesn't push it, and also does not order anything for himself.

And he doesn't ask why.

I wonder if he will begin to suspect what I fear.

When dinner is over, we return to the limo, which drives only a couple of blocks and then slides to a halt in front of a grand building, soaring arched windows gleaming with blazing light in the night. Red ropes, red carpet laid over the stairs. Someone opens the door, and Logan emerges. Camera flashes sparkle blindingly. He waves, smiles, and then assists me out of the limo. I try to smile, cling to his arm, and tell myself to breathe.

*Logan, Logan, who's your date?*

*What's your name, sweetheart?*

*Who is she?*

*Are you two an item?*

*What are you wearing?*

Questions come hard and fast, and Logan ignores them all, nudges me into a walk.

*Who is she?*

*What's your name, sweetheart?*

I do not have a real, legal identity. I have no ID card. No social security number. I suppose that information exists somewhere, but I don't know where. Or how to get hold of it. Some research online told me these are the basic ways to establish one's identity. And I do not possess that information.

*Who is she?*

How would he answer that?

Am I his girlfriend? Are we an item?

This is utter foolishness. Appearing in public, with Logan, where there is media, press. Cameras. Questions.

Former clients, even, perhaps.

In the theater lobby itself, there are more cameras. More posing.

I barely put on makeup.

I'm not wearing panties.

I did my hair hours and hours ago, and I only ran some light mousse through it, finger-styled it. Not expecting to go anywhere, to meet anyone, much less appear at a very public event where I would have my photograph taken a hundred and fifty times per second.

I'm panicking.

Grip Logan's arm with all the strength in my hand, and force breath into my lungs. Force myself to breathe. Expand chest, contract. Breathe in, breathe out.

"You're okay."

"What the *fuck* were you thinking, Logan?" I hiss this, nearly sotto voce.

"Fake it, Is. You're gorgeous. Flawless."

"I am utterly unprepared for this. What if someone recognizes me as Madame X?"

"We're together now, Isabel. Your name is Isabel de la Vega. That's all that matters now. I won't let anything happen to you."

I feel the back of my neck prickle. Turn, and there is Jonathan. A former client, and sort of friend. Tall, handsome, in a perfectly tailored tuxedo, with a stunning blonde clinging possessively.

A shocked expression mars Jonathan's handsome face.

Moves to stand in front of Logan and me. Mouth works, but no sound comes out.

"Hello, Jonathan." I smile. Pretend to be at ease. Fake it till I make it.

"Madame—"

"I go by Isabel now." I speak over Jonathan.

More shocked silence. "Isabel." Extends a hand, ingrained manners taking over.

I take the proffered hand, intending to shake it, but Jonathan turns my hand palm down and kisses the back. It is an archaic gesture, strange, and out of place. But the way Jonathan does it, it comes across gentlemanly, respectful. I am impressed.

"Pleased to meet you, Isabel." This is said with a dash of irreverent humor.

Jonathan's date is confused. "Jon? How do you know her?" Jealousy, barely restrained, a French accent.

"Isabel and I are . . . former business associates."

"Oh." The blonde relaxes, jealousy assuaged.

True enough, I suppose. Our true relationship to each other would be nearly impossible to explain, even if either of us were inclined to discuss Indigo Services.

Jonathan remembers his manners, once again. "Oh, sorry. Isabel, this is my girlfriend, Brigitte." He says it *Brih-ZHEET*.

"Pleased to meet you, Brigitte."

"You as well." I am still receiving a cold stare from Brigitte, despite the gorgeous man at my side, arm around my waist, scanning the crowd.

Jonathan extends his hand to Logan. "I think we met, a while back. At the auction."

Logan shakes, firmly, briefly. "Yeah. Logan Ryder."

"Jon." Just Jon. No last name, none of the pretense I saw when Jonathan was my client. He is at ease, confident. Well dressed, polite.

A success, then.

Jonathan and Logan are discussing something to do with business. I've tuned out, thinking about Jonathan when we last met, the arrogant posturing and callow shallow hubris, now turned into pride and confidence and an attractive charm. How *I* did that. *I* taught him that. Perhaps Comportment will be a success after all.

I vacillate often, sometimes thinking it will be the best thing I've ever done, and other times that I should just give it up as impossible.

I let Logan lead me to our seats.

The opera is not what I expected. It is beautiful, rapturous. Transporting. Logan, however, is impatient.

And even as much as I enjoy the music, the spectacle . . . seeing Jonathan shook me. Gave me pause. Reminded me.

So I am distracted.

It is over before I know it, and I am following Logan through the crowds, down the steps, to our limousine, which is waiting for us, door open, driver with a hand on the door.

The ride home is quiet. Silent.

Neither of us speaks.

Logan's hand rests on my knee. The closer we get to home, the higher up my thigh his hand goes.

When the driver halts outside Logan's home—*our* home—he is nearly touching my core.

And I am in a fit of confused, weltering emotion.

Aroused.

Aware that I am—that I might be—

I can't even think it, can't even think the word. Don't. Won't. Can't.

I push that aside. I know I have to face it, but not now.

I'm thrown off by Jonathan. Seeing him with Brigitte, a stunning girlfriend who is clearly possessive of him. Not by Brigitte, but more just . . . Jonathan. By all he represents. The only one of my clients I've ever really cared about. I'm not even sure why Jonathan's presence tonight has thrown me off as much as it has.

I feel dizzy.

As if life is whirling around me, as if the entire world is rushing in crazed circles just beyond my reach, and I cannot quite find a way to join the frenzy, stuck somewhere in a silent, lonely bubble, at the eye of a hurricane.

Even Logan seems . . . distant.

As if our connection has faded, or changed.

Lessened, or vanished.

Been broken, perhaps.

We are inside now.

I don't remember coming inside.

Logan is in front of me. Looking down at me. "Isabel?"

I blink. Look up at him.

I am afraid of losing him. I'm afraid I've ruined us. That my weakness for you, Caleb, has broken whatever potential Logan and I may have had. The thought of having to make my way without Logan is . . . impossible. Too painful to consider. I couldn't do it.

And the way he's looking down at me, as if I'm . . . delicate—it makes me panic.

Like he doesn't know me.

And if Logan doesn't know me, who does?

Who am I?

Isabel.

I'm Isabel.

Am I pregnant?

The thought strikes, just as Logan speaks again. "Talk to me, Isabel."

"I—"

No thoughts come. No words.

I can't tell him. I don't even know yet.

"I—I feel lost, again."

"You're right here. With me."

"But I feel like . . . like there's an ocean between us."

He presses up against me. "I know I said I needed time. And I did. I've had time. That's what this afternoon was about. I'm okay with it all. As okay as I can be. We're here. We're together. We work, as a couple. Even without sex, you and I work, as a couple. Even without sex, I enjoy your company."

"But I feel like there's space between us." A dam is cracking open, words pouring out I hadn't known existed within me. "Like the connection we had is . . . not gone, but—different. The way you look at me, the way you touched me this afternoon. It was . . . different. And I just feel . . . off. Everything feels off, ever since Caleb let me go."

"Isabel—"

"Nothing is right."

"Isabel—"

"And there's so much I—so much I need to say, but I don't know. So much I need to do, but I don't know how. I need an identity, Logan. Even just legally. I'm not really a person, legally. And . . . inside, I'm just—I'm a mess. And I don't know how to fix it. I love being here, with you. Living with you. Sleeping beside you. Eating with you. But tonight—it was . . . I don't know."

"Listen, Isabel—"

"I feel like there's so much in the way between us. Caleb is between us. My weakness, where he's concerned. What happened. The fact that he shot you. Almost killed you. Cost you your eye. That's my fault. You can say what you like, but that's how I feel. And that scares me, that there's so much between us, so much inside me I don't know how to express, even to myself. I want us. I want you. I want how easy it was, before. I'm afraid I—I'm afraid I ruined things."

"Goddammit." This is under his breath.

And then he kisses me. Abruptly, almost violently. He takes my face in his big warm hands, and his lips crash against mine. His tongue steals between my teeth.

Heat suffuses me.

I collapse forward, and my arms wind around his neck. I cling to him. Just touching him, thus, it centers me.

I have to touch him. Feel him. Feel *us*.

I am pushing at him. At his clothes. At his tuxedo jacket. It softly thuds to the floor in the foyer. His back is to the door; the alarm is beeping. Logan reaches past me, jabs at the green-lit buttons, and the alarm goes quiet. Cocoa is whining, barking.

Nothing matters.

I am obsessed. I need him. I need his skin. I need to know that *this*, the physical, mental, emotional connection that binds us, I need to know it still exists. And right now, the only way I know how to find that is by touching him. Filling myself with his body, his scent, his heat, his hardness. To feel him. To know. To relearn him.

I have his tie untied. Tossed away. Tear at the buttons. I hear one pop and clatter on the floor.

"Whoa, Isabel, honey, slow down a second—"

I kiss him silent. Shove the shirt off his shoulders, and he fumbles with the cuff links, shoves them in his trousers pocket. I have his belt gone now, the buckle jingling onto the floor at my feet. The double clasp and button closure of his trousers, the zipper. He kicks off his shoes and he lifts his feet free, and now, finally, God finally I have him bare, naked in my hands. His abs, his broad back, his hard round ass, the hot rigidity of his cock. I caress him all over, just touching him. Lean in, and kiss him. His shoulders. His throat. His tattoos. His scars. Fondle his erection, grasp him. Stroke him.

Logan gently but firmly pushes me back, stares at me, confused. "Isabel, babe. What's going on?"

"I need you."

I don't think, don't hesitate. Unzip my dress and step out of it, nude now except for my heels, earrings, and necklace. A moment, as he stares at me. Nipples peaked, core wet. I can smell my own desire.

"Logan, I *need* you," I repeat.

"Why do you seem so . . . desperate?"

"I don't know why, but I am. I'm desperate for you. I need you."

I reach for him, cling to him. Kiss the shell of his ear. His temple. Tug his hair free of the ponytail and spear my fingers through his blond wavy hair. Drag his mouth to mine. Kiss him with every molecule of my being.

"Is this good-bye, Isabel?"

"No," I breathe. "*Fuck* no. It's—It's . . ." I pull back but don't let go of him, cling to his hair and his cheek. "It's me saying, 'Love me,' Logan. Love me. Please . . . just love me. Show me. Remind me. I need us. I need *us*."

He bends at the knees, grabs the backs of my thighs, and lifts. I wrap my legs around him, lean in and devour his breath. Touch my forehead to his as his back hits the door. We groan in unison as he fills me. He moves to kiss me, but I steal it from him. Take the kiss from him. Bite his lower lip as he impales me, seats deep, sunk to the root. Hips to hips. Mouth to mouth. Heart to heart.

"This is what you need, Is?"

"Yes, God yes."

He moves. Carries me to the kitchen, sets me on the island, buttocks right at the edge. Grabs my hips, and pulls. Fills me with a thrust. Breathes onto my lips, groans, and kisses me. Pulls back, his one brilliant blue indigo eye on me, staring at me. Letting me see into him, as he always does, when we're like this. When he's inside me.

Still wearing my black high heels, I use my feet to pull him against me. As if he could get closer, as if it were possible to go deeper. It's not, but I try. As if him being deeper will unite us more. As if feeling more of him, as if being filled more completely by him will bind us more tightly. As if to love him thus—wildly, desperately, furiously—could erase my sins, could cure my addiction.

It won't, but I try.

Oh god, God, gods—I try. To erase, with Logan. To cure, with Logan. To remake myself, with Logan. He is inside me, but yet I am in him. Wound up, delved deep, tangled up, woven in. I writhe then and feel his cock slide through my stretched and burning and aching core, and I lean forward. Collapse against his chest, lips to his breastbone. Curl my hand around his ass and pull. Urge him.

"Love me, Logan."

He moves then. Thrusts. Pulls me closer. I lean back, close my eyes, push my hips against his, angle away. Hook my high heels around his calves and clutch the cool hard round bubble of his muscular buttocks and let him move. Just feel it. Feel him move. Feel him fill me.

But it's not enough.

I push at his chest.

He lifts me, pulls out of me, and sets me down. And now I push him again, shove him to the couch. He falls backward to the cushions, and I fall onto him. Straddle him. Kneel over him. Drape my breasts against his face, drag my aching nipples against his mouth. Reach down between us and guide his cock to my entrance. Don't waste a moment, not a single second. Impale him into me. Sink down on him. Grip his shoulder with one hand and the back of the couch with the other. Knees in the back of the couch, taking my weight. Lift up, sink down. God, so deep. So full. So thick. So much. I lean back, stare down at our bodies as I rise, watch his shaft slide out of me, gleaming and wet and slick and wide, and watch as he thrusts up and buries himself into me, watch as that thick beautiful erection disappears into me. He has my breast in his mouth, tongue lapping at my nipple. Licking my tits. I arch my back and beg him without words to never ever stop doing that.

I ride him, frantic, frenetic, and wild. He grunts, moves with me, but this is all about me. I'm taking this. I need this. This is mine. I cling to him, both hands now. On his shoulders, almost gripping his throat. His hair is loose and wild, in his face. I leave it that way, obscuring him. The patch is black through yellow strands, his eye is ultrablueblueblue. His skin is golden, his hair the color of the noon-day sun. Body hard and lean and strong and perfect, and all mine.

I kiss him, quickly. "You are mine."

He laughs. He *laughs*. "Yes, Isabel. I am yours."

His hands grip my hips and urge me to move harder, faster, to sink him deeper. And this, his hands thus on my hips, it is him saying without words—*and you are mine*. He doesn't need to say it, and if he did, I would hate it. I've heard those words far too many times from someone not him, and I cannot hear them again, not from Logan. He knows. He sees. So he says it another way, he tells me with his hands. He slides his big rough palms up my torso to cup my big, heavy, bouncing breasts. *Mine*. He brings one breast to his mouth, kisses it, devours my nipple, the areola; *mine*. The other; *mine*. Hands grazing now down my sides, cupping up under my buttocks, gripping them, lifting me, letting me fall down to bury him deepdeep-deep, so deep; *mine*.

Then—while we move, while he drives up into me, while I sink down on him, while my tits sway and bounce in his face, while he stares into me with his one good eye, the one eye now more arrest-ing and piercing than ever—he puts a thumb to my lips, a palm to my cheek, his fingers through my hair; *mine*. Grips my hair in rough fistfuls, suddenly, and kisses me so hard I forget to breathe, and thank God for that because in this moment with Logan Ryder I'd rather kiss than breathe, need his kiss this kiss more than oxygen, more than life, more than anything, however elemental.

Because this, us, we are elemental, thus. Bonded, connected, soul to soul;

*MINE.*

A jealousy, a possession going both ways. Ownership freely given, rather than taken.

I will myself to him. I would with all my soul belong to him and only him forever.

Our movements become ragged. Mine, his, ours. I feel his breath come as gasps. His grip in my hair and on my hip goes bruisingly beautifully rough. If I was loving him—not just moving, certainly not *fucking*, but *loving him*—wildly before, now I am primal. Feral. Mad. I even make sounds that aren't quite human. Sounds of need, sounds of utter abandonment. Bliss. Perfection. Beauty. Raw love being created between us.

He is growling.

I am whimpering and whining and snarling and clutching at him everywhere.

A hand in his hair, fisted in his sun-locks. Biting his lip. Eating his breath. Sucking down nipping dipping kisses.

I feel him come, and I explode around him in that precise moment. I feel him release, hear his lion's roar of ecstasy, and I give my own orgasm vent. Loud, crazed. We are clinging to each other. Mouth to mouth, kissing as if kissing were breath, were life, and we were drowning without it. He comes and comes and comes, and I am thrashing above him, squeezing him as he orgasms, undulating above him, driving him deeper and harder as I come so hard I see stars, go dizzy, nearly faint with the shattering power of it.

When he has finished his orgasm, and I have also, I grip his hair in both hands and yank his face back so he cannot but look at me.

He lets me do this. Enjoys it. Stares up at me unblinking, unwavering, and roams my body with his hands while I gaze into his soul.

"I love you, Logan." I whisper it, raggedly. "I love you."

A moment, fraught, rife.

And then we're twisting and falling and I'm lying on his chest and his arms around me and holding me tight and he's holding me together. Keeping all my pieces together.

"Isabel . . . Isabel." A thumb across my temple. A palm on my back, broad and warm and comforting. "I love you."

In that moment, I feel like just maybe things might be okay, somehow, someday.

# SIX

wake in our bed. Covered in blankets, still naked. A glance tells me it's after eight in the morning, and—

I barely make it to the bathroom.

After rinsing my mouth and brushing my teeth, I look at myself in the mirror. Front view, side view. Palm on my stomach. My still-flat stomach. I know nothing about such things. If I am—if . . . God, I still cannot even think it to myself—when I know, just by looking at myself in the mirror?

How do I find out for sure? I have no identification. No money. If I am ever to have any independence, I must have these things. I don't think Logan realizes. That I don't have an ID, that I've never had my own finances. Or how much I want those things.

I shower, wash away the evidence of last night. I smile to myself, thinking of that.

I am dressed, scrubbing my hair dry, and there's a knock at the door. Cocoa, lying on the floor of the bedroom, lifts her head off her paws, growls low in her throat. Hackles rise at her shoulders.

She stands up, slowly, lithely, in a move that reminds one she is descended from predators. She prowls to the front door, growling. I follow her, put a hand on her collar, and peek through the peephole.

A man in a brown uniform, holding a large square envelope. There's a truck parked in the street, emergency flashers blinking, *UPS* written on the side.

Another knock.

I open the door, holding on to Cocoa's collar, but loosely. I trust her to protect me. She's leaning against my knees, putting herself in front of me. Growling at the deliveryman, who glances down at her, nervous. I would be, were I on the other side of a growling, distrustful Cocoa.

"Isabel de la Vega?"

"Yes. How can I help you?"

He hands me the package, then extends a device with a screen and a small stylus. "Sign on the line, please."

"What is this?"

"Package for Isabel de la Vega. All I know."

"Who is it from?"

"It's from someone named . . ." A glance at the top left corner of the label, and then the package is handed back to me. "Caleb Indigo."

I take the stylus and sign my name, slowly, carefully.

"Have a nice day, ma'am." And then the carrier jogs to the street and is gone in a rumble of diesel fumes.

I stand in the open doorway, staring at the package.

From you.

What is it? What could you possibly be sending me? I almost don't want to open it. But I must.

I close the door, move as if in a dream to the kitchen island. Set the package down. Find the tab on the back side and pull it open.

Reach in, withdraw a small pile of papers. The paper on top is white, and smells old. There are three words across the top: *Acta de Nacimiento.*

Birth Certificate.

I see my name. My father's name. My mother's. The whole thing, naturally, is in Spanish, but I somehow translate everything without even thinking. Without trying. My brain just . . . does it. How bizarre.

The next item is a small blue card with *Social Security* across the top. My name, and a number, three digits, a dash, two digits, another dash, and four more digits.

My social security card?

The next item is larger, square, white paper with black inked designs printed around the edges. Across the top is *The United States of America*, and beneath that is *Certificate of Naturalization*, the first two words and the third separated by a gold leaf image of the U.S. seal. In the bottom left corner is a small photograph of me. Young, fourteen. Long black hair braided and hanging over my shoulder. A shy smile. That damned blue dress, I can tell I'm wearing it in the photo, by the hint of my shoulders visible. The damned blue dress. There is my signature, near the top. Neat, careful; the way I signed for the package.

Holding these items, I half expect to have a flashback, a memory. But . . . there is nothing.

There is a money order made out to the Commissioner of Motor Vehicles in the amount of fourteen dollars.

One last item flutters out of the package when I upend it. A small scrap of yellow paper, torn from a legal pad. The handwriting is beautiful. Perfect. Uppercase letters, slanted a bit, each letter printed so neatly it is almost calligraphy. But the words are scrawled diagonally across the scrap of paper, completely disregarding the ruled lines, meaning the note was scribbled quickly, dashed and torn off.

ISABEL,

I OBTAINED THESE FOR YOU. THEY ARE BRAND-NEW COPIES OF YOUR ORIGINAL SPANISH BIRTH CERTIFICATE, YOUR U.S. SOCIAL SECURITY CARD, AND YOUR CERTIFICATE OF NATURALIZATION. IT IS ALL YOU WILL NEED TO OBTAIN AN ID CARD. MERELY TAKE THESE THREE PIECES OF IDENTIFICATION TO THE DMV—DEPARTMENT OF MOTOR VEHICLES. YOUR BOYFRIEND WILL KNOW WHERE ONE IS.

CALEB

Your name is signed messily, the *C* curling and looping, huge, almost entirely enclosing the other four letters, which are printed uppercase.

There is no explanation as to how you got them, no explanation as to why. Just the five sentences, your name, and my name.

Terse, brief, efficient.

And the word *boyfriend*; I can almost feel the sarcasm, the vitriol. The letters of the word are darker, as if the hand holding the pen was gripping more tightly, pressing down harder upon the paper.

I open Logan's laptop, type in *DMV*, and a list pops up. There is one not far from Logan's home. I memorize the address, the intersection, the blocks intervening, memorize the route I will need to take. I want to do this myself. Logan would take me, and will be upset I did it alone. But this is for me to do.

Thank you, Caleb.

I don't know why you saw fit to provide me with this information, but you did. And I am grateful.

I replace the items in the package, find my shoes. They are flats, like ballet slippers. Comfortable, plain. I am wearing tight-fitting blue jeans and a plain green V-neck T-shirt, a knitted white wool cardigan over it. Comfortable clothes. Simple. Plain cotton briefs, and a supportive but comfortable bra. My hair is messy, but it looks good this way. No makeup.

I am Isabel. I do not need Valentino shoes or Chanel dresses, or Carine Gilson lingerie.

Almost out the door, my hand on the knob, about to close it, the key Logan gave me in my pocket, I hesitate.

And then go back inside. Open the laptop, pull up Google. Let out a shaky, shuddery breath.

Type in three words: *free pregnancy test.*

A moment as the computer thinks, and then it brings up a list of options. One, Avail NYC, is near enough to the DMV that I can walk there as well. I click the link to go to the website. See that I have to make an appointment, so I follow the directions and make an online appointment for later today. Close the tab, lower the lid of the laptop with shaking hands. My heart is whacking painfully in my chest. It's just a precaution, I tell myself. It's not true. It can't be.

I know better. I know when I'm lying to myself.

I leave Logan's house, putting Cocoa in her room, setting the alarm, and locking the door behind me.

It is a much longer walk than it seemed when examining the map.

One-oh-four!" a voice calls out.

A slip of paper in my hands reads 104, so I stand up, move to the owner of the voice. A black woman. Short, thin, middle aged, hair cropped short and dusted with gray, large gold hoop earrings dangling from earlobes. No eye contact.

"Help you?"

"I need an ID card."

"Not a driver's license?"

"No. Just an ID."

"Got the application done?" I hand over the application I filled out while I was waiting. "You'll need to provide two forms of identification. Social security card, a utility bill, something like that."

I place the three forms I have on the counter. The woman retrieves two at random, the social security card and the certificate of naturalization. Not at random, actually. She probably doesn't read Spanish, and a document from a foreign country probably doesn't count anyway.

Fingers clack on keys for a while and then a pink lacquered nail gestures. "Stand there for the photograph." A moment of adjusting equipment. "One . . . two . . . three." A bright flash.

More typing.

"Fourteen dollars, please." I hand over the money order. "Here's your temporary ID. Your card will arrive within two weeks."

"Thank you—"

"You bet. Have a nice day. NEXT! Number . . . one-oh-seven!"

And just like that, I have an ID.

I make sure I have all of my papers, place the temporary card with it into the DHL envelope. Orient myself, and begin the walk to the Avail clinic. It also is much, much farther away than it seemed on the map. By the time I get there, my feet ache, and I just want to go home.

But that is more likely because I don't want to do this. I don't want to have to face this truth. My knees shake as I sign in and take a seat in the waiting room. My hands shake. My stomach flips. I am fighting tears.

After a few minutes of waiting and filling out a form—the answers to many of the questions I leave blank, because I just don't know—a door opens and a young woman stands in the doorway, holding a clipboard. "Isabel?"

I stand up, and the young woman smiles at me. Twenty-two, perhaps. Bottle blond, on the heavy side of curvy, a kind, comforting smile and a welcome presence. "Hi, Isabel. I'm Abby. Come on back."

I follow her. I'm too nervous and terrified to even say hello back. Abby leads me to a room with an exam bed, closes the door behind us. "So, Isabel. You're here for a pregnancy test?"

I nod. Try to breathe and can't.

Abby sees my trembling, my obvious terror. Puts a small, cool hand on my shoulder. "It's going to be okay, okay? We're here to help. Just take a deep breath, let it out. . . . good. Now, can you tell me when your last period was?"

A digital thermometer under my tongue; a cuff Velcroed around my bicep, a gauge measuring something while Abby glances at a watch.

"Um. Last month. Middle of last month."

"So how long since your missed period?"

"About . . . three weeks?"

Abby nods. Unstraps the cuff, hangs it in its place. Retrieves a small clear container from a cabinet, writes my name on a label. Hands it to me. "I just need a small urine sample."

Abby shows me to the bathroom and I obtain the sample—which is a bit trickier than it sounds. Return to the room, and hand Abby the sample. There is something bizarre and embarrassing about handing a perfect stranger a cup full of my still-warm urine. But Abby seems totally at ease and unconcerned. Vanishes with the sample, promising to return within a few minutes with the results.

I sit on the exam bed and kick my feet, too nervous to sit still. Too afraid. Still not thinking about what it means. What I'll do. I can't think of anything. My mind is racing so fast with a million fears and thoughts and worst-case scenarios that I shut it all out and refuse to think at all. Blank. Staring into nothingness, breathing slowly in through my nose, out through my mouth, trying not to cry.

Abby comes back. Sits on the small stool, hands folded together resting on crossed legs. "So, Isabel. The results came back positive." A smile. "You're pregnant."

I swallow hard. Blink back tears. "Is . . . could there be a mistake? A false . . . um, a false positive, perhaps?"

A shake of bottle-blond hair. "No, honey. There's no such thing as a false positive when it comes to pregnancy. False negatives are real, and if the test had come back negative we'd give you a blood test, which is much more accurate if it's early, still. But your last period was three weeks ago, which is kind of a long time in these kinds of scenarios. So, it's conclusive."

I am handed yet another clipboard and pen, told to fill out more forms. I do so quickly, and Abby leads me to a different room, this one a counseling room. The counselor is a woman, white, with gray hair tied in a bun; kind, wrinkled eyes; a soothing, soft voice. Mary, from social services.

"Are you alone?"

I shrug. "I . . . at this moment, yes."

"Do you know who the father is?" This is asked gently, so as not to sound judgmental, I suppose.

"Um." There are only two options. "Yes." There should only be one option.

"But the father is not here with you?"

"It's . . . complicated."

"I see. Well, you have a few options, at this point, Isabel: abortion, adoption, or keeping it."

"I—"

Mary lays out several pamphlets. "If you choose to abort the pregnancy, there are several different methods available to choose from—"

"I'm sorry, I'm sorry—" I hold up my hands, stopping Mary's explanations. "I just . . . I need some time. Can I . . . I need to think about this. I need to talk to—"

"Of course, of course." Mary stacks the pamphlets, adds a few more on adoption and parenting, and stands up, hands them all to me, a thick stack of pamphlets explaining all of the various options for what to do now that I know I'm pregnant.

I'm pregnant.

I'm pregnant.

I feel faint. Dizzy. I have to sit down, put my head in my hands and breathe.

"Are you all right, Isabel?"

I force myself to my feet. Breathe. Breathe. The dizziness clears. I push it all aside, shove it back down. Can't think about it yet. Not until I'm home and alone. And sitting down.

"Yes. I'm fine. I just . . ."

"It can be scary and overwhelming, I know. But you have options. We're here to help, Isabel. If you need to discuss your options with someone besides your partner, come back here. I'm here to help you understand your options and I will help you choose the best thing for you. Okay?"

"Yes, I—thank you, Mary. I have to—I have to go." I put all the pamphlets in the envelope with everything else.

---

don't remember walking home.

Logan is waiting for me, sitting on the couch, cell phone in hand. When I walk in, he jumps up, strides over to me. Quick, jerky, angry strides.

"Where the hell have you been, Isabel? I was worried sick."

"I had . . . I . . ." What do I say? "Caleb sent me some information. My birth certificate. Social security card. Naturalization certificate. So I went to the DMV to get my ID."

He grabs me by the shoulders, holds me. Stares into my eyes. "Goddammit, Isabel. You should have waited. I would have gone with you." He blinks a few times. "Why would he send you that stuff?"

I shrug. "I don't know." I pull away. Turn away. "I'm sorry I worried you, Logan. I just—I had to do it alone. It was important that I did this myself."

He sighs, behind me. "I get it. I was just . . . you weren't here, no note, nothing. I came home early to take you for lunch, and you were gone. I thought—" His teeth click together, he cuts off so abruptly.

"You thought I'd left you."

"The thought crossed my mind, yes."

I turn back to him. "I wouldn't, Logan. I would never just vanish like that."

"I know. I just—you were just gone, and my mind started going in circles. I thought maybe Caleb had shown up again, snatched you."

"I'm sorry."

He crosses to me. Wraps his arms around me. "It's fine, Is. You're here. I'm fine. It's fine."

I shake my head. That's not what I meant. "I'm sorry, Logan. I'm sorry, I—I'm so sorry." I'm crying.

He holds me at arm's length, ducking to try to catch my gaze. I shake my head and lean into him. "Hey, hey. What's wrong?"

"I'm sorry, I'm sorry, I'm sorry—" It's all I can say. I'm hysterical, hyperventilating.

"Isabel. Calm down. Breathe, okay? Breathe for me. In through the nose, out through the mouth. Just breathe."

I breathe. Push down the panic.

Yank myself out of Logan's arms, pace away, the couch, stop. Grip the back of the couch for support. Turn and look at Logan through tear-blurred eyes.

"I went one other place, too." I toss the DHL envelope on the couch cushions. Breathe, breathe, breathe. "A clinic."

"What . . ." He takes a step toward me. "What kind of clinic?"

I bite my lip. Summon the words. Force myself to say it out loud. Two words.

"I'm pregnant."

# SEVEN

oly shit." He stumbles.

Stares at his feet for a moment, wipes a palm across his face. And then he's in motion. Wrapping his arms around me. Pulling me around to sit on the couch. On his lap on the couch. My cheek to his chest. Hand on my back, rubbing in soothing circles as I sob.

"You're pregnant. How long have you known?"

"I just took the test."

"But if you took the test at a clinic, you've been worried about it for a while, then. Right?"

I shrug. "I suppose. I was worried. I missed my period three weeks ago. The doctor at the hospital thought I might be pregnant, actually. So it's been in my mind all this while. And I've been getting sick in the mornings lately."

A silence.

"Holy shit. You're pregnant." A silence. "We're having a baby."

"Logan." I realize something, a factor I'm not sure he's thought of. "I—The time frame. I don't know—"

He takes my face in his hands, lifts my face up so I'm looking at him. There's nothing but love in his eyes. "I'm not an idiot, Isabel. I *know*." He kisses me, quickly, softly.

"Logan, it may not be—"

"You were with both him and me in the same span of time. So it could be either Caleb's or mine. That's what you're saying. And I'm saying I know."

"And you're not—you don't—?"

"What did you think I'd do? Kick you out? Tell you to take it to him? Say, 'Not my problem'? I love you, Isabel. I'm here. We're together. No matter what happens." He pauses. "Is it easy for me to accept? No. I'm not sitting here saying, 'Hey, cool, the woman I love is having a baby and we don't know if it's mine or the man who's cost me five years in prison and my eye.' It's not cool. It's not fine. Thinking about it in those terms makes me a little crazy."

"That's what I'm—"

He doesn't let me finish. "But what I'm not going to do is condemn you or hold anything against you or push you away. It'll take time to come to terms with, but I'll do that in my own way, on my own terms and in my own time. And I'm not going to get all nasty with you over it in the meantime."

This just makes me weep all the harder. "I don't understand you, Logan, and I certainly don't deserve you."

He touches my chin, and I meet his gaze. He speaks softly. "Doing the right thing isn't always easy, Isabel. You know that. But it's always an option. It's a choice. To be a good person is a choice, day by day. I had to choose—still have to choose each and every day—to not hate Caleb for everything he's done to me, to not seek revenge. I have to choose, in this case, to continue loving you, no matter what. That means accepting the reality of difficult circumstances. I'm not going to abandon you or push you away. It's hard, yes, but my love for you is stronger."

I cling to him. "I love you, Logan. I was so scared. So worried about what you'd say, what you'd do."

"His, mine, I don't care. It's *ours*. We'll handle this together." He goes silent. "Have you decided if you're . . . keeping it?" This sounds like an afterthought. Something he realized I may have considered.

"I haven't gotten that far, Logan. I don't even know . . . what to do. What to think. What I want. I want to not be pregnant. I want to not . . . I want to not be such a horrible person that I don't even know which of you is the father. How awful is that? What kind of horrible woman am I, that I'm pregnant and don't even know who—who . . . who the—the father is?"

I break down, then. Truly break down.

Sobbing. Mucus dripping. Chest heaving. Hyperventilating. Unable to function, to see, to move, to do anything other than just . . . break.

Shatter: to break suddenly and violently into pieces.

Logan just holds me. Lets me break, and clings to me through it.

I don't know how long I break, there against the wall of Logan's chest. How long he holds me. How long it takes me to shatter completely, until there's nothing left of me.


have no recollection of being picked up, carried, and set down in our bed. But I come to awareness, eventually, and I'm there, in our bed. Logan is spooned behind me. I can tell by his breathing that he's awake.

I lie silent a long, long time, letting my mind work. Letting my thoughts and emotions just flow, flicker, flit-stream.

How is it even possible? I am on birth control, and I have been for a very long time. You brought me to the same clinic in your office building, where I lived, where you live, where I had the chip removed. There was an examination, you watching like a hawk all the while. And then the doctor inserted something into me. Birth control, the doctor explained. An IUD. The process was a little uncomfortable. There was some pain, some dizziness, nausea. Normal, I was told, considering my young age and that I had never given birth before; it will pass. And it did. I had regular checkups by your private doctor thereafter. Once a year, that same doctor would perform an overall examination. You even had the doctor replace the IUD a year ago, as it had reached the end of its efficacy term.

Perhaps it came out? I don't know. I never thought to check. I should have, I was told to, but I never did.

Or, perhaps, it just didn't work. Nothing is ever 100 percent effective, I remember the doctor saying as much.

I slip out of bed and go into the bathroom, check for the IUD; it's still in place, which I assume means it failed.

In the end, though, it doesn't matter how it happened. It did. It's real. I'm pregnant. A human being is growing within me.

What do I do? The counselor at the clinic outlined three basic choices: abortion, adoption, or raising it myself. Which do I choose?

Abortion? Terminating the pregnancy?

I consider it. But something within me rebels against that idea. No. Not that.

So, adoption, or delivering the baby and raising it.

Adoption, delivering the baby to term, and giving it away for someone else to raise. Could I do that?

No. My heart rebels against that just as strongly. If I am going to carry the child for nine months, I could not then give it away. Give *her* *or him* away. Say, as Logan put it, *Not my problem?* I couldn't. I just couldn't.

I'm scared. I'm terrified. I don't know how to be a mother. I don't know how to raise a child. I don't even really know who I am, yet. Maybe I never will. How could I then raise a person, teach that child to be the best he or she could be? What could I teach them? What do I know? How to be addicted to a man who doesn't love me. Doesn't care for me. Just wants to possess me.

*Is that true, though?* A sinister little voice whispers, deep inside me. *What about the last time you were with him? He kissed you. He made LOVE to you. As Jakob. What if . . . ?*

No.

No.

No.

Even if you COULD love me, if you did, it wouldn't be enough to overcome all that I have endured at your hands. Even though you have given me a life, given me somewhere to live, even though you were there for me, caring for me when I was helpless and had no one. It isn't enough. It can never be enough.

And nothing you could ever feel for me, nothing you could ever do or say could ever match what Logan feels for me. The way he makes me feel. The way I feel about him.

I am complete, with him.

I have an identity, a future, potential, with him. I am *someone*, with him.

With you . . . I will always only be Madame X.

A possession.

I have to tell you.

The life growing inside me could be yours. I don't think there's any way to know until I give birth. Will the baby have blue eyes and blond hair, like Logan? Dark eyes, dark hair, like you? Like me? What if the baby's features aren't distinctive enough to tell me who the father is? What then?

Does it matter?

If I told you—*when* I tell you—what will you say? Will you want it? Want me? Would you insist I get an abortion? Try to force that on me? Manipulate me and twist me into it? If I had still been Madame X and this happened, I came up unexpectedly pregnant, what would you have done? Let me have the baby? Let me raise the baby on my own, alone, perhaps stopping by once in a while? I don't know. I don't know what you would have done. What you will say. What you will do.

I just don't know.

So I can't abort the baby—God, my heart twists in painful knots just thinking that. I can't. I can't.

And I can't give the baby away. That too hurts to even think.

So I am keeping the baby.

As if a human being is a stray dog to just . . . *keep*. It is a life growing within me. A soul. A mind. Talents. A smile. Hugs, kisses.

*Mama is a warm weight on top of the blankets, on the edge of my bed. Her arm is over me, her fingers toying with my hair. She's singing a lullaby to me, the same lullaby she's sung to me every night for my whole life. I am too old for lullabies, probably. But I don't care. I love these moments, when I am clean and my hair is damp on the pillow, blankets pulled up to my chin, Mama's breath on my ear, her voice singing sweetly, softly, a song her mother sang to her, and so on down the generations. So Mama tells me, some nights. An age-old song. I feel myself start to fade, to fall into sleep. I welcome it. My window is open, and the sound of the ocean crashing against the shore is another lullaby.*

*I hear her humming now. The tune only. Stroking my hair. "Duerme, mi amor."*

*Fading in and out, listening to the waves. Later, I hear my door creak.*

*Heavy footsteps. Papa's cologne. His hand, warm and heavy on my shoulder. Whiskers on my cheek, breath smelling faintly of the red wine he and Mama drink when they think I'm asleep.*

*Kiss to my cheek. "Te amo, mija."*

*I am too nearly asleep to even murmur.*

*Now that Papa has kissed me good night, I can sleep.*

I smile to myself. They loved me, my mama and my papa.

I will love this one—my hand goes to my belly. I will love this one.

"I'm keeping the baby." I whisper it.

Logan's hand slides over my hip, his fingers tangle with mine, over my stomach. "Good."

"I'm so scared, Logan." My voice quavers. "I don't know how to do this."

"You're not doing it alone, Isabel."

"But I don't . . . I don't know how to be a mother. I barely even remember my own. A few snatches of memory. Her cooking for me when I was a little girl. Her singing an old lullaby to me in Spanish. But . . . how do I mother a child? I'm not—I don't—"

"Love, Isabel. That's how. Hugs, kisses, lullabies. Be there. Just . . . love. The rest we'll figure out together, as we go. That's all anyone has ever done, I think. I don't think anyone is ever ready for a baby, sweetheart. No one really knows what they're doing. You just . . . do the best you can. Love them, be there for them, take care of them to the best of your ability. That's all you can do."

"But what if . . . what if it's his?"

"Will he want it? Will he want, like, joint custody or something, if it is?"

"I have no idea, Logan. I don't even know how to tell him. I don't

know if I ever want to see him again." I shake my head against the
pillow. "He has answers. He knows things about me. There's a history, there, somewhere. He *knew* me. I know he did. But . . . if I see
him again, I'm afraid of what will happen. Me changing has changed
him. I don't want to . . . to see him anymore. Even if I never find out
the answers, I don't want to see him. I am Isabel now, yes. But I am
also the woman who was Madame X. I am both. Madame X is still
a part of who I am. So is he. But now . . . so are you."

"We're a part of each other."

"It's all so . . . messy."

"Life is messy, Is. We're all just . . . fumbling around out here.
Living, doing the best with what we've got. It's never easy, and it's
never simple."

"I wish it were."

"So does everyone else."

"Not everyone has been through what I have."

"True. And I'm not trying to make light of that. Just saying,
you're not alone in this mess called life."

"I have you."

"Exactly." He pulls at me, so I'm on my back. I turn my head to
look at him. He's removed the patch, and the space where his eye
used to be is a wrinkled, scarred hole. It's strange, but it's part of
him. "Listen, Isabel. I promised you I'd love you, no matter what. I
do. I will. I'm making that promise again. I love you. No matter
what. Okay? You want to tell him, I'll go with you. You want to stay
clear of him, we'll make sure you never see him again. We'll move
to freakin' Thailand if we have to. Okay? I'll take care of you."

"And the baby?"

"And the baby."

I can't help crying again at that.

And again, he kisses me. Kisses the tears away. Wipes them with the broad pad of his thumb. Kisses my lips.

It's going to be okay.

t is early in the morning, and we are having breakfast. He shoots me a glance, sets the newspaper down. "Babe?"

I lower my mug of tea. "Yes, Logan?"

He snorts. "You gotta loosen up, honey." He straightens his spine, makes a tight, sour face, raises his voice to a falsetto, and captures my inflections precisely. "'Yes, Logan?' Like for real, if I say, 'Hey, babe,' you should say something simple and *normal*, like . . . 'What's up, buttercup?'"

I frown at him. "What does that mean, 'What's up, buttercup?' It strikes me as trite and empty."

Another laugh. "It is. Which is why it's funny. Just . . . try it. So let's start over." A pause, and he clears his throat. "Hey, babe?"

I slouch in my chair, make a grumpy face, affect as deep a voice as I can. "Yo dude, what's up?"

A big broad shout of genuine laughter. "Exactly! I love it!"

I straighten. "Now that we've gotten *that* out of the way, what is it you wanted to ask me?"

"You ever see the touristy stuff around here? Like, the Statue of Liberty and all that?"

I shrug. "Probably before, but not recently that I am able to recall."

He slaps the table with his palm. "It's settled, then. Time for a field trip!"

"Really?"

"Really. I'll take the day off and we'll just hang out and do the tourist thing. I've never really done it myself, for as long as I've lived here. You just . . . take it all for granted, you know?"

I shake my head. "Not really."

"I suppose you wouldn't, huh? It's like, you live here, you work here, and the tourist stuff will always be here so there's no point in going to look at any of it, because you *live* here. So you never end up going to see it." He pulls out his phone, glances at me. "I'm gonna get us an Uber so I don't have to worry about driving. You'll want a sweater or something for when we're on the ferry."

"Ferry?"

"Well yeah, how else are we gonna see the statue? It's way out in the bay, right?" A shooing gesture. "So go get some sturdy walking shoes on and grab a sweatshirt. The Uber will be here any minute."

I do as instructed, putting on a pair of running shoes and a zip-up hoodie, by which time Logan has locked up Cocoa and is waiting outside by the Uber car, a black Mercedes sedan. He locks the front door, and we're off.

I'm excited, actually. A day off, out with Logan. Exactly what I need, really, especially since I've already dealt with the morning sickness today.

Our first stop is a pier on the Hudson River, where Logan buys us a ticket for the full tour of the island. We find seats on the upper deck, in the open air, and wait for the boat to fill. Within fifteen minutes or so, the ropes are thrown off, a horn sounds, and we back out of the slip, pivot, and trundle out into the river. Another couple of minutes, and then a voice fills the air, coming from a PA system, narrating our journey, describing landmarks of the island on our left telling us which number avenue we're passing and explaining how the number of the pier corresponds to the street number nearest it. I pay close attention, sitting on the inside of the row, closest to the water, feeling as giddy as a little girl.

Mile by mile, however, a strange sensation grows within me. Familiarity. As if I've been here, before. The sun is midway up toward the zenith, beating warm on my face, and the boat is rolling gently, an elderly, stentorian male voice guiding the tour. Behind us, a woman and her two young boys chatter to each other in Spanish:

"*Mama, where is the Statue of Liberty? Are we going to see it soon, Mama? Can we go up in it?*"

"*No, 'Jandro, we are going to go past it, but not on it. I think the man will tell us when we will be able to see it.*"

"*Can we get some food, Mama? I'm hungry. It's been hours since breakfast.*"

"*My God, Manuel, you only think of your stomach. We have to save our money, so we cannot get anything to eat just yet. We will have lunch after the tour.*"

I hear their voices, feel the sun. I'm floating.

Dizzy.

Something sparks, tumbles in my mind.

Clicks.


*M*   *ama is on my right, Papa to my left. We are up on the very top of the boat, sitting as far forward as we can. I am excited, flush with exuberance, but I am trying to keep it in, to be more like Mama, who has her hands folded on her lap and her ankles crossed beneath her, under the bench. She is calm, quiet, watching the buildings of Manhattan float past us.*

*We are really in New York! I am as excited as I am frightened. I know no one. I have no friends. We have no family. Papa speaks the best English of any of us, and mine is a close second to his, but Mama speaks barely any at all. I think it is okay for her, though, since because she is so very beautiful most men will do whatever she asks, even if she is asking it in Spanish, and they speak not a word. They'll trip over themselves just to get a smile from her. I've seen it happen. She wanted a bottle of water but couldn't figure out the money. The paper bills were all too big and they all looked the same, but the coins were too small and all looked different, and she was worried about getting cheated. The man trying to sell us the water didn't speak any more English than we did, but he was a man, and a man with eyes for a beautiful woman. So when Mama let out a frustrated sigh, smiled that smile of hers, and held out the money to the man, he made the correct change for her. I am good at math, so I counted it, because really it's very simple, and tried to tell this to Mama, but she just shushed me. But she got the bottle of water, and the correct change, and all she had to do was smile.*

*That's Mama.*

*Papa is more trusting. He would have given the man the money and trusted him to make the right change, and wouldn't have realized he'd been cheated until much later, when it was too late. But Papa knows this, which is why he let Mama buy the water. Because he is smart about being stupid.*

*That is most men, I think.*

*Or so I have observed.*

*We have only been here two days, Mama and I. Papa came first, a month ago, and found us an apartment to live in near where both he and Mama worked, registered me for school, and signed us up for our citizenship classes. He'd even managed to get a few days of work in but hadn't had a chance to see anything fun. So the moment Mama and I arrived in the baggage claim area, Papa piled our suitcases onto a trolley and led the way to our car. It's not a new car, and not a very nice one. It has rust on it, and there is a crack in the windshield, but Papa said it was a cheap rental just for the day, because taxis cost too much money and the subways are very confusing, the roads only marginally less so.*

*Papa was very excited, babbling a mile a minute, talking about how our new apartment is nice, very nice, but of course not so nice as our home back in Barcelona, but still nice.*

*Even now, despite the fact that there is a tour guide, Papa is talking,*

talking, talking, pointing out buildings he recognizes, laughing at what I assume was a joke the tour guide made that I did not quite understand.

Eventually, as she always does, Mama quiets him. "Luis. You are babbling, my love. Hush, please, and let the tour guide be the tour guide."

Papa pretends to be grumpy and embarrassed, but he reaches his arm behind me and Mama reaches up, holds on to his fingers with her own. I roll my eyes at their display and get up, move to the front of the boat.

"Isabel, please be careful," Mama says.

"I will," I say, stuffing down the impulse to say something rude and childish about how I'm not a child that I need a reminder to be careful.

As soon as I am up, Papa takes my seat and Mama leans into him, tucks her head against his shoulder. I sigh and look away, turn my attention forward, hoping to see the statue. There is nothing to see yet, though, but the island on our left and the place called New Jersey on our right, and water between. I like the wind in my hair, because it reminds me of home—of Spain.

This is home now.

I feel a pang in my chest at that. This is home.

I'll never see Maria or Consuela again, my best friends since I was a baby. I told them I would write letters, but in my heart I know I probably won't. I'll be busy with school, and trying to make new friends, and learning to speak English. Maria and Consuela were jealous of me for getting to move to America, but I think maybe it isn't going to be as fun and exciting as everyone thinks.

It is scary. This is a huge place, this New York. Everything is so tall, so wide, so fast, so new. There are millions of cars, taxis, buses, trucks, and there is the rumbling of trains underfoot and the crush of people, so many people.

And they are all so rude, so unfriendly. As if they cannot be bothered to even look at me, because their lives are so important, so much to do. At home—back in Spain—people would smile at you as you passed them. You might see someone while you're sitting at lunch in a café, not even someone you know, but you could become friends with them, talk to them. Smile at them, at least. And no one was in as much of a hurry as they are here. You take too long ordering food or even walk on the sidewalk too slowly, people get so irritated, push past you, yell at you to hurry up. I do not understand why everyone is in such a rush here.

I am not sure I like it, really.

Even though I am a little excited to see the Statue of Liberty in person. I've seen it in American movies a thousand times, but now I'm about to see it for real, right in front of me.

And then it happens, the tour guide tells us we'll see it on our left first if we're on that side, but no matter which side we're sitting on, everyone will get a good look. I am in front, in the best spot to see it as we approach. There it is! Huge, so big, so much larger than it seems even in the movies, soaring so high into the sky, impossibly vast. It strikes something deep inside me, the statue. It is just a big green woman with a torch and a book, but it means something. It inspires something in you, something beyond being the symbol of America, the symbol of so-called freedom. I don't know the words to capture my own emotions, but I am full of thoughts and words and pictures and hope, so full my chest hurts as if they're all trying to rupture out at once.

I forget myself, that I am fourteen and not a little girl anymore. "Mama! Papa! Do you see it!"

She smiles, that soft bright smile she gives only to me. "Yes, mija, I see it. It is very big, isn't it?"

Papa just smiles, and watches Mama and then me, as if capturing the moment in some internal, mental camera. Remembering. But not the statue, not the trip . . . us, Mama and me.


We came here," I say, when the memory breaks and I am once again myself, an adult, here and now, with Logan. "My mama and papa and I. On this tour."

Once again, the tour guide makes the announcement that the Statue of Liberty will be visible soon. I am compelled forward, to the bow once more, hands on the railing, eyes scanning the river for the first sign of the statue. I feel Logan beside me, and he puts his arm around my waist. He's quiet, letting me experience it in my own time. Letting me feel it, I think.

There it is. God, so vast. Arm raised high, torch flames looking as if they could flicker alight at any moment, sleeve tumbling down her arm, the other hand wrapped around that big book, on which— so says the guide—is written the date of the Declaration of Independence, July 4, 1776. Two days after my birthday. Her full title is *Liberty Enlightening the World*, and she represents Libertas, the Roman goddess.

I am dizzy from the overlap of memory and reality.

I could close my eyes and be fourteen.

I could turn my head and see Mama and Papa.

I am so tempted to turn my head, to look. But I do not. It is just a memory, a precious memory. I lean into Logan, and focus on each breath.

"You remember something?" he asks.

I nod against his shirt. "Yes. But I'm not sure how to put it into words. I mean, it's a simple memory, really. Us, the three of us, on a boat just like this, about to see the statue. Being a young girl in a new place. I think we'd just come here a few days before. I was unsure of so much. Trying to be adult about it, but really, I was just fourteen."

"A big change for anyone, much less a girl at that age."

I nod. "Yes, exactly. It was very scary. I didn't understand—oh, so many things. Why everyone was in such a rush, for one, and why everyone seemed to be so rude, for another."

Logan laughs. "Ah, New York. Those aspects of this city are a culture shock for people born in the States, much less someone like you from a much slower-paced, friendlier place like Spain."

"What was it like for you, when you moved here?"

He tilts his head to the side. "Oh man, it was . . . kind of the same, honestly. I mean, I'd already been stationed in Kuwait and fought combat missions in Iraq, flipped houses in Chicago. So . . . I wasn't a kid, you know? But it was still a culture shock. Everything happens so fast, here. Like you said, everyone is in a rush, you're always getting jostled and told to hurry it up. Plus, there's just . . . so *much*. You could live your entire life in this city and there'd still be things you've never seen, places you've never been, restaurants you've never heard of."

"I get that feeling too, the little of it I've seen."

"It's weird, to me, how you can have been here since you were fourteen and still know nothing about the city."

"Not by choice."

"No, that's for sure. I get it. It's just . . . weird." A shrug. "Twelve years, and it's like you're seeing it for the first time."

"Because I am, really."

"And that's why we're here, babe. I want your memories of New York to be of me, of us. I want . . . I want to give you good memories."

I melt into him. "Every day I spend with you, it's a good memory."

"Good answer, sweetheart, but we gotta make you some new ones, some *real* memories. That's what today is about."

I watch the statue drift past us as we glide around it, across the bay and to the opposite side of the island. We sit again, once the statue is out of sight, and the rest of the trip is quiet, slow, and peaceful. I hold Logan's hand and listen to the tour guide, and enjoy the sun on my face.

By the time we've returned to the dock, it's well past lunchtime, and my stomach is grumbling, so Logan hails another Uber and has us taken to Times Square, another place I've never been, or don't remember coming. The driver deposits us at the edge of the square, and we get out, make our way on foot through the bustling crowds to the giant red staircase. I look around in awe at the myriad flashing lights and mammoth screens and endless advertisements, finding it hard to breathe from the grandeur of the place, the chaotic wilderness of lights and lives and frenzied exuberance.

There are thousands of people, just like us, taking photographs, posing for selfies, pointing, just sitting and taking it in. After a moment, Logan leads me across the square, consulting his phone now and again. A map, directions to something. A restaurant, I assume. Indeed, he guides us unerringly to a little place not far from the square itself, called Ellen's Stardust Diner. It doesn't look too impressive from the outside, and indeed, the interior is that of an aging diner, vinyl seats and Formica tables. But once we're seated and we've ordered food, I see why he brought me here.

The servers all sing.

I smile the entire time as a flamboyant young man with bouffant red hair climbs up on a little catwalk between a row of booths, microphone to his mouth, singing an old show tune for all he is worth. And then, after a moment, a girl starts singing a different song, and while she's singing she's inputting an order and carrying a glass of soda to a table, and then she's dancing past the tables and shaking her butt and holding the end note until I begin to wonder if her lungs can possibly contain any more oxygen. The whole lunch is like that, me watching the waitstaff singing and forgetting to eat, while Logan watches me.

And then, once we're done eating, Logan leads us back out to the square, and to a theater a block away, where he buys tickets for a show called *Aladdin*. A real Broadway show? I'm so excited for that it's hard to contain it, and I find myself wishing the day would pass more swiftly, so it would be seven o'clock sooner. But then, I don't want to miss anything else Logan has planned for us.

Which, apparently, entails shopping.

We walk to Fifth Avenue, and when we reach the intersection and stand on the corner, he sweeps his hand at the array of shops, a grin on his face. "Pauper me, Isabel."

"Pauper you?"

"Yes, love. This is Fifth Avenue, honey, one of the most expensive streets in the world, along with Rodeo Drive in L.A. and Rue St. Honore in Paris. I'm giving you *carte blanche* to go into any store and buy anything you wish." He winks at me. "Every girl's dream, I think."

"I don't even know where to start, Logan. I've not done much shopping."

He tugs on my hand. "Well then, let's start simple—with a woman's best friend."

With that cryptic remark, he leads me into a jewelry store—Tiffany and Company—which makes more sense of the comment: diamonds. I spend a few minutes just perusing, and I'm overwhelmed.

"I don't know, Logan. They're all beautiful, but . . . maybe this sounds bizarre, but I don't even know what I should like."

He laughs. "That is pretty weird, Is. But it shouldn't be too hard; just look at the stuff, and if something grabs your eye, point it out and I'll buy it."

"Just like that?"

"If you like it, yeah, just like that."

So I look again, this time just letting my gaze flit and float from piece to piece. I'm starting to wonder if there's something wrong with me, because nothing catches my eye. But then . . . I see a necklace in the shape of a key.

I point it out, and an elderly woman behind the counter drapes it over a black felt stand for me to examine. My heart is pounding, for some odd reason.

And then, when I touch it, I understand why.

The moment my finger touches the diamond-encrusted key—

*I am a little girl. In my mother's room. The sea crashes somewhere in the distance. I shouldn't be in here, but I just want to look at Mama's box. It is a hand-carved thing of polished reddish-brown wood, and it has all of Mama's keepsakes and jewelry in it, which I want to look at. There is a little brass lock in the front, keeping it closed.*

*I tug on the lid, but it is locked.*

*"You want to see inside, mija?" Mama's voice comes from behind me.*

*I startle, spin. "I just wanted to look, Mama. I wasn't going to—"*

*She lifts the box in both hands, holding it reverently. Sits on the bed, pats a spot beside her. "Come, sit." She smiles down at me. "This is a very special box, Isabel. You know why?"*

*I nod. "Because it has your jewelry in it."*

*Mama shakes her head negative. "No, mija, although that is true. Even if the box were empty, it would be special. And if someone were to tell me I had to choose between the box and all the gold and silver and diamonds and pearls in the world, I would choose the box."*

*I am confused now. I touch the lid, carefully. It just seems like a wooden box, not even a very well-made one.*

*Mama laughs. "Would you like to hear the story?" I nod, of course. "Your papa made this box, many years before you were born. Now your papa, he is the best goldsmith in all of Spain, as you and I both know. But he is not so good with wood. But still, he made this box, and he made it just for me. It was the only gift he ever gave me, until after we got married, but that was fine with me. You see, I don't know if you know this or not,* but when I was young, there were a lot of young men who wanted to marry me. I told them all no, which made my parents upset, but they were all so dull. Rich and handsome, perhaps, but boring and stupid. And then I met your father. He wasn't rich, and he was—well, handsome to me, but not like the other boys. His hair was always in his eyes, and he didn't play football like the other boys. But I liked him. He was apprenticed to a goldsmith, which meant he worked very hard all day, every day. We spent a lot of time together, all of his time he could spare from work, and from sleep. I grew to love him, but of course I couldn't tell him that. I had to wait for him, because back then, that's how it was done. I was waiting, Isabel, for so long. And you know, I knew he loved me too. He was silly with it, like boys get. And you know, men get even sillier than boys, when they're in love. But don't tell your father I said that. I was waiting, and waiting. And one day, when I was very impatient because I hadn't seen my sweet Luis in almost a week, he finally showed up in my parents' courtyard, holding this box.

I was excited, thinking he'd come to propose, or to give me a very fancy gift.

But no, it was only the box. A simple, not very well-made box. I was confused. But your father told me that, even though he loved me, he couldn't ask me to marry him, even though he wanted to. He had to finish his apprenticeship first, and then he had to find enough work to support us. My father respected that, and of course he liked it because he hoped I'd find another, wealthier boy to marry in the meantime.

"Luis told me the box was a promise. A promise that he would marry me, one day. Of course, I took the box. Yes, I told him, I would wait for him. I tried to open it, but it wouldn't open. It was locked."

Mama reaches into the front of her shirt and pulls out a brass key on a red ribbon, lifts it off her neck, and hands it to me; it is still warm from her skin.

"Luis told me that he had already made the ring he would propose to me with, and that it was in the box. He'd saved and saved all of his money, rather than taking me on fancy expensive dates or buying me presents, so *he could buy the diamond and pay his goldsmith master for the gold, so he could design and build the ring. Again, I tried to open the box, but of course, it was still locked. And that was when Luis showed me the key. 'When I ask you to marry me, Camila, I will ask you by giving you this key. And if you accept the key, you are not only accepting the key to this box and the ring inside, but the key to my heart.'"*

*I stare at the key for a long, long time. "So this is the key? To open the box?"*

*Mama nods. "Yes." She turns the box on her lap so it faces me. "Go on, mija. Open it."*

*I insert the key, twist; the lock disengages with a tiny quiet snick. Mama lifts open the lid, and I gasp. Inside, lying in little felt trays, are gold rings, gold necklaces, gold bracelets, gold earrings. Each piece is unique, and ornate, and beautiful. Handmade by my own papa.*

*"Each of the things in the box your father made me, and gave to me on the anniversary of the day he asked me to marry him. He got down on one knee and held up the key to me, holding it in both hands like he was a knight and I was his queen."*

*"And you said yes?"*

*Mama laughs. "Well, of course, silly girl! We had you, didn't we?" She closes the lid, turns the key to lock the box, and then holds the key on her palm. "This key, mija, it is worth more to me than anything else in the whole world, except your papa and you."*

*She hands me the key, and this time I look at it more carefully.*

*It is just a brass key, plain, burnished, simple. There is but one simple set of teeth on the stem, rounded, old, worn. The bow of the key, where one holds it to turn it in the lock, it is the most beautiful part of the key. It is a circle, but within the circle is an ornate flower blossom, symmetrical, four petals at the four compass points of the circle, connected by delicate filigree, at the center a knotwork design.*

*"I don't think there are many women in the world who can say they*

*have the literal, physical key to their husband's heart on a ribbon between their breasts,* mija. *Which makes me the luckiest woman in the world, because your father's heart . . . it is what makes my own continue to beat every single day."*

jerk my hand away, gasping.

The memory sears me, sits heavy in my heart. God, the love my mother had for my father . . . it is staggering.

And this key, the ornate, diamond-encrusted thing on the pedestal, it reminds me of that key. Obviously so, because it sparked such a powerful memory merely by touching it.

Logan lifts the necklace in his hands, moves to stand behind me. I feel my mother, in that moment, I feel the way she would move, if my father were to fasten a necklace around her throat. She would gather her thick hair, black as raven's wings, in her hands, drape it over one shoulder, tilt her head forward. Papa would fasten the catch with his thick but nimble fingers, and then he would gather Mama's hair in his hands, and she would lean back against him, look up at him, craning her neck to peer into his eyes.

My hair is too short to gather into my hands, to drape over my shoulder, but I feel Logan behind me, feel his fingers working to fasten the clasp. And I am my mother in that moment, leaning back against the man I love, twisting my head up to look into Logan's face, feeling the love in his eyes.

Logan accepts a little hand mirror, and I look at the key, hanging just so between my breasts. It is a beautiful thing, the key. Made of platinum and white gold, with hundreds of tiny diamonds lining each side from bow to stem. The petals of the flower within the bow are each large teardrop diamonds, and the center of the blossom is a stunning square yellow diamond.

Logan spins me in place. His eyes ask the question.

"This, Logan. Please?" I wish I could explain the meaning, but I cannot. Not yet. I need a moment or two to process the memory, to internalize it.

I just need a moment alone with the memory, before I share it.

I hear Logan speaking to the clerk. The price staggers me—twenty-two thousand dollars. I expect him to haggle, at least, but Logan pays it without a squabble, handing the woman a card to swipe, signing a slip, and then he's guiding me outside.

I lift the key, gaze at it. "I'm sorry, Logan, I didn't know it would cost that much."

He laughs. "Are you kidding? I'm glad you found something you like." He tips my chin up so I'm looking into his one bright blue eye. "I have money, Isabel. Plenty. More than plenty. You could shop for weeks and not put a dent in it. So don't apologize."

"All right. I just was shocked when she told you the price."

"It means something to you?" He says it somewhere between a statement and a question.

I nod. "Yes. I . . . remembered something else."

"You don't have to share it, if you're not ready, Is. I'll never pry, okay? I'm just happy you're not only making new memories with me, but getting old ones back too."

I am near tears. Blink them back. "I don't know how to thank you, Logan. For the necklace, but also for—today. The ferry ride, getting a few memories back. I cannot tell you what it means to me."

"That's thanks enough, Isabel. I love you. Anything I can do, I will." He shrugs. "But honestly, it just seems like luck, sort of, you know? I wasn't setting out to get you your memories back, since there's no way to know what will or won't trigger something."

"It's not luck, Logan. It's you. You . . ." I have to think hard about what I'm trying to say. "You're bringing me to life."

He touches the key where it rests between my breasts. "Aside from what it obviously triggered for you, it's apropos, you know? Because I don't feel like I'm bringing you to life, I'm just . . . opening doors for you. Unlocking the life that was already there, so you can live it."

He takes my hand, and we walk for a while. Finally, while in line in the Godiva store, picking out chocolates, I feel ready to share the memory.

So I tell it to him as I remembered it, and I can recite my mother's words verbatim.

When I'm done, Logan and I are outside again, munching on truffles. Logan is quiet a few beats, and then he laughs softly, shakes his head. "Goddamn, that was smooth. Your pops had *moves*, Is. He literally proposed to her with the key to his heart? That's romance right there, man." He bends close to me, licks chocolate off the corner of my mouth, and then kisses me. "I can't promise I'll be able to come up with anything *that* romantic, but I'll sure as hell try."

"I don't think anyone could live up to the standard my father set in that regard, Logan. And I don't need you to try. Just be you. Love me, and that will always be so much more than enough."

He tugs me flush against him, his palm warm and strong against my spine. "You make it easy to love you."

"I nearly got you killed. I cost you your eye. How does that count as easy?"

"Men have fought wars over the love of a woman, Isabel. And trust me when I say you're the kind of woman wars are fought for."

It's easier to shop after that. He follows me from store to store, sometimes suggesting we go into a certain one. I buy dresses, skirts, tops, shoes, everything wildly expensive. Logan never bats an eye. I've been keeping a loose tally, and if my math is correct, we surpassed a hundred thousand dollars quite a while ago. Logan is heavily laden with bags, half a dozen in each hand, a huge one hanging off his shoulder.

I take pity on him, though he's not uttered one word of complaint, and indeed, he seems to be actively enjoying watching me splurge.

"I think I've spent enough of your money, Logan. Let's take this stuff home."

He glances at his watch. "Sounds good to me. We've got to get changed for dinner and the show anyway."

We catch another Uber home. Set the bags down, sort through them, pick an outfit for tonight, strip for the shower . . . and up on the counter, beneath Logan, which has us running late for our dinner reservation. Not that I mind.

Dinner is a fancy affair at an upscale place somewhere in what Logan tells me is Hell's Kitchen. I don't recall the name, or the cross streets. I don't really care, not today. I'm all about the experience, letting Logan take care of the details. I follow him on foot from our home to the nearest subway station for my first subway ride. It is a revelatory experience, sitting in the inward-facing seats, holding on to the bar, watching the wide variety of people. Old, young, white, black, brown, Asian, rich, poor, clean, dirty, self-absorbed, alert. There is nothing connecting any of them—any of *us*—except this moment on this train.

We are ascending the stairs to street level now. I wind my fingers through Logan's and share a slice of my thoughts. "When I lived in the condo in Caleb's tower, there would be many, many hours of my life that were just utterly . . . empty. One can only read for so long, you know? One of my only pastimes was to look out the window and watch the people coming and going. There was never any lack of passersby, so I could stand at that window for hours, just watching them go past. I would imagine lives for them, create entire stories about them. I still do it, sometimes. If I'm having trouble processing my emotions, or I'm just overwhelmed, I'll end up people-watching, and imagining stories for them. I would create these elaborate histories for the strangers walking under my window, I think, because I had no history of my own."

Logan nods. "There's a word that sort of encapsulates that idea: *sonder*. It's the realization or understanding that each person passing by you or sitting next to you on the train or whatever, that everyone has their own life, their own complex network of friends and relatives, their own stories. I picture each person having a thread that follows them, and it's a tangled, knotted, interwoven thread with a million individual skeins, but if you could follow that thread, it would eventually, somehow, intersect with yours. Sometimes it's just that individual moment, where you and that person occupy the same space for a single heartbeat, and other times that person might be more intimately connected to you in a way you'd never have imagined."

"*Sonder*. I like that word."

By this time, we're at the restaurant, where we're told it will be a bit of an additional wait, as we're a few minutes late for our reservation. Logan leans close to the hostess, an attractive young woman wearing a dress that reveals more than it covers, has a brief whispered conversation that also involves a surreptitiously passed bribe. I don't know what he said or how much he bribed the hostess, but it clearly worked, since she leads us to an empty table immediately.

When we're seated and Logan has ordered us a bottle of wine, I question him about it. "What did you say to the hostess? And how much did you bribe her to get us this table?"

Logan laughs. "Oh, I didn't bribe her. I just showed her my business card." He slides one out of his wallet and hands it to me. It bears his name, a cell phone number, an e-mail address, and nothing else.

"So? I don't understand."

He taps at the bottom of the menu: *Owned and operated by Ryder Enterprises, LLC.* "This was the very first business I started, when I moved to New York getting out of prison. I figured a restaurant was a safe bet for an ex-con, right? As long as the food and the service is good, the environment quiet and the atmosphere pleasant, the clientele won't care whether or not the owner has an arrest record."

"So you own this restaurant?"

He shrugs. "Yeah. I actually worked as the manager for the first year it was open, too. I had limited capital, and I didn't want to blow it all right off the bat. So I took it slow. Got directly involved, made sure this place was stable, made sure I personally hired a quality manager, good waitstaff, a great head chef. Once I was sure this place would turn a profit, I started sniffing around for my next venture, but I stayed involved here still, more as the owner than the manager, at that point. Now, with all the other shit I've got going on, I'm rarely here, but I figure since I own the place, I might as well take advantage of it, right?"

"I thought you sold off businesses once they were turning a profit?"

He shakes his head. "Not all of them. One of the most important things as an entrepreneur is to make sure you always have multiple streams of income. Never rely solely on one venture, if you can help it. Diversify, diversify, diversify. So I've kept ownership of . . . oh, a dozen or so various enterprises. This place, a chain of auto parts stores out in the Midwest, Detroit, Chicago, Milwaukee, that region. There's a security firm for B-list celebs out in Hollywood, um . . . God, it's hard to remember them all. I don't have anything to do with the day-to-day running of ninety-nine-point-nine percent of them. They're all owned under the overall umbrella of Ryder Enterprises, which is, basically, a management corporation. I've got a whole staff of efficiency experts, transparency officers, troubleshooters, sales account managers, shit like that. Unless there's a major, major problem, I just file the taxes and rake in the profit. Oh, there's a chain of cinemas down south, small-town, single-screen sorts of places. Um, a couple different gas station franchises, three—no, four, luxury car dealerships, one here in Manhattan, one in Atlanta, one in San Diego, and . . . shit, where's the last one? Seattle."

I wrinkle my brow as I sip my wine, the one half glass I'm allowing myself. "I thought you flipped other businesses? I'm confused again. What is it you actually do, Logan?"

This gets me a laugh. "After I got out of prison, I had a decent chunk of start-up capital stashed down in the Bahamas, one of those private, offshore, numbered accounts. I'd been siphoning my income there via a complicated network of transfers while I was working for Caleb. Security, you know? I needed to know, if something went wrong, that I'd have some cash to start over. Well, good thing I did that, because obviously, something went wrong and I had to start over. And I started over by starting small. This was a floundering restaurant when I bought it. It was a sushi place, I think, and not a great one. So I gutted it, remodeled the interior, gave it a new identity. Upscale, a simple but elegant menu, efficiently run, good service. I sank maybe a quarter of my capital into this place between the purchase and the remodel, but it started turning me a decent profit within three years. It was stable and climbing toward the black by the end of the first year, though, so I knew I was good to start looking for my next endeavor, which was the car dealership here in Manhattan: BMW, Lexus, and Range Rover. High initial cost, but quick returns." He searches my face. "Am I boring you?"

"Sort of, yes," I admit. "I'm not a businesswoman."

"Okay, short version, then." He takes a swallow of wine, pauses so we can order our dinner, and then starts over. "I started out buying businesses, anything I could find that I could afford and that I thought would turn a quick profit. Once I'd gotten my investment back from each business I bought, I would invest in another. And meanwhile, each business would be turning me a profit, increasing the cushion between my investment and my income. I would invest, restructure if necessary, get involved to make sure it was running, and then I'd move on to the next venture after I was sure the company could run without me. I did a lot of traveling in those early years. I was an independent business owner, essentially, and that was it. But after a few years, my income was enough and my diversity of businesses broad enough that I figured it'd be safe to let that spread of companies be my stability, so I set up Ryder Enterprises, the management company, to run them without my input. And then I started doing what I do now, which is what you saw, what I've told you about—flipping corporations. Mostly stocks, tech, investment, securities analytics, high-dollar, white-collar sorts of stuff. See, there are millions of businesses out there, thousands just here in New York. And at any given time, there are always some that are barely making it. I buy them up at a bottom-dollar price, since they're about to go under, and then I either jigger things internally so they'll start turning a profit, or I disassemble them and transfer their accounts to a different company, usually one I own, which I then sell at a profit. You ever see *Pretty Woman*? I'm kind of like Richard Gere's character in that movie, just . . . hopefully less of a dick than he was."

"What about the people who work for the businesses when you tear them apart?"

"Well, that's what sets me apart. I always make sure there's somewhere for everyone to land. I've got a whole team dedicated to referrals, connecting employees to headhunters, things like that."

"So this restaurant, the gas stations, and the movie theaters, you just own them?"

"Right. They're income stability. So even if I make a colossal blunder, make a bad investment and lose a shitload of money, the Ryder Enterprises spread of companies can sustain me in comfort." He bobs his head side to side. "Can sustain *us* in comfort, I mean."

I expect Logan to have our bill comped, since he owns the restaurant, but instead he pays it and leaves a rather significant tip for the waitress, who I don't think had any idea she was serving the owner.

And then a long walk block after block back to the theater district. We take our seats just as the house lights are lowered.

The show is . . . unlike anything I've ever experienced. Bursting with energy, music that soars and sweeps and hints at the Middle Eastern origins of the story. The dancing! The singing! It's all too much, and I want to sing and dance with them. The Genie, especially, is a delight, such wild, joyous, frenetic energy, presence that dominates the stage, the whole theater.

I am raving as we leave the theater, chattering more than I think I have since I woke up from the coma. Logan is listening, attentive, but seems content to let me talk, to merely enjoy this admittedly rare bout of effusiveness from me.

It is past ten o'clock now, but the city is still manic, bustling. Lights flash and blink, voices rise in a pleasing din. A policeman on a huge black horse trots past, watchful, alert. The crowd of people leaving the theaters takes over the streets, so the cars trying to ply their way from one avenue to another must inch slowly between the gaggles of theatergoers. I chatter about my favorite songs, about the Genie, about how fun the show was, how Logan has to take me to see as many shows as he can spare the time for.

All the while, Logan has my hand and is taking us somewhere specific.

To a place in the heart of the theater district called Junior's. It is crammed with people, every table occupied, and the hostesses are telling people it's a twenty- to thirty-minute wait minimum. Logan puts his name in and then finds me a seat, stands in front of me. I've run out of words by this time, though, and now we're quiet.

But I like this, too, that we can sit together in silence, content to merely *be*.

It seems Junior's is famous for its cheesecake, and Logan doesn't have to ask me twice to convince me to order a piece of chocolate cheesecake. Which, when it arrives with Logan's coffee and my tea, is mammoth. More cheesecake than I think any one person should be able to eat all at once; that is my thought when it arrives, at least. But yet by the time I've set down my fork, I've eaten very nearly the whole thing.

Cheesecake eaten, Logan pays the bill and yet again leaves a fabulously generous tip, and then leads me back to Times Square, which at night is a simply magical place. The lights, the way the TVs shine and flicker and shift, the advertisements for all the shows, the contagious air of vivacity that infuses the crowd . . . it is truly magical. We sit on the steps and watch people, and I take the time to process everything I've experienced today. The ferry, the memories I regained, the key necklace, which is now nestled between my breasts, exactly the way Mama wore hers.

I am sitting a step below Logan, between his knees. I lift up, twist, and kiss him until someone hoots at us, and someone else tells us to get a room. I smooth my palm over the stubble on his cheek. "Logan, I know I already said this, but thank you so much for today. It was . . . I think this was the best day of my life."

Logan's eyes go down to my cleavage, but the speculative gleam in his eyes tells me he's looking more at the key, and I wonder what he's thinking.

Marriage?

I'm having a baby, possibly his.

And possibly . . . not his.

So what do I want?

To belong to Logan forever, of course. To be utterly, irrevocably his. To know that no matter what else life throws at us, we will belong together, side by side, hand in hand, lives tangled and braided and inextricably woven together.

Yes, I want to marry Logan.

And I cannot wait to discover how he will ask me. Because he will. I know he will.

It's just a matter of when, and how.

I am not impatient, I realize. He will ask me in his way, in his time. And it will not disappoint, because Logan is incapable of disappointing me.

Love is patient, I remember reading somewhere.

# EIGHT

ess than forty-eight hours later, early in the morning. Four thirteen A.M., so says the digital clock on Logan's bedside table. There's a pounding on the door. A fist, hammering wildly. Cocoa goes nuts in her room, clawing at the door, barking like a demon. Snarling. Logan is out of bed, tugging on jeans, jogging to the door.

"Shit," I hear him mutter under his breath.

I'm in one of his button-downs, the hem coming to midthigh. Behind him, peering past him, as if I could see through the door. But the sinking lead ball in my stomach tells me who's on the other side.

Logan's curse tells me.

He jerks open the door, puts his body into the crack. "The fuck you want, Caleb?"

"What is *mine*." Your voice is mad, animal snarl.

"Dude. We've been over this. You let her go, remember? You let her go. She's with *me* now. It's what she wants. Just . . . let her go. Please. For her."

A moment of silence, and an explosion of violence. Logan is

knocked backward, and you are lunging through the doorway. I shrink back against Cocoa's door. She's wild, barking, snarling, scrabbling. Tearing the door down like she did when Logan was gone.

Not this. Not again.

Logan is up on his feet, bleeding from his lip. "Back off, motherfucker. Just leave before this gets messy, huh?"

But you are lightning, you are a striking serpent. Pistol whipping out, a black blur, the point jammed up into Logan's chin. "I will *not* miss a second time, Ryder."

You twist the barrel into Logan's flesh. Turn, see me. Your eyes flash, your lip curls. "X. Get over here. *Now.*"

I rise to my feet. Straighten my spine. "No, Caleb. It's over. I don't want to see you anymore. Never again."

"Isabel." This, from you, is a plea. Low, vicious, desperate. "You *must.*"

"No." I gesture at Logan. "I love him. If you kill him, you will have to kill me as well."

"Isabel—" Logan grunts.

"No. You shut the fuck up, Ryder." Your voice is a rabid, grating snarl. Rough, unstable. To me, then: "Isabel."

You wander away from Logan, but the gun stays trained on him. To me. Stumbling, nearly. Uncharacteristically uncoordinated. Not drunk; your eyes are lucid. Mad. Crazed. I don't even know. I glance at Logan. Plead with him silently to stay put. I will not allow you to shoot him again.

"You don't need the gun, Caleb." I make sure my voice is cool, calm.

"You'll come with me?"

"No."

"Then I need the gun. You are mine. You will come with me." Your voice is . . . not yours. Not Caleb's. Almost as if you are regressing. Becoming Jakob, somehow. Someone less refined, less in control. The Czech is showing through in your rhythms and diction.

"I can't, Caleb. I do not belong to you. Not anymore. I'm with Logan now."

A snarl. The gun levels at Logan. "Then he is dead. He should have already been dead. He does not get to have you. Only I."

"Caleb, please." I touch his wrist. Urge him to lower the gun. "Please don't do this. Don't."

Your hand latches onto my wrist. You jerk me hard, so I fly through the air, land against you. "Mine—only mine. Not his."

"Caleb, let go. You're hurting me."

"Let her go, asshole!" Logan shouts.

Cocoa's claws are gouging through the door.

Logan lunges again, and you fire. Miss. A hole appears in the wall to Logan's left.

"A warning, only. For her. Back." You grab me by the throat.

Twist me so my back is to your front. The gun jabs at Logan. Your fingers pinch against my throat. I cannot breathe. I don't think you realize what you're doing.

"Let her go, Caleb," Logan murmurs, careful now. Voice low, slow, soft. "Let her go. You're hurting her. You're choking her."

You glance down, let me go with a start. But then you grab me once more, this time one of my wrists, the other, pinioning them in one of your hands behind my back. Propelling me to the door.

"Caleb—" I start.

"Silence." You push me to the door. Let me go. Twist in place to cover Logan with the gun. "You. On your knees."

"Not gonna happen, man. You can shoot me if that's your game. You did once, already. I survived that."

"You will not survive a bullet in your brain," you say, and jerk open the front door.

The alarm has been blaring this whole time. I didn't even notice until now. I don't think anyone has.

Logan watches with agony on his face, watching Caleb take me away yet again.

"Caleb, wait!" Logan pleads.

"No waiting. She is mine." This is not you. This is Jakob, someone I do not know. Someone I can predict even less than I could Caleb.

"You don't understand, Caleb. It's Isabel . . ." He steps around front, accepts the barrel of Caleb's gun to his forehead. "She's pregnant."

You go stone-still. Your eyes search Logan. I, between you, see this. See the hunt for the truth in your eyes on Logan's.

"No." You shake your head. A denial. A refusal to accept it.

"Yes, Caleb." I whisper it.

"His?" You turn your gaze to me.

"I—I don't know." I despise myself for having to admit this. "It could be either of yours. There is no way to know, yet."

A moment of frozen, fraught silence.

"*Kurva.*" This, in a language I do not know, from you; Czech, most likely. It has the tone of an epithet. "A baby?"

"Yes." I turn in place, look up at you.

"*Kurva*—a baby." You look down at me, as if I am a creature you have never seen before.

There is a depth in your eyes, a wrecked, mortal agony in those dark brown pools that is awful to see in a man ordinarily so closed off and stoic. You search my face. Hands at your sides, gun held casually, easily, forgotten.

"Isabel . . ." This, from you, is a whisper. A plea. A moment of weakness. A caress, with a word. Softness from a stone. Love, even, from a razor blade.

And then, without a word, you're gone. Just . . . gone. You turn, and flee. Run swiftly, desperately. Round a corner, and gone.

Logan and I both stare after you.

Logan wraps his arms around me, hauls me inside. Carries me. Sets me down on the couch. Lets out Cocoa, who sniffs me and then Logan, tail wagging, murmuring softly, whining.

"What the hell was *that*?" Logan asks, taking a seat beside me and curling his arms around me, pulling me against his chest.

I shake my head. "I . . . I don't know. He's coming apart."

"He certainly seemed . . . unstable."

"It was frightening. That was not Caleb. That was nothing like the man I've known these last six years. He is always so . . . in control. Strong. Stoic. Emotionless." I gesture vaguely. "That? That was . . . I am worried. For him. For me, for us. I never quite knew what he might do, but now? After seeing him that way . . . I am afraid."

"Understandable. That was one of the weirdest things I've ever experienced." The next is more to himself than to me. "It's almost as if he has multiple personalities or something. To be so completely unlike himself . . ."

"What is that?"

He glances at me. "What? Oh. MPD, multiple personality disorder. It's where a person goes through something so extremely traumatic that the mind sort of . . . compartmentalizes, in a way. Cuts out the part of the mind that contains those memories. But instead of just suppressing or repressing them or whatever, the mind will create a different personality, an entirely new psychological entity that is tougher, that can deal with the trauma or whatever it was. If . . . Jakob—the guy born in Prague—went through something really truly awful, he might have created Caleb as a way to deal with it. If Jakob felt overwhelmed and weak and victimized and out of control, he would have created a personality like Caleb, you know? Someone strong, dominant, in control. And now, losing you, somehow it has fractured Caleb's hold on Jakob, if you know what I mean. Like Caleb has been in control this whole time, and now Jakob is breaking through."

"You think that is the case?"

He shrugs. "I mean, it's all speculation. Only a trained psychologist could really diagnose something like that. It's just a totally wild guess. Caleb could just be losing his shit in the more normal sense. Just . . . cracking up."

"It worries me, either way. I never caught even a hint of any of this from him until recently."

"No way to really know, unfortunately. And he's not your problem, anymore. Your concern now is being healthy. Taking care of this baby."

I breathe out slowly, a shuddery breath. "The baby." I put my hand on my belly. "It doesn't feel real. And I don't . . . I don't even know what to do next."

"Well, we get you a doctor, number one. Make sure you're healthy, all that. And then, number two, I think you should talk to someone. A therapist. Try to make some kind of sense of . . . everything. And eventually, you need to make some decisions regarding your future, and our future."

"What decisions?"

"Well, you've been staying here sort of out of default, because there was nowhere else. But is that what you want? How do you want to structure your life? Do you want to keep living with me here? Do you want to keep working on getting Comportment off the ground, or does being pregnant change that?"

"God, Logan. That's too much. Too many questions. I don't know. I don't know any of that!" I feel stifled, my lungs compressed, my mind crammed so full of such a wild whirling maelstrom of thoughts and emotions that I can't think, can't sit still, can't take anymore.

I shoot to my feet, pace away. "I need to get out of here. I feel crazy. It's all too much." I clutch my head in both hands, feeling as if the crushing weight of everything that is my life is about to explode out of my skull. "I can't be here anymore. I have to—I don't know. I don't know."

I could scream from the burden of it all. Caleb, Logan, the baby, my past—and the lack thereof. The brief snippets of memory that hint at a wonderful childhood, and the not-so-pleasant glimpses at something far more nefarious between Caleb and me. Lies. Truths. Illusory tapestries woven with skeins of both lies and truth. Six years, nine years. A mugger, a car accident. Did I know him before? Did he cause the accident somehow? Has all this been a plot of his devising? How can I care for a child when I am not even a person, but a ghost, a shred of a soul lost in limbo? I am no one, I am nothing. I am the *Starry Night*, and *Madame X*. I am a shaven-headed girl in a hospital bed. I am a blank slate, a tabula rasa on which a mysterious man named Caleb Indigo has inscribed his imprint. I am Rapunzel, locked in the tower, raven-haired instead of blond. I am Belle, prisoner of a Beast, a thing of shadows and magic and primal carnality. The least of the threads that comprise me is Isabel.

Logan is beside me, grabbing me, turning me to face him. "Look at me, Isabel." He tilts my chin up with a fingertip. "Breathe. Take a breath. Look at me, and take a moment."

I focus on breathing, focus on Logan's gaze, the brilliant indigo soothing me. He found his patch at some point, the brown leather one. I don't remember him putting it on. Truth be told, it's a relief when he puts it on. I feel horrible for it, but looking at the bare, raw, healing wound is . . . too much. Too hard to look at. It makes my stomach churn to know how close he came to death.

But that train of thought only upsets me more.

Am I crying, yet again? I have wept so much, of late.

I feel listless. I see you, over and over and over. The man in the tower, dressed impeccably, the master of his world. The rutting beast, the controlling, dominating sexual conqueror, the man who can ensnare my mind and my body and my emotions, bend me to your will, get me on my knees and on my back. The silent aggressor, the man who will always get your way. The man in room three, on your knees behind Rachel, fucking her from behind, your eyes on me, Rachel's eyes on me. Rachel enjoyed that, knowing I was watching. So did you. I see you, Caleb. I do not see Jakob. Not until the night in my room, a month ago. When you did not fuck me, did not control me, but kissed me and made love to me, and spoke my name with something like reverence. The way you shut down abruptly when I spoke the name "Caleb" rather than "Jakob." You were not you, then. That was a man I could have loved. Perhaps that was the man I *did* love, when I was Isabel, the first time, the sixteen-year-old Isabel, the errant, school-skipping girl infatuated with an older man. I see you, the mixed-up, unstable, violent creature who was just here. Yelling, cursing in Czech, tripping over your own feet. Running away.

"Enough." Logan lifts me in his arms.

I let him.

He deposits me in the bathroom, on the closed lid of the toilet. Starts the shower. Adjusts the water. Pulls me to my feet, unbuttons the shirt. Guides me in under the spray. This isn't sexual. I wish it were, I would like the distraction from my thoughts. But it's not. Instead, he washes me gently, shampoos my hair, rinses it, and wraps me in a towel. Dries me, dabbing and patting and rubbing. Guides me to the bedroom. I sit on the edge of the bed and watch as he grabs clothes from the closet and the bureau. His clothes, mine. Underwear, T-shirts, jeans, socks. Several days' worth of clothing. And then he dresses me.

I am little help, my mind has shut down. I am content to do whatever Logan wishes, let him take me wherever he wishes to take me. I cannot bear anything more. He slides underwear up my legs. Slides my arms through the straps of a bra, and I cooperate in fastening it the rest of the way. Hands me a pair of jeans and a sweater. I put those on while Logan showers, a military-fast shower. Three minutes, at most. Emerges naked, hair damp. Dresses with military efficiency, ties his hair back, packs the clothes into a black hard-sided suitcase. He doesn't fold the clothing, however, but rolls it into tight rolls. I notice this, and find it odd. And then, packed and dressed, he makes two phone calls. One, to Beth. Arranging for Cocoa to be looked after for a few days, and to make sure the office knows he will be out of touch and out of town, to handle whatever comes up as best they can, leave a voice mail in case of emergency. The next call is, from what I can tell, to arrange a flight somewhere. Leaving now, today.

What time is it? Morning? Night? I don't know. I glance at the clock on the bedside table: 5:05 a.m. Fifty-two minutes since the first knock on the door.

In the car, then. Logan's Mercedes SUV. Radio off, heat on. The air outside has a chill to it, and the interior of the SUV is cold. It is still dark.

A long, long drive in silence. Logan drives with his left hand, holds my hand with his right, fingers tangled. Eventually I lean my seat back and drowse, but do not let go of his hand.

I wake up, and we are parked . . . I don't know where. Nothingness as far as I can see. The sky is gray now, a tinge of orange-pink on the horizon. A building off to my right, long, high, impossibly large. Blue lights in lines and rows all around. To my left, an airplane. A jet, but not a large one. Small, only four or five windows, and an opening with a staircase that can be rolled away. Lights blink, and engines roar.

Logan opens my door, and someone else fetches the suitcase from the trunk. Up the stairs, Logan's hand on my back. The interior of the jet is luxurious. Six pairs of seats, in rows of two, an aisle between. Each seat is deep, upholstered in creamy leather. Plush carpeting. A huge television. A woman in a uniform, waiting, hands clasped behind her back.

"Welcome, Mr. Ryder. My name is Amanda. It will be my absolute pleasure to serve you and your guest this morning. Please, be seated. Can I get you coffee, to start?" Her voice is bright and cheerful.

I take a seat in the middle row, against the window. I only pay partial attention to Logan talking to the flight attendant. A mug is pressed into my hand; tea, piping hot. He has coffee when he sits down beside me.

"Isabel?" His voice, sun-warm, worried. "You haven't said a word in a long time."

"It's all too much."

"Sleep, then. We have a long flight ahead of us."

I should ask where we're going, but I don't seem capable of curiosity at the moment. I watch dawn break out the window as Logan speaks with the captain, discussing flight patterns or something like that. Logan buckles me in. The plane taxies, and then velocity presses me into my seat, my stomach sinks, and we're airborne. Up, up, up over the clouds.

When we are no longer climbing, Logan unbuckles me, places a pillow on his lap, takes my now-cold tea from me, and pulls me to lie on his lap.

I float, drift, sleep.

I wake up in Barcelona, Spain.

# NINE

A silver convertible BMW is waiting when Logan leads me out of the plane.

At first, nothing registers. Not when Logan inputs an address into the navigational system. Not when we leave the airport behind. It is hot, and the wind in my hair is soothing.

Nothing on the drive away from the airport registers as familiar.

But then, after what feels like an eternity, something flickers inside me. Like a lightbulb being screwed into a lamp whose switch has been turned on, so that the bulb flickers to life, dies, flickers again. The sea is to our left. The beach, separated from the road by a wide swath of dune grass. To our right, white condo buildings, three and four stories high, screened in by palm trees and bushes. This is what causes the flicker, the dim gleam. The sky is wide and endless and blue, dotted and hazed with clouds. There are people on the beach, families and couples and singles. A cyclist, a group of them. Someone running on the side of the road.

I know this place.

I have been here.

I have driven down this exact road. I have seen this condo before, that hillock of dune grass–covered sand leading down to the azure rippling waves of the Mediterranean. I do not remember, not precisely. I just . . . *feel* it. In my bones and my blood and my soul, I feel it. It is not painful, as I expect it to be.

It is . . . soothing.

Comforting.

I have never felt at home, before, but the sea, the sun, the sand . . . it feels familiar.

Logan pulls off the main road onto a smaller side street, which in turn leads to a narrow avenue wreathed in shadows cast by a bower of tall trees. A few meters down this avenue, and then into a driveway leading to a condo building. There is a keypad; Logan consults his phone, taps in a few numbers; a gate trundles aside, admitting us.

Reception, Logan speaking in halting, uncertain Spanish. Mangling it. *"There is a holding for one rooms, please, under name of rider."*

The receptionist, a woman, puts on a strained smile, attempting to decipher what he's saying.

Without thinking, I cut in, speak the first words in many, many hours. In Spanish. *"We have a reservation, I believe. Under Ryder, R-Y-D-E-R."*

Logan stares at me, stunned. "You speak Spanish?"

"Apparently." I duck my head. "I figured it out with Caleb. He said something, telling me a story about how we met, one of his lies, or maybe the truth, I don't know. He said something in Spanish, I could understand it. He said something else, and I understood that too."

"So just now, I was—"

"Making rather a mess of it, yes." I try to smile, to lessen the sting of the insult.

He just laughs. "Yeah, well, I used to speak it sort of fluently, but that was twenty years ago, and it was street-level Spanish—Spanglish more than anything. Enough to know when I was being insulted by my Hispanic buddies and insult them back."

"Much different than what is spoken here, I presume."

"Yeah, I'd guess."

The receptionist has our keys, speaking to me now, runs a spiel about incidental charges and room service and the elevator, hands me the key. I realize, as Logan carries the suitcase and leads the way to the elevator, that the receptionist was speaking rapidly, and that I followed her effortlessly, without even realizing she was speaking Spanish. How is that possible? I didn't even know I knew it until very recently. It has been six years, at least, but I am perfectly fluent.

The human mind is a strange and mysterious thing, I think.

Logan swipes the key card, shoves open the door. The room is bright, sunlight coming from outside, through the sliding glass door. Evening light, golden-crimson sun settling into the sea.

I move as if in a dream to the door, slide it open. Step out on the balcony.

Waves crash.

A seagull haws.

Chatter, in Spanish: *Mama, Mama! I made a sand castle, come look!—No,* mijo, *it's not time for supper yet, you just had a snack—She was talking about her cousin, who went on holiday to Greece last winter, and met a much older man. She's still seeing him, I hear* . . .

Oh, the ocean.

The soft, steady crash of waves on sand. The way the blue ripples endlessly, curling into white and breaking on the shore. The wheeling of gulls, tipping on a wing to flutter to the sand, scooping up some prize, yipping in triumph, defending against other thieving gulls.

The flicker in my mind brightens.
Whiteness.

*he sun is hot, blazing hot. Baking my shoulders and the top of my head. My feet are cool, though. The waves crash and wash up over my feet and calves, licking up to my knees. I am sitting in the dark brown wet sand at the water's edge, digging a hole. Digging, digging, digging. It's futile, of course. The ocean rushes up and over me, into the hole, filling it and caving in the edges, smoothing away the hole so there's barely even a divot remaining. And then I dig, dig, dig all over again, watch the hole vanish as if by magic. Behind me, a sand castle sits half ruined, partially obliterated by my own feet, after an hour of careful, painstaking construction. I was a giant, of course, and the castle was full of nasty little mortals. They had to be crushed, of course. I am hot enough to consider going in the water now. It will be cold, and the salt will sting my eyes and crust my skin when I get out, but it's worth it to cool off.*

*Behind me, I hear a giggle. It's a low, soft sound. Happy, delighted, amused. Mama. I stand up, brushing sand off my butt and hands. Turn, watch Mama and Papa. She is lying on her back. She is lovely, so elegant. Sexy. I learned this word at school recently, and I think my mama is sexy. Her bathing suit is rather small. I would never wear anything like that, I would be too afraid of people seeing me in my underwear. That's all it really is, Mama's bikini. She looks like a supermodel, I think. Her hair is loose, because it's always loose unless she's washing dishes. It's so long it comes down to nearly her bottom, and it's black as a crow's wing. Straight, thick, glossy. Her tummy is flat, but her boobies are big, and so is her butt. I've heard kids talking at school, and that's how women are supposed to look, they say. I wonder if I will look that way? Probably not. I'll never be as beautiful as Mama.*

*She's laughing because Papa is kissing her. She's lying on the big blan-*

ket Abuela made by knitting. Or crocheting? I don't know. She made it before I was born, and we always bring it to the beach with us. Mama is on her back, one knee up, the other leg straight out on the blanket. Papa is lying almost totally on top of her, like I saw them doing that one time by accident, only this time they have their clothes on. He's kissing her, all over. All over. Her mouth, her neck, her shoulders. She's laughing and laughing, telling him to stop, but not really. She doesn't actually want him to stop, I can tell, so I'm not sure why she's saying so. She's slapping his shoulder with one hand, but her other hand is in his hair. Adults are confusing. She tells him people are watching, that I'm watching.

He just says, "Let her watch, then, my love. She will see that her parents are in love."

More laughing, more kissing.

Yuck. But it's not yuck. I used to think it was gross when they kissed like that, but I'm old enough now to know that it is supposed to be romantic. Luisa's mama and papa don't kiss at all, she said. Sometimes they even sleep in separate rooms, because they argue so much. So maybe I'm lucky, because my mama and papa are in love and kiss each other and make each other laugh, and sleep in one room every night, and sometimes I hear them laughing and making lots of weird sounds late at night. I think that's having sex. Luisa said she saw her mama doing that with a man who wasn't her papa, and that's just weird. I'm not sure what sex is, but I know men and women do it together when they are in love, and maybe when they aren't, too. I'm not sure.

I am very hot now. Too hot. And Mama and Papa are just kissing now. No laughing. No saying stop. Just kissing, their faces so close, tilting their heads this way and that, Mama's fingers in Papa's hair, as if she's afraid he'll stop and she doesn't want him to get away.

So I go in the water. Tread out through the waves, up to my hips, and that's where I stop. I have to jump in now. But it's cold, and I always have to tell myself I'm brave enough to do it. Sometimes Papa will run up behind *me when I'm not paying attention and throw me in, and laugh, and tell me I have to just do it, or I'll think myself out of jumping in.*

*I look back, and Papa is still kissing Mama. But now she has her foot around his leg, and I think they will be kissing for a very long time.*

*So I jump in. Just jump. Deep breath, and jump. The water is cold, shockingly cold at first. But then I'm swimming under the water and I'm already used to it, and it feels wonderful.*

*I swim for a long time, chasing waves and pretending I'm a surfer like I saw on TV. I don't notice anything, forget everything but the water and the waves and the sun. I glance back at Mama and Papa, but they're sleeping. Under a blanket, even, which is weird considering how hot it is. But we're totally alone on this part of the beach, so who cares? Adults are weird, and I don't bother trying to figure out why they need a blanket in the summer.*

*It isn't until I feel the water start to surge and pull that I notice anything is amiss. I look up, and suddenly the sky is gray, and it looks heavy, as if the clouds are full of pencil lead and might break open. It is windy, too, and the waves are big. Too big. They crash over me, push and pull me, knock me under. I surface, kicking and pulling with my hands as hard as I can. I am a good swimmer, a regular old fish, like Papa says. But the waves are so strong, and I'm getting farther and farther from shore. A riptide, I think.*

*I finally get a breath, manage to spit out the salty water, and scream.*

*But I only get a little scream out before another wave pounds onto my head and spins me in a somersault, twisting me under the water until I don't know which way is up. I surface again, flailing now. I am very afraid, suddenly. I am having trouble breathing, and my legs and arms are tired, and the glimpse of shore I get through the smashing waves is far, far, far. I try to scream. Choke on water, spit it out, coughing, and scream again. Kick, kick, try to move with the waves, like a surfer. Like a fish, or dolphin. But the waves hit me like fists, over and over, and I am struggling, but weakness is like a heavy blanket tangling me up. Making it hard to kick, to pull with my hands.*

*To stay above the waves.*

*I can't. I am under. Not breathing. Trying to swim, but I can't. Fear is a knife in my heart. I'm not going to make it back up this time.*

*And then I feel a hand. It wraps around my hair and pulls HARD. My head breaks up over the surface, and then there's an arm under my armpits and a shoulder against my face.*

*"I've got you,* mija," *Papa says. It's Papa. "I've got you. You're all right. Kick your feet, okay? Kick with me."*

*I kick. I'm choking on the water, but now Papa's arm has me lifted up above the water, so I can finally catch my breath. I'm so tired. I try to kick, but my legs won't work.*

*"I can't, Papa." I sound small, and weak, and afraid.*

*"You have to, Isabel. The storm is coming. You have to kick . . . you have to help." He sounds out of breath too.*

*I look around and see that we are very far from shore, still. The sky is so dark it is almost like night, and there is rain pattering and pitting on the water, tickling my face, warm, and blowing in sheets by the wind. The wind, it is angry. The waves are like mountains.*

*I kick. I kick as hard as I can, to help Papa save us both.*

*"That's good,* mija. *Keep . . . kicking. We'll make it. Just keep—keep kicking."*

*It seems like we swim forever, Papa's strong arm under me, keeping me above the waves. I feel his legs kicking hard, tirelessly, ceaselessly, scissoring over and over and over. His other arm pulls, stabs out, pulls. He's gasping rhythmically, breathing hard. He's tired, too.*

*And then I feel sand under my toes. I put my feet down. "Papa, we made it. I can walk now."*

*He lets go, and I splash. It's at my chest, and the waves are big, and* strong, but Papa is so tired. I can see it, in the way he staggers to his feet. I am brave. I am strong. I will walk the rest of the way. But the waves keep hitting me, and I have to grab on to his hand for balance, or I will fall and go under.

The rain is falling very hard now. Like warm bolts hitting my head and my shoulders. It is raining so hard now that even walking is like swimming.

Papa glances down, sees me struggling to keep up. He lifts me in his arms, like a baby. I don't mind. I am tired, so tired, and fear is still worming through my blood, making it hard to breathe or to think or to move.

I feel him set me down, and Mama's arms are around me, her wet hair against my cheek, and she's crying. "Oh my baby, my baby. I thought I'd lost you."

"Papa saved me, Mama."

"I know. Your papa is very brave."

I open my eyes to see her looking up at him. Her eyes shine, and I can see tears on her face even though the rain is running all over her. Papa falls heavily to the sand beside us, puts his long strong arms around both of us, and we all just sit there in the rain together, breathing and glad to be alive, and on the shore.

Thunder booms like a cannon, and lightning lights up the dark gray skies.

"We have to go," Papa says. "The storm is getting worse."

We take Abuela's blanket, our now-sodden towels, the cooler full of juice and wine and crackers and cheese, and run for our car. We get in, wet still.

When we are almost home, Mama lays her head on Papa's shoulder. Swivels a little to look at me.

"You scared me, mija." It is as close to a scold as I've ever gotten from her.

"I'm sorry, Mama. I didn't realize it wasn't sunny anymore, or how far away I was. And then I couldn't get back."

"You shouldn't ever swim out that far by yourself anyway, even in good weather. Only if Papa or I are with you."

*"Well, I wanted to swim. It was hot and the sun was still out, then."*
*I frown. "And you and Papa were busy kissing under the blanket."*

*Mama hides an embarrassed smile against Papa's bare shoulder. "Next
time, come and get one of us and we'll swim with you. Okay?"*

*"Even if you're kissing like you don't want to ever stop?"*

*Mama laughs. "Yes, mija, even then."*

*I wonder what it would be like to never want to stop kissing someone?*

They loved each other." I am startled to hear myself speak.

"What?" Logan is behind me, arms around my front, cupping the front of my hip bones, chin on my shoulder.

"My parents. They loved each other very much."

"You remember something?"

"The beach." I point to the sand. "I was . . . oh, young. A little girl. We were at the beach. I went out to swim, and a storm blew in suddenly. I got pulled out and couldn't stay above the waves. I was about to drown when my father rescued me."

I stop, think. Capture the memory, savor it.

"I remember the fear. Being underwater and knowing I wasn't going to make it, and then Papa grabbed me. Even with him, we almost didn't make it back to shore. But . . . more than the almost-drowning, what I really remember is Mama and Papa. It's so strange how vivid the memory is. It's like I'm *there*, again. I remember what I was thinking, what I was feeling. Much different than even the memories I have postamnesia. But what really stands out is them. My parents, being in love. They were like kids, I think. Always touching each other. Kissing."

"Want to go out there?"

"In the water?" I twist to look at him.

"Yeah."

"Why are we here, Logan?"

A sigh. "Maybe being here will jog things for you. That's what I was thinking. You grew up here. And when you said you needed to get away, I thought, *Why not Spain? See if she remembers anything.*"

"It seems you were right. I don't know if I'll remember anything else, but even if that's all I remember, it will be worth it. Knowing my parents loved each other, and me . . . ?" I let go of the balcony railing and press my fingers between Logan's. "I didn't bring a bathing suit."

He just laughs. "*You* didn't bring anything. I packed for us, remember?"

He tosses the suitcase on the bed, opens it, rifles through the stacked rolls of clothes until he finds a pair of bright orange swim trunks, and then again until he comes up with two different bathing suits for me. One is a white one-piece, and the other is a rather skimpy pink-and-blue two-piece, little more than a few pieces of string and patches of fabric.

I hold up the two-piece. "Really, Logan?"

He shrugs. "I told her a one-piece and a two-piece. Didn't pick 'em, remember?" His eyes light up. "You could try it on for me, though, right? You don't have to wear it out if you don't want to."

"I'm pregnant, remember?" I suddenly don't want to put on either.

"Babe. You're not showing at all." He takes the bikini from me, tosses it into the suitcase. "But don't worry about it. You're gorgeous, no matter what you wear or don't wear. We're here to relax and get away from all the bullshit, so don't stress about the bathing suit."

He kisses me, a quick peck, and then grabs his trunks and moves toward the bathroom, peeling off his T-shirt on the way.

I watch, shamelessly, as he pees, then shucks his jeans and underwear. He does all this in the bathroom, but with the door open, so I'm able to watch in the reflection of the mirror. He turns as he's pulling up the trunks, just in time for me to watch as certain por-

tions of his anatomy vanish. I don't think I'll ever get tired of looking at him, I realize.

I strip, tossing my clothes on the bed. Eyes on Logan, his on me.
His hands find me, when I'm naked.

"Start that, Logan, and we'll never get to the beach."

"It'll still be there in an hour or two," he murmurs, palming my
ass and kissing me on the jaw.

"True . . ."

And then, somehow, my fingers find the strings of his trunks
and are tugging the knot apart, and then he's naked with me. Pushing me backward to the bed, lifting my knees over his shoulders,
mouth to my core.

I writhe off the bed, wrapping my legs around him, pulling him
closer. I'm greedy for what his tongue can do to me, and soon I'm riding his tongue and fingers through one orgasm, two . . . I'm nearing
a third when I finally manage to pull him away, pull him up, pull him
over me, lift my hips to his. We find each other, him sliding inside me
smoothly, slowly, as if our bodies were puzzle-made for each other.

As he moves, I kiss his jaw, his cheekbone, his temple. My fingers
slide up his face, up the right side, encounter the leather of his eyepatch. I brush it away, toss it aside. Feather kisses up his right cheekbone, to his temple. Over his empty eye socket. Telling him without
words that he is beautiful, even thus. Especially thus.

He moves harder when I kiss him like that, so I bring my heels
up to my buttocks and lie still, let him move above me, let him have
me as he wishes to have me, and I focus my attention on touching
and kissing his face, his neck, his shoulders, his jaw, sliding my
fingertips over his skin, stubble skritching under my nails.

When I feel his rhythm falter, when I feel him tighten and throb
within me, when I feel him surging hard and rough and wild, I press
my lips to his ear and whisper his name, again and again and again,

and then I whisper *I love you* in the other ear. I palm his buttocks and urge him to move harder, pull him against me, hook my legs around his back and move against him.

I do not come with him.

I don't want to.

I want to only feel him, take him.

He has given me so much, loved me so unconditionally, accepted me, forgiven me, taught me to be *me*.

He comes hard, grunting against my breasts. I carve my fingers through his hair and hold his mouth against my nipple and pull him to my lips and kiss him as he comes, bite his lip and suck his breath into my lungs and cling to his neck and writhe beneath him to milk his orgasm until he's limp above me, giving me his weight.

"Jesus, Isabel." He is gasping, still, his face on my chest, between my breasts. I love his weight on me, thus. "You rock my world harder every single time we do that."

"You haven't just rocked my world, Logan. You have utterly changed me. You have rescued me."

"Love don't quit, baby."

"No, I'm realizing that it does not." I move beneath him, and he slides off me, pulls me against his chest, as if to cuddle. I have other ideas. "The beach, Logan. I want to swim."

I do, very much. The sea is calling to me. I want to feel the sand in my toes, the wind in my hair, the water around my ankles.

"Let's go, then."


I opt for the two-piece. I feel naked, but when I try it on and look in the mirror, even I must admit I look rather stunning. And Logan can't keep his eyes—or his hands—off me. Thus, the two-piece.

Now we're standing on the side of the road, waiting to cross. There is a fence between the road and the back of the condominiums, with gates here and there to allow residents and guests to come and go from the beach. A couple of cars pass, and then we cross, dancing through the dune grass and down to the shore. The sand is hot until we reach the water's edge, and that's where I stop.

Water lapping at my toes, up to my ankles. Wet sand pulling at my feet, sliding and shifting with the receding waves. The sun is low, sending a path of reddish-gold light on the ocean.

Logan is quiet, holding my hand. Watching me.

I wade slowly deeper, and Logan comes with me.

The memory from earlier is vivid in my mind. It is all I can see, all I can feel. I almost expect to be able to turn and see Mama and Papa on the sand, on Abuela's blanket, kissing. I turn, in fact. But the beach is empty, except for a few singles and couples drifting along the shore in the distance.

I wade in deeper. To my thighs, to my hips. The water is cool at my waist.

"I always used to stop here. This deep. I had to work up the courage to jump in." I blink; salt stings my eyes. "Papa would sometimes push me in, if I was taking too long."

"Like this?" Logan says.

And then wraps his arm around my waist and throws us into the water. I come up spluttering, but laughing.

"Yes, Logan. Exactly like that."

And now that I'm in the water, I'm home. More than anywhere I've ever been since waking up from the coma, I'm home. I dive back under, down to the sea floor, trailing my fingers along the rippled sand. Kick hard, draw at the water with cupped palms, swim long and hard until my lungs burn, and then I plant my heels in the sand

and kick off. I break the surface, roll to my back, and drift on the waves. The sea is calm, gently rolling. I feel Logan beside me. Just watching. There, but silent. Giving me this moment.

I float for a while, eyes closed, remnants of the sun's heat bathing my face.

I drop my feet to the sea floor and turn to face Logan. "Thank you, Logan."

He's left his eyepatch in the condo, but, in this moment at least, I can look at him without feeling the squirm of guilt.

"For what, babe?" he asks.

I push up against him. Kiss him. "This." I gesture around us. "For bringing me here. I feel . . . at home. At peace."

"Good. That's what I wanted."

"How can I ever thank you? It seems impossible." I run my hands over his wet hair. "You've given me so much. Done so much."

"That's love, honey. It's life. It's . . ." He shrugs, at a loss for words. "All you have to do is love me back."

"I do. Very much. I never thought to even wonder what that was, that it even existed, until I met you. I knew only one thing, and that seemed to be all there was in life. And you've shown me so much in such a short span of time." I kiss him, taste brine on his lips. "I remember . . . from earlier, my memory of being on the beach with Mama and Papa, I remember how they couldn't seem to stop touching each other, kissing each other. They kissed like they never wanted to stop. And I remember this thought, wondering what it would be like, kissing someone and wanting to never stop."

Logan cups the back of my head and kisses me senseless. Tongues tangling, our lips and teeth colliding, his hand pulling me closer, stealing my breath. A moment of surprise, and then I kiss him back, and it lasts for an eternity. We stand in the water, in the path of light spread by the crimson sunset, kissing as my parents once kissed, as if there were nothing else in all the world but the kiss. As if the kiss were all.

"Never stop, Isabel." Logan's whisper is soft and sweet. "Please, never stop."

"I couldn't, not even if I wanted to." I plaster myself against his body, cling to him, breathe him, taste the sea on his skin, the sun on his lips, the love from his fingers, the adoration on his tongue. "I don't want to ever stop."

# TEN

We spend a week in Barcelona. We swim, we make love, we sleep tangled around each other. We live free, soaking up the sun, bathing in love.

It is the happiest I have ever been.

The happiest I will ever be, I think.

# ELEVEN

I have almost managed to forget about you.

Almost.

We have moved, Logan and I. He sold his row house, and we spent a month hunting for something that suited us. We looked at other row houses, other brownstones. We looked at condos, ground-floor apartments, penthouses. I expected us to choose something like Logan had, something quiet and private with a backyard. Instead, however, we chose the penthouse of a condo building in the heart of Greenwich Village. The entire upper floor, with a private rooftop terrace. It is nothing like the echoing monstrosity of your home, a fact that I love, smaller and cozier than that, yet larger than Logan's previous place. A beautiful kitchen flowing into an informal dining area, a breakfast nook tucked into a corner. The living room is sunken a few steps down from the kitchen and bedrooms, which strikes me as odd, but I find I like it, for reasons I can't quite enumerate. There are four bedrooms; one for Logan and me, one as his home office, one to be a nursery—that still makes my hands shake and my stomach flip, because it isn't real yet, and is still terrifying—and one for Cocoa. The master bedroom has an en suite bathroom, and there is one more shared between the other three bedrooms. The master bedroom is isolated, set above the rest of the unit so it over-looks the rooftop terrace. The front of the room is a wall of movable, adjustable-tint glass, which leads to a balcony that in turn descends via twin curving staircases to the terrace.

Cocoa loves the terrace almost as much as I do. As soon as we let her out, she runs laps around the perimeter for a few minutes, barking like a fiend, and then puts her front paws up on the ledge of the waist-high wall and stares down at the street, tongue lolling, eyes excitedly scanning the sidewalk below, tail swinging a mile a minute, and that's where she'll stay, just like that, until you make her come in.

Logan sells his old place with all the furniture included, both to fetch a higher price and because he wants us to choose everything for our new home together, from silverware to bedsheets. The only things we bring with us are our clothes and the contents of his office; everything else stays. And we spend days, weeks even, pick-ing out curtains and couches, silverware and wineglasses, bedsheets and cooking utensils and everything in between.

I never realized how much *stuff* it took to make a house a home.

And I savor every moment of it, every decision, down to the small-est, most arbitrary thing. It is normalcy, and it is glorious.

I have decided to put on hold the preparations for Comportment. Even if I do not feel it yet—aside from the change in the foods I like to eat, and the morning sickness—I am pregnant. I have seen a doc-tor, with Logan, and verified the clinic's verdict. Took measure-ments and did an ultrasound, a blood test, all sorts of medical procedures to ensure that I am healthy, and the baby is growing as it should be. It is early yet, but the doctor said all is progressing as it should be. I am taking prenatal vitamins, continuing to exercise and eat healthy.

All this means that trying to get my own business off the ground is not feasible, as yet. Perhaps it never will be. Or perhaps, when I am ready to reexamine the notion of going into business for myself, I will have new ideas, a different business plan. For now, I am content to be Logan's girlfriend, to live in our own home that we chose for ourselves. To run, and watch movies with Logan, and make love with him in every room, on every surface both vertical and horizontal.

Thus, learning to live life as a normal woman, I manage to nearly forget about you.

To forget the questions.

The doubts.

The inconsistencies.

Everything.

It all gets shuffled to the back of my mind, set aside. Not important, now that I am discovering the sweetness of normality.

But, in that inexorable, mysterious way you possess, you appear when least expected, and do something absolutely unpredictable.

Yet, really, when it happens, I am not surprised at all.

It is you, after all:

You kidnap me.

# TWELVE

t is rather unnecessarily dramatic, the way you snatch me.

Right off the rooftop terrace, in broad daylight. Just past ten in the morning, in fact.

I am reclined on a lounge chair, my feet up, sunglasses on, clad in a robe and a bikini so revealing I'd never wear it out, only here, at home, for Logan, or alone on the roof. I am reading, sipping herbal tea, enjoying the sunlight of what promises to be one of the last warm days we will have for some time. Cocoa is beside my chair, her chin on my thigh, snoring.

I hear a helicopter, and think nothing of it. This is New York, there are helicopters going overhead all the time. But when the volume of its whumping rotors grows, I become curious. Sit up, look around. Cocoa's ears prick and twitch, and she too seems disconcerted. Growls deep in her chest. I watch as the hackles on the back of her shoulders lift.

Something is amiss.

I wrap my thin robe around myself and cinch it closed, tie the belt. Set aside my mug. Clutch my cell phone, ready to call Logan if needed.

The rotors are close now, but the aircraft itself is still somewhere out of sight. Cocoa spots it first, and barks at it. But not the bark she has for another dog, or strangers, or squirrels, or birds. This is her fierce, defensive bark, frightening and feral. The helicopter is swooping low over the rooftops, moving fast. Too fast. News and medical helicopters, even the few police ones I've seen, none of them have flown thus, barely clearing rooftops, scudding with precise and unerring speed toward this rooftop.

And I know.

I am in motion as soon as I realize who is in that machine, but it is too late.

The helicopter flares to a stop barely a dozen feet overhead, the down-blast of the rotors nearly flattening me. A door slides open, and two ropes drop to the rooftop. Cocoa is a brown blur of fury, moving to stand in front of me, teeth bared in a snarling rictus. Black-clad figures slide down the ropes, and one levels a handgun of some sort, aims it. There is a quiet thump, and Cocoa whines, collapses. I cry out, grab for her, find a dart protruding from her neck. Hands grab me. I fight, thrash.

A gloved hand goes over my mouth, silencing my scream before it can leave me. The hand is replaced by a gag, a length of cloth tugged between my mandibles and tied tight.

My cell phone is tossed aside.

I am lifted off the ground. My hands are wrenched behind my back, and something hard is wrapped around them with a *zzzzzh-hhhrrrrippp*, binding them painfully together. My vision is obscured suddenly, something thick and black draped over my head. A black bag, or a pillowcase, something totally opaque.

Terror claws at my heart.

More ropes are tied around me, but this time in a kind of impromptu harness, under my armpits, around my thighs near my groin on both sides, back up around my armpits, low around my waist beneath my belly, again and again in a swiftly and expertly woven pattern that assures there is no pressure on any one part of my body as I am hoisted off the rooftop. Up, up, up. I am glad in that moment for the bag making it so I cannot see myself being lifted off the ground.

I dangle and sway in the air as I am brought up and up. Hands grab me, pull me in, set me down. Untie the rope harness. Sit me down, and buckle me in, a five-point harness, *click-click—click—click-click*, all centered over my torso.

The noise of the rotors is deafening.

Perhaps thirty seconds have passed, total, since the aircraft halted to hover above me.

No one speaks. A door closes and the noise of the rotors is quieter. I feel the helicopter resume forward motion, and then it is banking. Even without the use of my eyes, I can tell that we are moving with horrifying speed through the canyons of the city.

I am still wearing my sunglasses, I realize. It is an odd thing to notice in such a situation. But it just reinforces the speed and precision of the snatch.

Perhaps twenty minutes of flight, at most, and then I feel forward motion become downward motion. I feel touchdown, a gentle bump. My harness is unfastened, hands lift me and set me to my feet. Hands guide me across what I guess may be another rooftop and through a doorway. I hear a door close behind me, and the sound of the helicopter is muted.

The hands on my biceps guide me, turning this way and that, and then halt. Elevator sounds. A brief downward journey in the elevator car, the only sound that of my captor's soft breath. I am nudged forward, and I take three steps. Hear the elevator door close behind me. A sense of wide space, echoing of my breath within the bag, my bare feet shuffling on some kind of cool hard floor.

"Here she is, sir." A deep, accented male voice. European accent, of some kind. German, possibly. I am not sure.

Then your voice. "Thank you, Kai."

"Of course, sir."

"I've added a bonus, to ensure that you and your men remain . . . discreet."

"Discretion is the byword of our business, Mr. Indigo."

"It had better be. You wouldn't want me to have to buy your silence through . . . other methods."

Kai's voice, behind me, is cold. "That would be unnecessary, and ill advised, sir, even for you."

"Good-bye, Kai."

"*Auf wiedersehen.*" Bootheel-clicks recede.

Silence. I can only breathe through my nose and fight panic and fear, and hope my knees do not give out.

I feel you.

In front of me. Close, so close I can feel your body heat and smell your cologne.

"I apologize for the dramatics, Isabel."

I would not say anything even if I weren't gagged.

You breathe, just breathe. Looking at me, I assume. And then I feel a touch. Hear you inhale. Your nose, sliding along the curve of my neck. Your fingers, then, tracing the V opening of my robe.

"What are you wearing beneath this, I wonder?"

You loosen the knot, tug the belt open, and the edges of the robe slip aside. Your fingertips brush down the sides of my throat, to my clavicle, along my breastbone. Gentle, tender. Your fingers shake on my flesh. I am breathing hard past the gag. Blinking furiously in the darkness within the bag blinding me. You nudge at the robe, and it droops off my shoulders, baring me. Now the scant coverage of the bikini leaves me feeling utterly naked.

"Ah . . ." An appreciative sigh. "So lovely, Isabel. Far too lovely to be covered."

*Snick.*

A terrifying sound. Metallic. Sharp.

Something thin and cold touches my chest, my cleavage, right between my breasts. I stop breathing. Hold completely still.

The sharp edge does not pierce or cut as it traces the outline of my breast. A quick jerk between my breasts, and the string holding the tiny cups of the bra is severed. My breasts fall and sway loose.

I resume breathing then, but now my breathing is ragged with fear.

The blade tickles lower. Down my side, to the knot at my hip. Another quick jerk, and the string is cut. The bottom falls around my feet, and I am naked.

Gagging on my panicked breathing.

"Hush, Isabel. Be calm. You know I'd never hurt you." Your breath, your voice, a whisper in my ear. "I couldn't mar such perfection."

Your presence recedes.

I hear a *click*, the snap of a camera shutter. Ticking of smartphone keyboard keys. The *bloooop* of a message being sent, and received.

*Bbbbbrrrrriiiinnnnggagg!* Your ringer, so familiar, the old-fashioned metallic blat of a rotary landline phone from decades past.

"Logan." A pause. "Calm down, Mr. Ryder. As you see, she is unhurt. And she will remain unharmed. But if you leave your office, you will never see her again. No, you idiot, I won't kill her. I will merely . . . keep her. I have, as of this moment, every intention of returning her to you in the same condition I received her. The photograph is merely proof of life, I suppose you could call it. I'm not going to hurt her. Nor you, for that matter, although I do have eyes on you, and those eyes are in possession of a rifle, capable of putting a bullet between your eyes from a mile away. Remain where you are."

Another pause, as you listen. I can hear Logan on the other side, yelling, tinny, distant.

"What do I want? A moment with Isabel, that's all. To talk. Just she and I."

Logan's voice.

"I will have her returned when we are done with our conversation." You sigh, a sound of long-suffering. This is pure Caleb, calm, in control. "Your dog? She is unhurt as well. The dart merely contained a dose of sedative. She will wake up in a few hours none the worse for wear. And now I must let you go, Mr. Ryder. Remember, stay where you are. Stay in that very room, if you please. Do not leave for anything. In fact, it may be best to not even stand up, for now."

And then you are in front of me, again, close enough to smell.

Silence, for a long, long time. An eternity, in which you are there, in front of me, not touching me, not speaking. I don't know what you are doing.

And I can only endure it.

At long last, I feel your hands tugging at the hood. Removing it.

The light, even with sunglasses still on, albeit askew, is blinding after the total darkness.

I blink, and feel you adjust the sunglasses so they sit properly on my face.

My robe is still draped behind me, hanging from my bound wrists.

You are impeccably dressed. Three-piece charcoal pinstripe suit, tailored to fit your trim waist and wide shoulders. White button-down, a crimson tie, knotted but loose around your throat, topmost button undone. Hands in your hip pockets. Just eyeing me.

I glare back. Pretend to bravery I do not in any way feel.

"Isabel. Oh . . . Isabel. You are, as always, lovelier than ever." You step closer. Closer, yet. I am unable to slow my breathing, then, when you press up against me. Inhale against my throat once more. Back up, run your palm up my side. Cup my breast and release it. "Pregnancy suits you, I must admit. It adds a softness to your already full figure."

I am still gagged. I want to vomit at your touch. It is an immediate and instinctive reaction. And surprising.

Yet . . . welcome, considering my former addiction to you, my former susceptibility to your sorcery.

A tear escapes, slides down my cheek, appears beneath the rim of my sunglasses.

You reach up, wipe it away with a thumb.

"I'm sorry, Isabel. I'm sorry for all this. I . . ." You turn away, scrub your fingers through your hair. "I couldn't help myself."

Back to me, then. An abrupt whirl, two harsh paces. The hand still in your trouser pocket flies up and out, a black something clutched in your fingers, and then there's that horrible *snick* as a blade snaps open. I stumble backward, screaming past the gag.

You grunt in irritation. "Oh, shut up and hold still, would you? I said I would never hurt you. Surely you understand that much, at least."

It's a quick, efficient move, the way you slide the flat of the blade between my cheek and the gag. Twist, so the blade bites into the gag and parts it. I feel a sting, however, and you frown. Lick your thumb, and wipe at my cheek where the tip of the knife, razor sharp, nicked my cheek.

You lean in, kiss the wound.

I flinch away. Work my jaw.

Tears blur my eyes. "What do you want, Caleb?"

"You heard what I said. To talk, that's all."

"You could have called me."

You laugh. "Oh no. That wouldn't do at all. You and I, our history? It deserves so much more than a mere phone call."

"But this?" I am cold with fury; you hear it in my voice.

My hands are still bound. The robe hangs from my wrists. My breasts are bare, my core exposed, and my thighs tremble with the furious, fearful knocking of my knees. I do not know any longer what you are capable of. Anything, I think. Anything at all.

You still have the knife out, and you spin the blade in a circle on your palm, a casual demonstration of mastery and familiarity with the weapon. You approach. Your motions are those of a predator, smooth gliding steps of a panther, a prowling lion. Your eyes rake my body. You move around to stand behind me, slink your knife-wielding arm around my neck, trace my cheekbone with the dull back edge of the knife. Your other hand toys with me, flicks at my nipple, cups my breast, smooths down my rib cage, flattens possessively against my hip.

"You are my siren, Isabel." Your voice is a rough murmur against the shell of my ear. "Your body sings a song I have never been able to resist. Yet I am not so fortunate as godlike Odysseus that I can bind myself to a mast as he did to resist his siren. I have only my will, and where you are concerned, my will is entirely insufficient."

I still have not even registered where I am; I look around, trying to not even allow myself to process your words. Not your home, not the cavernous penthouse at the top of your tower. This is somewhere new. Windows all around, a mammoth, gaping, totally empty space. Windows, and light. Floor-to-ceiling glass walls, showing Manhattan in all four directions. Behind me, an elevator shaft.

The only feature of the entire room, which is the footprint of a skyscraper. Tens of thousands of square feet in every direction. Bare concrete underfoot.

"Did you hear me, Isabel?" You tap my cheekbone with the tip of the knife, gaining my attention.

"Yes, Caleb." I step forward, pivot in place. "Or should I call you Jakob?" It is a test, to see how violently you react. It is a dangerous game, I think.

But you do not react. Perhaps you didn't hear the last part. I do not know. You move up close to me, so the tips of my breasts crush against the front of your suit coat. You lean in, as if to kiss me. Brows furrowed, eyes tormented, but lucid. Instead of kissing me, you touch your forehead to mine. I don't dare move, because you still have the knife, and you are reaching past me with it. Around to my back. I am not breathing, not moving. Don't even blink as you breathe on my cheek, touch your ear to mine, your chin to my shoulder. Looking over my back, watching your movements as you slip the knife blade between my wrists, and . . . flick.

The plastic binding my hands together parts, and I am free.

The robe pools onto the floor.

You close the knife blade. Pace in caged-tiger circles around me. Pocket the weapon. Gazing at me. Your eyes, my God your eyes, they are haunted, blazing with pain and need. Your mask has slipped, Caleb. The emotion within you is a cauldron. No . . . a caldera, crumbling to reveal an active volcano beneath, ready to erupt.

Your chest rises and falls heavily, as if you have recently run a marathon. You are gazing at me as if I am the source of all life, and you are a dying monster, ravening in the shadows, hungering for the sweet morsel of life just beyond its reach.

I remain utterly motionless. Watching you pace in circles around me. Naked. Vulnerable. Terrified. Confused.

And then you move up behind me. Touch my spine. Trace each knob downward. Feather your palms, yes, lovingly over my bottom. Cup my hips. I do not move. I hate your touch. Hate it. But you are manic, unbalanced, and I fear you. So I must allow it, I think. I want to go home to Logan. I want to feel the baby in my belly grow.

As if reading my mind, you press your front to my spine, and your fingers dance around my sides, between my ribs and my arms. Your palms flatten against my belly. It has begun to bump, just a tiny little bit.

"Is it true?" You murmur this, ever so gently, in my ear.

"Yes."

"How far?"

"Thirteen weeks." My voice shakes.

"And you do not know if it is mine or his?"

"No. There is no way to know. Not until after the birth." There is, actually, but my doctor said the procedure came with risk, and wasn't worth it. I agreed. But I'm not about to say this.

"I don't suppose it matters." You turn away from me. Pace away, long quick angry steps.

And then back. Kneeling in front of me. Eyes wide, wondering. You press ten gentle fingertips to my belly. Gently, reverently.

"But . . . if you carried my child inside you . . . ?" You breathe this, as if it is too wild a notion to be believed. "*My* blood, beating within you. *My* bloodline, growing in your uterus."

"Stop, Caleb," I whisper. "Please, just . . . stop."

"If it were mine, what then?" You stand up. Stare down into my eyes.

"I don't know. I don't know what then."

"I have tried to let you go, Isabel. Time and again. I try. But I just . . . cannot." You turn away again, as if ripping your gaze from me, painfully. Rub the stubble on your jaw with a palm. "I can't.

And now that you're pregnant, now that you may have my son or daughter growing inside you—how can I let you go?"

I risk a step closer to you. "You have to, Caleb. You *must*. It is all there is *to* do. Find it within you, Caleb. Please."

"*I can't!*" This, desperately. Shouted, spittle flying. "Do you have *any* fucking clue what I've been through because of you, Isabel de la Vega?"

"No, Caleb, I do not. How could I? You've lied to me at every turn. Hidden the truth from me. Locked me away from myself, from my life, from my past." I breathe out slowly, trying to regain some measure of calm. "You *knew* me, didn't you? Before the coma? Before the accident. You knew me."

Your gaze sharpens. Slices into me. "You've remembered something, haven't you?"

"Yes."

"Tell me."

"*You* tell *me*, Caleb."

A frustrated sigh. You turn away, snatch my robe off the floor. Bring it to me, hold it open for me. I slide my arms in, and you tie it closed, reluctantly, reverently. You have never behaved thus. As if I am something precious.

Always I felt like just . . . a possession. A watch you were jealous of, but that held no real emotional value to you. As if you possessed me merely so no else could. Owned, but not cherished.

This, the way you look at me now, the way you touch me now . . . if you'd shown this side of you all these past years, perhaps there could have been something for us, between us. But it's too late. Too late.

You cling to the belt, the knot, for several long moments, and then, as if physically forcing yourself to do so, you release the belt. Breathe in, out, again, and again. Just staring at me. As if plumbing the depths of my soul through my eyes, seeking something.

And then you turn away, walk the many paces to the window. Assume that familiar pose, one arm barred horizontally on the window, your forehead resting on your arm, in the crook of your elbow. Other hand lifted to the glass, fingers tapping a rhythm. Weight on one leg, the other knee bent.

Staring into the past.

I put my back to the window a few feet away from you, sink to sit on the floor.

"You were just a girl when I first saw you. Fourteen, not yet fifteen, but nearly. You were in the process of blooming from an awkward girl into a lovely young woman. I knew, the moment I saw you, that you would be . . . stunning. A Helen of Troy, a woman for whom armies would go to war. But then, you were just a girl. No tits, hair in a sloppy braid, staring wide-eyed at the big bad city, this place, this modern Babylon. You were with your parents. I knew you'd be stunning, because you looked just like your mother, and holy mother of God, that woman was gorgeous. More than gorgeous. A woman to kill for, to die for. A true Spanish beauty. Long thick black hair, firm, dark, unblemished skin even at her age, forty or so. Eyelashes so thick you could almost hear them as they swept against her face. And her body, your mother, Isabel, she had the body of a goddess. Your father was a damned lucky man. He was a rather handsome man, himself, however. A little older than her, I think. Forty-five, nearly fifty, perhaps? Going a little silver at the temples, but it gave him that distinguished air, you know? Tall, straight, strong. A good bit of stubble, not quite a beard. You were between them, your mother on the inside, you, and then your father nearest the street. All three of you were fresh off the boat, so to speak. You were literally clutching your visa in your hands, still. You'd gone straight to Fifth Avenue, like all the tourists do.

"I passed you. But that moment, when I first saw you, I will never forget that moment for as long as I live, Isabel. You looked at me, and you saw me. Your face told the tale. You thought I was handsome. So I smiled at you, and you ducked, looked away, blushing, giggling. I saw then how beautiful you would be. And I knew, once you came of age, that I would have to have you. But not until you were of age. I was no pedophile, no predator of young girls. In my world, I had men like that . . . eliminated with extreme prejudice. If a man came to me looking for young girls, he would vanish. I would see to it. I had no patience for such filth. Did not, and do not."

You tap the window, fall silent for a while. I wait, knowing you will continue. Needing you to continue.

"I was a pimp then. There is no other word for it. But I was good to my girls. I took care of them. Kept them off drugs. Fed them, clothed them, gave them somewhere safe to live and do business. Made sure their clients were clean, and not rough. Made sure no one abused them. And I never took advantage of their services myself. At least, not without paying for it like anyone else. I was not a good man. I am not, and never have been. Never will be. But back then? I was . . . bad. I was on the rise. Twenty-five years old and so very angry at everyone, at life. I was making money hand over fist. I was hungry for respect, for success. I was ruthless. If someone got in my way . . . well, they regretted it. But I had standards. Rules. A code. All of my girls were at least eighteen, and they knew, each and every one of them, what they were getting into. I never coerced them or forced them. I made sure they were loyal to me and only me, yes, but . . . they were not victims. And you . . . I'd never seen anyone like you. You were sweet. Innocent. Young, then, too young. But you . . . you *saw* me, Isabel. You looked right at me. And you didn't do so with fear or disgust. Not like everyone else. You should have. And if you'd been able to see what I truly was, you would have. But I was selfish, and I liked the way you looked at me.

"I kept tabs on you, on the three of you. Nothing nefarious, I just . . . kept track. You went to school in Brooklyn. Your father worked at a jewelry store, a little place owned by a very distant cousin, I think. Or a friend of a distant cousin. I don't remember anymore. Your mother worked for a hotel, cleaning rooms. It was demeaning work for a woman meant to be an empress, but she did it with vivacity and determination. For you. So you could have shoes and clothes and some money to spend. Your father and mother both worked very long hours to put a roof over your heads and food in your bellies, which meant you were much alone. You had no friends that I ever saw. You never left school with anyone, you never met anyone outside of school. Once school let out, you would go to the library. But you'd stop for a snack on the way, at the same bodega every time. You liked your sweets. You'd get a Coke, and a Snickers bar. I had the feeling, when I watched you, that you got these things as a form of rebellion, that your parents wouldn't approve, which is why you did it. You'd stay at the library for long, long hours, reading. I never knew anyone to read so many books as you. You'd just sit in the stacks, nose in a book, from when school ended until late at night. Your father rarely came home before midnight, and your mother nearly that, and they'd both be gone a few hours past dawn. Seven, eight at the latest. You were . . . very independent. You'd take yourself to school, take yourself home. I assumed you made your own breakfast, lunch, and dinner. Always alone."

"It sounds as if you kept very close track of me indeed, Caleb."

You do not bother to turn, to look at me. "Oh yes. It was unhealthy, and I knew it. But I couldn't help it. My work suffered. I fucked up a rather important deal because I was watching you rather than doing my due diligence. But I couldn't help it."

"Why? What was it about me?"

A sigh. "Just . . . you. Everything. I do not know if I can explain

it, even now. Something in you spoke to something within me. I
was impatient for you to grow up, for you to be . . . ready for me. I
never interfered in your life, nor that of your parents. I wanted to.
I wanted to drive you to school so you wouldn't have to walk. I
wanted to feed you. Stop you from eating trash. A body like yours,
or rather a body such as I knew you would have one day . . . it
deserved better treatment than you were giving it. You were just a
teenage girl, so you knew no better. But I wanted better for you."

Another sigh. Knuckles tapping on the window. Toe tapping on
the floor.

"What was it about you?" you repeat. "What *is* it about you now?
I don't know. I'd never even spoken to you. But I . . . *knew* you. I
knew you. I knew the books you liked. Classics, fiction, philosophy.
Hemingway, Voltaire, Rousseau, Sartre, Tennessee Williams, Haw-
thorne, Shakespeare, the Romantics . . . you read so much, so
widely. You possessed so much intelligence, so much raw beauty
and potential. I wanted it all. I wanted to . . . shape you. It wasn't
sexual, not then. As I said, I am not a predator. Not of that sort, at any
rate. If I was not, as I have already said, a good man, I was not so
depraved as to prey on fourteen-year-old girls."

"I believe you, Caleb," I say. And I do. I do not know why, but
I do.

You turn, finally. "You believe that?" Eyes narrowed, jaw muscles
flexing, a breath. "You believe that I never meant you harm? That
I did not then, and do not now?"

I must consider my next words carefully. "I believe that you were
not a predator of young girls. That is what I meant."

You hear what I do not say, however. "But you do not believe the
rest?"

"Given all that has occurred between us, it is difficult. You shot
and nearly killed Logan—you *meant* to kill him. You kidnapped me

out of my home. You tranquilized my dog. I was bound and gagged and blindfolded. You have mixed truth and lies and omission for so long that I do not know how to believe anything you say."

You frown at me, stare at me. "I suppose I cannot fault you for that." You brace your spine against the glass, cross your arms over your chest. "But believe, if you are able, that everything I'm telling you is the truth. Nothing left out, nothing false."

"I will try."

"That is all I ask."

"I have a question, though."

"What?"

"Why now?"

You let your head thud back against the thick glass, let your eyes slide closed, as if summoning an answer from deep within. "It is time. For many reasons."

"How illuminating." My voice is flat, sarcastic.

You snarl. "You wish the truth?"

"Yes—"

"Then do *not* mock me, Isabel. Do not forget who I am." You pivot, resume your earlier pose, leaned against the window, facing out, but now with your arms still crossed. "We met for the second time by accident. If you believe nothing, believe that. I hadn't meant to ever come face to face with you again until you were at least eighteen. But then, I believe it was the day after your sixteenth birthday—you saw me in a café, and approached me. I tried to be rude, hoping you would go away. For your own good. I was not ready for you, nor you me. But you were persistent. You sat down at my table, ordered an espresso and a *pain au chocolate*. You carried on as if we'd always known each other. You told me your name, and asked me mine."

You pause for so long I wonder fleetingly if you've fallen asleep.

But you continue, only now your voice is so low I can barely hear you. I move closer.

"You are responsible for Caleb Indigo, you know. I've never told anyone that, but it's true. You asked me my name, and I panicked. I didn't want you knowing who I was. I didn't want you finding me, finding out that I was a pimp, and a former prostitute myself. It wouldn't have been hard for you to find out. None of it was secret. I don't know. I just . . . panicked. When I was a prostitute working for Miss Amy, there was a man. A client of hers, and thus, of mine. He was a vicious, brutal son of a bitch. Completely cold. Never gave away anything. Nothing. His name was Caleb. He would show up for an appointment with me, and he would just . . . use me. I was never a small or weak person, but he—" Your voice cracks. You suck in a breath. "I envied him his ability to obscure all of his emotions, all of his thoughts. When you asked me my name, his came to mind. So I told you my name was Caleb. 'Caleb what?' you asked me. You were wearing the blue dress. You know the one. Indigo. Not just blue, but indigo. And thus, Caleb Indigo was born."

"That is difficult to believe, Caleb."

"I know. But yet it is true."

"The original Caleb. What happened to him?"

You make a sound, somewhere between a grunt, a growl, and a hum. A strange sound. Animal, rather than human. "I killed him. After Amy died and I went into business for myself, he came looking for me. I refused him. He tried to force it, and we fought. I won. Made sure no one would ever find him. Although a man like him, I don't think anyone would ever look."

"So you told me your name was Caleb Indigo."

"Yes. Because I was . . . I didn't want you to know Jakob." A brief silence. "So then we began meeting at the café. Once a week, twice. Sometimes more. I continued the charade of being Caleb. Acted out a persona that wasn't me. Pretended to an emotionless façade I did not feel. Never told you anything about me. I never touched you. It was clear you had a crush on me, an infatuation. I tried not to encourage it, and even made it clear you were too young. But I couldn't make you stop coming to our café, and I couldn't stay away, knowing you would show up looking for me. You made advance after advance on me, and I turned you away. Made you angry, time and again. But always you came back. You couldn't stay away and neither could I. This went on for months. And during those months, I found the Caleb persona useful. I pretended to be Caleb more and more. Caleb was . . . calm. Cool. Powerful. I could hide behind him. He wasn't the orphan, the homeless boy. He wasn't a whore. He wasn't weak. He was *in control*. I *liked* being Caleb."

A pause, a breath, and you clear your throat. Begin again. "And then something unforeseen happened."

"The car accident?" I asked.

"No, not yet. That was later. This was . . ." You breathe slowly in and out several times. "I was alone, late at night. Out walking. I'd been drinking. I didn't drink often, but that night I'd had a deal go wrong and needed to unwind. So I went to a dive bar far from anywhere I normally visited, and got drunk. Very, very drunk. I was stumbling home, and there you were. Walking home from the library. Of course, the library had closed hours and hours earlier. But you'd take the books you'd checked out to an all-night diner nearby and get a cup of coffee and sit and read. The waitresses all knew you, and they let you stay as long as you wanted. I walked by that diner. You'd just walked out, and you had your books in your backpack, and you were wearing . . . God, this outfit I would never have let you leave the house in. A short skirt, sandals, and a blouse that showed too much cleavage. You'd grown up in the two years I'd spent watching you, the months we'd spent talking in that café. Sprouted breasts, started wearing a pushup bra. Of course, even at sixteen you didn't need one, but you had no one to tell you no. Your parents loved you so much, but they had to work endless hours, because New York is an expensive and merciless mistress. So there was no one to tell you to put on different clothes. I remember that night. More vividly than any other night in my life, I think. I was behind you, and you . . . I don't know. You felt me, I think. You turned around, and you saw me. You seemed happy to see me. It was the best feeling, that joy in your eyes, meant for me."

I do not like where this is going. I do not like the hesitance in your voice. I am silent, still, frozen, as if only my ears function.

"We walked together. I remember the moment you took my hand. It was so innocent. But yet . . . so sinful. We were crossing a street. It was nearly midnight, and the sidewalks only had a few people on them, in that neighborhood. We were only a few blocks from your apartment building. I remember it. You put your palm to mine, and our fingers just . . . wove together. I think I stopped breathing, because I knew I should let go, but I was drunk, and I didn't want to. I let myself pretend we were just . . . two people. We held hands, and walked, and talked. Or rather, you talked and I listened. You were normally a quiet girl, I think, except with me. You saved all your words for me, it sometimes felt. Poured them all out on me.

"But then . . . you changed everything. For me, and for yourself. I stumbled. Tripped on a crack in the sidewalk, and—somehow, somehow—I ended up holding you in my arms. I'd fallen against the wall of an alley, and you were in my arms. You smelled good. You were so close. Your eyes were large, and I couldn't look away. And then you kissed me. *You* kissed *me*. And that was your undoing. You might have escaped me, if you hadn't kissed me. But after I'd tasted you, tasted the coffee on your breath, tasted the virginity in you, I knew. I just knew. You were *mine*. Sixteen, a virgin, and destined to be mine.

"I tried to resist you. Even after that. I pushed you off me, said something vulgar and demeaning, something about how I didn't fuck naïve little virgins."

A pin could prick the silence. A knife could flay it. A word could shatter it.

*He tasted sour, the way Papa's breath sometimes smelled, late at night. But this was different. This was Caleb, and I was tasting him. Kissing him. And he was kissing me back! It was beautiful. It was right. He was finally seeing me. His hand was on my waist, just above my hip. I wanted him to touch me where I'd never been touched. I leaned into him, pressed my chest against his, pressed my hips against his. Without words, I begged him to touch me. To show me how to be a woman, the kind of woman he wanted. He moaned, deep in his throat. It felt as if the moan were coming from deep within the earth, as if the ground itself were making the sound. His fingers tightened in my skin, gripping my waist. His tongue touched my teeth. I whimpered and opened my mouth, so I could taste more of him, so he could show me how to kiss with tongue. It was my first kiss, and it was everything I'd ever dreamed of. My first kiss, with Caleb! Oh, oh, oh . . . his hands were moving now. Downward. To my hips. Yes! YES! I whimpered again, and then his hands were palming my bottom, lifting me, pulling me harder against him. And I felt IT. A thick, hard THING between us, pressing into my belly. It felt so big, so hard, and I wondered what it would look like. I knew what sex was, of course. I knew how it worked. I even knew I was supposed to put my mouth on him down there and suck, and it was supposed to feel good for him. A blow job. Girls gave men blow jobs. And men did things like this, what he was doing to me. Holding my bottom, his fingers gathering the fabric of my miniskirt so more and more and more of the flesh of my buttocks was bared. I wasn't wearing panties. A dare, to myself. I LIKED it, too. It felt wrong. Naughty. But so good, the way my* thighs rubbed together, the way my privates felt every draft of air as I walked. The way I had to sit carefully so no one realized. I was a good girl, but I didn't WANT to be good. I was invisible at school. No one noticed me. I had no friends. No one even picked on me. I just wasn't there. I wanted to be seen, to be noticed, to matter. I used to matter, before we came here, to this country. America was not what I thought it would be like. Not as clean, not as magnificent. Not as wonderful. Mama and Papa were always gone now and never had time for me. No one had time for me, except Caleb, and he'd made it clear I was too young for him. So I tried to grow up faster, for him. I listened to conversations about sex, looked things up on the Internet. Learned to curse in English. Today, I didn't wear panties, because maybe he'd notice, maybe he'd realize I wasn't a little girl. And he had! He'd noticed! He was kissing me and touching my bottom—my ass— and I felt his cock. Maybe he would have sex with me. I wanted him to be my first everything. My first kiss, my first boyfriend, the man who took my virginity.

He had my skirt up around my waist, one hand huge and warm and rough against my butt cheek, gripping it. The other . . . oh God, oh God, oh God . . . it was moving around between us. Inches from my privates. I'd touched myself there, of course. Made myself feel amazing sensations. Made things explode inside me, like something was coming apart in my privates, in my belly. Maybe he'd make me feel that. Or even better. I felt his finger, right THERE, nudging ever so gently against the edges of my privates—

But then he stopped.

He grunted roughly.

"You're not wearing any panties." It wasn't a question.

"No," I whispered.

"Fuck."

He'd never cursed like that.

"What?" I asked. Tried to kiss him again, wanting him to keep going. Keep going!

*But he shoved me away. Hard. I nearly fell to the dirty ground, and he stood there, leaning back against the wall, the hand he'd been touching my privates with pressed to his face. He was staring at me. His eyes were narrowed to slits, and his chest was heaving up and down as if he'd just run a race.*

*"You're a virgin." Again, it wasn't a question. I heard the liquor in his voice. But he was lucid, coherent.*

*"Yes. But I'm ready. I want this. I want you, Caleb."*

*His eyes go dead. I don't know how else to think of it, other than that they just go . . . flat. Empty. Hard and cold. He stands up straight, shoves his hands into his trouser pockets. Arrogance radiates off him in thick, palpable waves. He takes a long step toward me, stops so his face is less than a foot from mine, staring down at me with those eyes like cold dead chips of stone.*

*"I don't want you, Isabel." He delivers this calmly, easily. I know it's a lie. "I don't fuck naïve little virgins."*

*My heart twists, and my eyes sting.*

*"I tried to be nice about it, but you just don't get it, do you? You're so naïve! You actually think I'd fuck you? I wouldn't even let you suck my dick. So just go home. Okay? Go home, and grow the fuck up, stupid little girl."*

*And then he turns and walks away. He does not stumble, does not waver or sway. He turns the corner, and he's gone, and I manage to hold back the tears for a moment, two, and then they pour down my face. I feel the pang, the ache, the hate, the twist of the knife in my heart.*

*I turn and go home, replaying every moment, repeating every word he said to me.*

didn't mean it." You whisper this. Never have four words felt so porcelain. Especially from you. "I didn't mean it. But I had to make you . . . stop. Make you go away. Before I ripped that skirt off your

delectable, too-young, sixteen-year-old ass and fucked you there in
the alley. You were all woman. Sixteen, and a woman. But yet, still
a girl. So naïve. So innocent. Yet so hungry to be worldly. The
makeup you put on when you came to see me, you caked it on. Too
much of your mother's perfume. I pretended not to see you as you
would approach our café, but I always saw you. You would stop at
the corner, and fluff your hair, tease it out. Tug your shirt down and
push up your tits. Pull your skirt up to bare more leg. As if seeing
more of your skin could tempt me any more than I was already
tempted. You were just pouring gasoline on a wildfire, but you didn't
realize it. I was Caleb, and Caleb never gave anything away. Caleb
did not feel. So you never knew just how close you came, that night,
to being fucked up against an alley wall like a common slut. I fantasized about it, about that night. Fantasized, dreamed of what I might
have done differently. How I might have held on to your ass and
lifted you up around my waist. How I would have slid my cock into
you and fucked you so hard it would have hurt you. A virgin, you
were, and you would have bled all over me. I'd never fucked a virgin
before, and I wondered how tight you would feel. I'd fucked so many
women, so, so, so many. All of them older, more experienced. Thir-
ties, forties, and beyond. Or younger women who'd already been
initiated into the world of hard and fast fucking, the way I did it. You
would have cried, maybe. Then I could have kissed away your tears
and fucked you gently, to show you that I could." You speak reverently, using words I've never heard from you, expressions and turns
of phrase and inflections that I didn't know you knew. You are fading
between being Caleb and Jakob. "I jerked off, thinking of all the
things I wanted to do to you. I fucked my whores, pretending they
were you. But I stopped going to the café. I stayed away from Brooklyn, where you lived. I stayed away. I stayed away, Isabel. For you, I
stayed away."

I believe this. It frightens me, so I believe it. You wanted me, sixteen-year-old me. And I wanted you, twenty-nine-year-old you. But you stayed away from me. Because you wanted to fuck me so hard I would cry. You stayed away. I wish you had succeeded.

"And then the accident happened. It was in Manhattan. I still to this day do not know why you were there, in Manhattan. What you were doing. It was late. Past midnight. Cold. Wet. A fall day, a few months after the kiss. I was good, I was being good. Staying away. Keeping you safe from me. Keeping you out of my world. I was walking. I liked to walk, back then. I would walk to get something to eat, I would walk to meet clients, I would walk just to walk, so I could think. Of you, most often. Walking out the desire to find you and take you home and keep you. I didn't wait for the light. There were no cars, and I was preoccupied, so I just crossed, as I have a million times. But a car, an older green Impala. I remember the car. The rust on the front left wheel well. A crack in the windshield, low, near the base. A rock chip that spread, most likely. I froze. The car was barreling toward me, too fast to stop. That moment, it changed everything. If I'd just moved, if I hadn't frozen . . . things would be different.

"The driver hit the brakes, swerved to try to miss me. The back tires hydroplaned on the wet cement, and the car kept coming toward me, this time sideways. I saw him, your father. Behind the wheel. I saw his mouth moving as he swore, or yelled, or something. I saw your mother in the front seat beside him. Screaming. And I saw you. In the back. I saw you.

"Why did it have to be you? Of all the millions of people in the fucking city, in the whole fucking world, why did it have to be *you*? Why you?"

Why me, indeed?

You seem to choke on your words, on your breath. Scuff the toe of your fine Italian leather shoe against the concrete floor. "It would have been okay. I threw myself out of the way at the last second, and your car missed me, spinning through the intersection. But a pickup truck came through the intersection right then, from the left. T-boned your car. You were sitting behind your mother, or it would have killed you. It sent the car flying, rolling. I saw it. I fucking—I watched your car go tumbling like a goddamned Matchbox toy. The truck—I don't even know what happened to the truck, or the driver. Never bothered to even find out. I threw myself out of the way, but I got clipped by the truck as it went past. The side mirror hit my head and knocked me out. When I came to, your car was upside down a hundred feet away. It wasn't even recognizable as a car anymore. There was glass everywhere, and blood. I picked myself up and went over to your car, looked in. I saw your parents in the front—" You stop. Breathe carefully. "That's the only time something I've seen has made me vomit. Everything I've done, seen, been through . . . but what happened to your mother and father in that wreck was . . . awful. There are no words. But you weren't there. You weren't there. The backseat was empty. I don't know if you crawled out, or were thrown out. Still don't. I found you a good quarter mile away. Crawling on your belly. Bloody, incoherent, but crawling with this unstoppable determination. 'Ayuda me,' you said. 'Ayudalos.' Help them. 'Mama, Papa . . . ayudalos.'" You whisper the last three words, as I may have. Desperate, broken. "I picked you up. Carried you to the hospital. There were so many other accidents that night that things got lost in the shuffle. Paperwork was accepted half finished. The ER was a nightmare on earth. People bleeding, paramedics coming and going, ambulances everywhere, nurses just trying to get people into triage. It was a fucking battlefield. They took you from me. Asked about insurance and I said I'd pay cash, no insurance. That's all they cared about. I filled out your name,

address, what little information I knew. Told them I was your boyfriend."

"So the mugger . . . ?"

"A lie."

"I don't understand."

"I know." You let out a breath. "When I came back the next day,
you'd been moved out of the ER, out of the ICU. I still don't entirely
know what happened. Reports got mixed up, I don't know. They did
the surgery on you, and you seemed to be healing. There were so
many accidents that night, other stuff, shootings, a stabbing, a million different patients, a million different people and families and
investigations. Yours got . . . shuffled. Lost. Missed. I don't know.
The car was totaled, and your parents were unrecognizable. Their
dental records weren't in the system because they were from Spain;
there was no ID in the car. Lost in the wreckage, forgotten at home.
Just another John and Jane Doe, dead in a car accident, with no family
to ask about them, no reason to look, not when there were murder
victims and whatever, mysteries to solve. And you . . . you were
alone. You went under the knife. You had your head shaved, all that
beautiful hair shaved off. A nine-and-a-half-hour surgery, with no
promise you'd recover. I came back the day after your surgery, and
you were fine. I mean, not fine, but alive. Awake. Not really coherent,
but alive. I don't know if you didn't remember the accident, or if you
were too scared to ask about your parents, or if you were just in a
daze from the anesthesia . . . I don't know. So much I don't know.
Maybe the surgery was never actually successful and the fact that
you weren't really lucid was a symptom of something wrong in your
brain. They made me go home, and when I came back the next day,
you were gone.

"I went nuts. They had to sedate me, and when I woke up again,
they told me what had happened. That you had gone unconscious,

internal bleeding, put into a coma to preserve brain function. The bleeding had been stopped, but you weren't coming out of the coma. I sat by your bedside for a week. They made me leave. Six security guards physically and literally carried me out, put me in a cab, and told him to take me somewhere else. I don't remember much after that. Days, weeks maybe, I don't know. Just . . . gone. I went on a bender, stayed drunk. I don't remember any of it.

"When I finally dried out, I went back to the hospital. You'd been moved again. This time to a long-term care facility. No one knew anything about you there except your name. And you were just a body in a bed. There'd been so many different floors, so many different nurses and doctors, charts moved around, whatever, by the time you were moved to the hospice, no one knew how you'd even gotten hurt. Or about me. I showed up claiming to be your boyfriend, and they let me in to see you. I bribed them, honestly. A nice little stack of hundreds, a sob story about how I just want to see my girlfriend. If you believe a lie, everyone else believes it too. I really did just want to see you. That's all I cared about. They let me in, and I sat down beside you, and I cried. I came back every day after that. Every day. I filled your room with flowers. I brought in a CD player and played music for you. I read books to you. I . . ."

Another timeless, endless, fraught pause. A pregnant silence. Your shoulders lift, and you let out a breath, as if you'd been holding it despite all the words you've spoken, more words than I've ever heard anyone speak all at once, let alone you.

"Jakob died in that room. Jakob starved to death. Wasted away. I ignored everything. When the various men and women who helped run the various parts of my little empire came to me, concerned that I was squandering everything I'd worked so hard to build, I sold it all off. Everything. I set all my whores free, as I told you. Set them up with houses and jobs and money. Piece by piece, Jakob vanished.

There was a time, then, while you were in the coma . . . it's just . . . emptiness. I was no one. You've spoken of being no one, Isabel. And I understand what that feels like. All too well. No one knew my name. No one cared. You were in a coma, and it wasn't likely you'd ever come out of it. You were the only person on the face of the earth who knew me. Everyone else was . . . gone. Not dead, but they knew Jakob. And Jakob was gone. Months . . . it was months that not one person spoke to me, not one person said my name. The staff of the hospice was efficient, but they had a thousand other patients and you were just a half-dead girl in a coma with a crazy, unresponsive boyfriend. They ignored me. I kept to myself, so they just let me come and go as I wished. I slept there, many, many nights. I slept there—*Jakob* slept there, and at some point Caleb woke up in his place."

I dare to break the spell woven by your tale. "How—" My throat seizes around the words. "How long? How long was I in the coma?"

The glass of the window echoes your words. Reflects them, with your image, back to me.

"Four years, three months, and nineteen days."

# THIRTEEN

F our years, three months, and nineteen days.

"You told me six months!"

"I lied."

"You told me there was a mugger!"

"I lied."

"You—you told me I had no name. That no one knew who I was. You told me—"

You whirl. *"I LIED!"* You scream it, spittle flying.

Your voice echoes like thunder, reverberates.

"Why?" I back away from you. Emotions are at a boil within me, rising up into my throat like magma welling up the chute of a volcano and bursting against my teeth like vomit. "Why?"

You sag backward against the window, like a hot-air balloon with the furnace extinguished. "I couldn't face telling you the truth. Your parents were dead. Cremated, I believe, or buried in an unmarked grave. Everything you knew was gone. You remembered nothing. *Nothing.* I couldn't just leave you there, without a single memory,

without even your name. No one to ever visit you. You'd just waste
away there. But what could I do? If I had told you the truth about
yourself, what good would it have done? Your family's apartment
was long gone, everything sold off or thrown away. I had no proof
of anything. You, as Isabel de la Vega, existed only in my head. What
would you do with that name, that identity? Nothing. It would be
useless information. Like knowing the capital of New York is Albany,
it would mean nothing to you. But for me . . . you were still Isabel.
The girl I . . ."

You trail off, an admission aborted. I wonder what you were
going to say? *The girl I*—what?

I am feeling so many things, I cannot even parse a single thought
out. Anger. Confusion. Compassion; yes, for you. I understand. In
your place, what would I have done? I ask myself this but come up
with no answer.

"And at first, you were merely this . . . body, alive, awake, but . . .
empty. I don't know how to even describe you, in those first days.
You couldn't speak. You were weak, your muscles essentially atro-
phied, although the staff had done at least the bare minimum to
keep you from getting bedsores and complete atrophy. You weren't
even really aware of yourself or me or anything. You were just . . .
there."

You push away from the window, wipe your face with your palm.
"During the four years you were in the coma, I built my empire as
Caleb Indigo. I created a whole new identity. New social security,
new driver's license, a credit history, work history. It will hold up to
even the most stringent investigation. I paid several fortunes to make
sure Caleb Indigo was a complete and real human being with a life
any detective or federal investigator would believe, no matter how
closely they looked. There are even actors on retainer with entire
albums full of doctored photographs and memorized, scripted mem-

ories of me, should someone go looking. Jakob Kasparek is dead, and
Caleb Indigo is alive. He's real. He's me. I'm him. I became him,
completely. I took speech therapy classes to eradicate my accent. I
took acting classes to more fully realize my new identity as Caleb,
to sell him as a person even to myself. Business classes to learn how
to be a legitimate businessman, not just a pimp or dealer. I built a
new empire from scratch. A better one. A legal one—well, mostly
legal. But that's a different story. This is about you."

"Is it?"

You don't hear me. "By the time you woke up, I was lifetimes
more wealthy than I'd ever been as Jakob. I was in the process of
building a tower, a skyscraper of my very own. When it was clear
you were awake and would not be suddenly regaining your memory, but that you were physically well, I took you out of the facility.
Against their wishes, and against the rather vigorous objections of
the doctor. That was the last time I signed my name as Jakob Kasparek. I signed you out, and they let me. I brought you to my partially finished tower and put you in an apartment, and brought
therapists to you, to help you relearn to speak, to walk, everything.
About this time was when I realized I couldn't tell you who you
really were. You were different. You woke up . . . different. I don't
know. The girl I had known was gone. You were twenty years old
and had no identity."

You glance at me, to make sure I'm listening. "I know you want
to hear me admit that I saw it as my opportunity to . . . I don't
know . . . create you to be the person I wanted you to be. And I suppose on some unconscious level there was an element of that. I
helped . . . sculpt your new identity, but you chose it all. I didn't force
it on you. I brought you to the museum as something to do, and you
didn't want to leave. I wheeled you in your wheelchair from painting
to painting, exhibit to exhibit. And you made me stop at the *Madame*

X. That was real. I didn't do that. It was *you*. I sent you books, brought them to you, box after box after box. I brought all kinds of books. Classics, modern fiction, histories, biographies, crime, everything. And you chose what you wanted. You read what you wanted. And for two, almost three years, all I tried to do was help you . . . find yourself, I suppose. I taught you things, yes. Manners, bearing, presence. How to intimidate people. How to read people. *I* did not create Madame X—not alone. That was us, Isabel. I had no reason to think you'd ever regain your memories. So while I accept as valid your anger over what you perceive as me lying to you, that isn't quite fair. But then, life is not fair, is it?"

"How old am I?"

You blink, roll your shoulders, as if to shrug off the mantle of the past. "How old are you? Twenty-six."

"And my birthday?"

You smile, a faint, lukewarm thing, as if you've forgotten how. "July second, 1989."

"And how old are you?"

"I was born in 1976, in Prague, what is now the Czech Republic. I am thirty-nine years old."

"So when we first met . . . ?"

"You were fourteen and I was twenty-seven."

"And when you first fucked me?"

"This?"

I lift my chin. "Yes, Caleb. This."

You sigh. Pass your hand through your hair. You look so much younger than thirty-nine. Thirty, at most, I would guess. "You woke up when you were twenty, nearing twenty-one. It took . . . something like two and a half years of therapy before you were fully functioning, before you had complete autonomy over your speech, over fine and broad motor control, all that. In that time you were learning, reading, becoming Madame X."

"Caleb."

"I waited three years, Isabel—"

"Was I a virgin?" I ask, cutting in over you.

You wipe your face with both hands. "Isabel—"

"*Was* I a *virgin*?" I demand again. "You told me I wasn't. And now you're telling me I was. I don't remember, and I can't believe anything you say, clearly. How am I supposed to sort the truth from the lies?"

"You were a virgin. That's the truth."

"Why lie about it?"

A shrug, almost insouciant. "I didn't want to risk bringing up . . . all of this. Answering the questions I knew you'd have if you knew you were a virgin when we first slept together."

"Call it what it was, Caleb—you *fucking* me."

You lean close, suddenly fierce. "Oh no, Isabel. That's not what it was at all. You wanted it. You wanted *me*. You didn't know me, not as the man you'd known before the accident, but your body knew mine. You *wanted* me. So don't think you can pin that on me. I'll take responsibility for the lies, but I never took from you anything you didn't want to give me, sexually. Not then, at least."

"How old was I?" I ask. "When you—when we first had sex?"

"You were twenty-three. The first time I touched you sexually was on your twenty-third birthday."

"Why then?"

"You needed time to regain full mobility," you say, with a sigh and a shrug. "And I needed to make sure you weren't going to suddenly regain your memories. I lived in constant fear of that. I always have. I've dreaded and feared this day, when I would have to lay all this out for you. Try to make you understand . . . everything. I waited. Six years, I waited. I wanted you from the first moment I saw you that day on Fifth Avenue. I *craved* you after you kissed me in the alley. I thought I might go crazy with the need for you. And then you were in the coma for four years, and I watched you age, day by day, yet remain the same. And then you woke up, and you were no one. So I had to help you rebuild yourself. Or not *re*build, but . . . create a self. I couldn't touch you. I knew I couldn't. You had no way of consenting, of knowing what you would be consenting to, and that was not something I took lightly. But as the years went by it became clear to me that despite not knowing me, not remembering me, your body remembered your attraction to me. That was the same. You wanted me. You didn't seem to know what to do with it or how to act on it or what it meant, though. So I resisted it. Fought off my need for you, every single day for three years. I bathed you when you were helpless. Dressed you. Fed you. Taught you to do all those things for yourself. I was faced with the temptation of your naked body every single day, but I couldn't touch you. Couldn't have you. You wanted me, I wanted you, but I couldn't have you."

You halt. Swallow hard. Turn away. Scrape your fingers through your hair yet again. Fist your hand at your side. Clear your throat.

"My vow, to you and to myself, was that I would wait until your twenty-third birthday. If you were totally well, independent, and in possession of all your faculties and motor skills, and still showed evidence of desiring me, I would allow myself to explore a physical relationship with you. But not until then."

"So that day in my kitchen, when you came up behind me, not quite touching me . . ."

"I was on fire. I was mad, crazed. I'd abstained from physical contact of any kind with anyone for three months prior, in anticipation of that day." You turn to face me, stare at me, seeing me as I was then, perhaps. "You . . . *hummed* with sexual energy. Vibrated with it. And when I got close to you, you fairly radiated with need. It took every ounce of self-control I had to go slowly. To ease into it. All I wanted was to just . . . *take* you. Bend you over that counter and fuck you so hard it would shake the foundations of the earth."

"That's how it felt to me, that day. It felt as if you just took me, as if you fucked me exactly that hard. You took possession of me that day."

Your gaze becomes anchored in the now, fierce, hot, and wild. "Yes. I did. I'd waited seven years for that day. I took care of you, saw to your every need. Gave you everything I knew how to give you. And yes, when it became clear you welcomed my touch, I took possession of what was *mine*."

You advance on me. Stalk toward me, predatory, hungry. I back away, gripping the edges of my robe and tugging them more tightly closed. I back up until the wall of the elevator bank is at my back, and I can back away no farther. You stop, inches from me. Hands at your sides. Chest heaving. Eyes burning into mine. You spoke of me radiating sexual energy.

In that moment, you radiate thus. You burn, you hum, you are a living conflagration of sexual need.

Tears prick my eyes. My stomach twists. My heart is spiked through.

Because my body . . . it reacts.

Comes alive.

I thought I was past this, but I am not.

I never will be, I do not think.

"You cannot deny it, Isabel," you whisper. Your lips brush against mine, a feather-light, not-quite touch, not-yet kiss. "You cannot deny that I . . . own . . . your . . . *body*. I own your past. I own your *soul*. And you *know* it."

You take my hips in your hands. I feel you erect between us.

Again.

Here I am, *again*. Facing you. Facing myself. Battling the demon that is my body's instinctive reaction to you. And I must face that it is not just my body, but some powerful portion of who I am that is reacting thus to you.

But I cannot do this again. I cannot. I cannot.

*Will not.*

"But you do not own my heart, and you do not own my future." I find it hard to breathe as I say this. Indeed, the words are gasped. Squeezed through the slivers of space between my tight-clenched teeth.

A breath leaves you. A single sigh.

I force myself to look at you. To meet your gaze. To know viscerally and down to the pit of my soul the gnashing pain in your eyes as you absorb my words.

Your shoulders lift. Brows lower. Your jaw flexes. Dark eyes go molten with . . . sorrow? Rage? Some potent conflation of both?

Your hand rises up from my waist.

Fingers curl. Fingers tighten around my throat. Your eyes on mine.

My airway is constricted. I cannot breathe. Stars burst behind my eyes.

"*You . . . are . . . MINE.*" This, from you, is a snarling hiss.

I am lifted up, off the ground. My vision narrows.

I do not fight you. This is the price I must pay. You gave me truth, finally. I believe every word you said, and more that you didn't say, the word writ large and bold and bloody between the lines.

Your chest heaves. A sound emerges from you, a feral growl emitting from deep in your gut.

I feel oxygen rush through my teeth, into my lungs. Your fingers unclench. Slowly, ever so slowly. As if some invisible force is prizing each of your fingertips from my throat.

My feet once more touch the floor, and I collapse to my hands and knees, gasping, clutching my throat.

Watching through tear-blurred eyes as you back away. Hand still raised, as if still wrapped around my throat. A step back, another. A third.

A moment passes, in which I attempt to breathe, and you merely stare at me, jaw flexing, eyes narrowed, a blaze of emotion bleeding through your normally-flat brown gaze.

And then you reach into your pocket. Bring up your cell phone. Dial a number. Hold the handset to your ear. "It is time." And then you end the call, replace the device in your pocket.

A tableau, then. You, staring at me, hands fisted at your sides. Me, on my knees, robe coming open, hair in my eyes, breath rasping painfully through a bruised windpipe. Staring back at you.

Hands lift me to my feet. Pull me away. I do not take my eyes off you as I am drawn onto the elevator.

I see you, as I so often have, through the narrowing perspective of the closing elevator doors:

Tall, straight. Broad shoulders. Night-black hair swept back. Tailored suit clinging perfectly to your godlike physique. Hands at your sides, fists clenched. I see them trembling, see the way your jaw muscles flex and tense. Your brow is furrowed. Your gaze is rife, fraught, wild, molten brown.

You are a god.

You have been *my* god.

And I am walking away from you.

I have turned away from you. Denied you.

Chosen my future.

I put my palms on my belly, cup the slight bump. You see this gesture, and you flinch. Your head rocks back on your neck. The doors close, and I catch one last glimpse of you.

I cannot be sure, but it seemed as if you were falling to your knees, head drooping.

I do not believe that, though.

I close my eyes and I see you. Standing tall. Imperious. Gorgeous, perfect, cold, a statue carved from living marble. A Roman god made flesh.

You are my god no longer.

# FOURTEEN

The helicopter flares with sickening abruptness to hover twenty feet above my rooftop terrace. A man kneels in the open doorway, holding a rifle with a scope butt to shoulder, scope to eyes. Trained on Logan, who stands on the rooftop, effortlessly withstanding the battering down-blast of the rotors.

There is a winch, thousands of yards of thick rope, and a sort of foothold attached to the dangling end of the rope. A harness made of rough webbing is fastened around my torso and thighs. The rope is lowered a few feet, and a second man gestures. I am meant to climb out of the helicopter and cling to the rope, bare feet on the round metal as I am lowered to the ground.

The man, wearing a black helmet that obscures his features, clips a hook connecting my harness to the rope.

With steady hands and a thundering heart, I inch on my bottom to the edge of the doorway. Touch the soles of my feet to the cold skid. Stand up on quavering knees, grip the rope in both hands. Breathe in, hold it, and out. Twice. And then step away from the safety of the aircraft to stand on a tiny circumference of ridged metal. Despite the hook and harness, I am terrified. But there is no time for fear, because the winch whines and I descend rapidly downward. My heart is in my throat, and I squeeze my eyes shut to block out the sight of the rooftop growing larger and the helicopter smaller.

Down-blast buffets me, sends me swaying side to side and spinning in circles.

My gut rebels, and I clench my teeth, swallow hard, breathe through the nausea.

And then warm rough familiar hands clutch me: Logan. I can only shake and shiver as he strips the harness off me with the ease of practice. A moment of noise and howling downforce, my cheek to Logan's chest, his heartbeat under my ear. The helicopter ascends, the wind dies down, and then we are alone.

And I weep.

Shoulders shake, tears flow.

Logan scoops me up in his arms and carries me up the curving staircase and into our bedroom. Lies down with me, pulls blankets over us. I focus on his heartbeat as the only real thing in the world:

*Thrum-thrum . . . thrum-thrum . . . thrum-thrum.*

"Isabel?" Logan's voice, low and warm. "Did he hurt you?"

I don't know how to answer. I can only weep harder. But why am I crying? Being kidnapped? The fear of the descent? Relief at being home? That I passed the final test, won the final battle against my need for Caleb? That I finally understand myself, my past, how it all fits together? For the haunting torment so visible in Caleb when he released me, sent me away?

All of it.

And I cannot put it into words.

"I'm here, Logan." I whisper it to the cotton of his T-shirt; it's all I can manage. "I'm . . . okay."

"What happened?" This is a low rumble, rough, unsure.

Perhaps someday I will be able to tell him all that Caleb told me. Perhaps. But not now. Not today.

"I chose you." My voice breaks on the last word.

Logan rolls me off him, and I open my eyes. Stare up at him.

One blue eye blazes with love. Azure eye. Deep-blue-sea eye. An eternity of blue.

Delicate touch to my cheekbone, tracing down. He brushes aside a lock of my hair. He is levered up on his elbow, leaning over me. He touches the scabbed red dot where Caleb's knife nicked me. His eyes ask the question.

"I was gagged," I answer in a whisper. "He cut it off."

He traces a line across my jaw. Down to my throat. Touches with a tender fingertip five individual points on my throat, four on the left side of my windpipe, one on the right.

I shake my head. I can't answer that one. "I'm fine." It's all I can say.

"He put his hands on you."

"I'm fine."

"*Isabel.*" Harsh, a scold, angry.

I curl my palm around the nape of his neck. Gaze up at him. Let him see the pain in my eyes, the confusion, the relief, let him have it all, have everything I can't say.

"Just love me, Logan." I whisper this as well, to hide what I suspect is a hoarse rasp. To speak too loudly does hurt; Caleb's fingers left marks deeper than the bruises.

But Logan, Logan: You are my comfort.

I want to replace everything in my whole life with You.

Paint You over the scars on my soul. Wrap myself up in You, curl up in the warmth of You. Soak You into my skin, into my heart. Drink You, to slake my thirst. Relive each nightmare, each hazy memory, and sear You over each one. I need You, Logan. I want You in every crevice, every pore, I want to let the light of Your love blast away the shadows.

I won.

I walked away.

And it feels like I lost, somehow.

It feels as if I have ripped myself open to get away.

And more than anything else, it feels as if Caleb ripped me out by the roots.

Logan descends upon me. Presses his soft warm wet lips to mine and the kiss . . .

this kiss,

our kiss,

You kiss me as if there will be no tomorrow, as if there was no yesterday, as if You have never kissed me, Logan, as if You have never made love to me, as if I might vanish, as if I am fading away right now and You must cling to me and clutch me closer and kiss me to keep me.

Kiss me, Logan.

Keep me, Logan.

I do not speak these words, but You hear them anyway, Logan.

His fingers delve into my hair, and his body presses down on mine. I relish the weight, savor the tang of his tongue clashing against mine. His lips break away from mine, and we both gasp, breathless. And then he kisses me again, and again it is freighted with despera- tion, given tectonic power by the unspoken plea in my eyes, dripping silent from my lips. The plea is in my fingers as I work the cotton of Logan's T-shirt up his back and rip it away, breaking the kiss for a wild frantic second. The plea is in the way I fumble with his jeans, in the way I tear at the knot of my robe, needing both of us bare, needing skin against skin more than I ever needed anything in all my life. Were I starving, I would need this more than food; were I about to succumb from thirst, I would need this more than water.

I need it more than I need to breathe, because I can breathe Your oxygen, fill my lungs with Your breath and never need to breathe again.

Somehow, someway, Logan's clothes are tossed aside, and he is above me, magnificent chest bare, pectoral muscles scribed into his flesh as if by a razor, abdominal muscles grooved and ridged and cut with the same blade. His shoulders are broad, wider than the earth, blocking out the heavens and the stars. His eye is the sky, his eye is the sun. Warming me, giving me life. The patch is one I've not seen yet, rich supple white leather, hundreds of individual strands woven in ornate, interlaced knots. It is a work of art. His hair is loose and long and the color of honey, the color of ripe wheat, curling around his shoulders, strands catching in the stubble of beard on his chin. His lips are reddened and swollen from kissing me. His hands, rough, work-worn, scars on knuckles, callused, touch me. Trace my curves. Breathe heat and need into my flesh. Cup my breast and then my cheek with equal passion. I breathe and gaze at him and give him my soul. My will. My body.

He presses his palm to my belly, to the bump wherein a life grows.

I smile at him, and he kisses the tear tracks on my cheeks.

And now his palm descends to tease my core, closer, closer, closer . . . and then to my thigh, teasing. Kneading the muscle of my upper thigh, up to cup my well-padded hip bone. I have gained weight. *Pregnancy suits you, I must admit. It adds a softness to your already full figure.*

I banish that voice. It has no place in this moment.

No place in my mind.

No place in my life.

Not any longer.

I breathe in and will the voice to vanish, breathe out; and there You are, Logan. Kissing the corner of my mouth, Your eye on mine, watching me, knowing the battle I fight, and letting me fight it myself, so that I may know the sweetness of victory and come back to now, to here, to You, to us.

And I do.

There is only silence, only Your breath and mine, and the whisper of Your hand on my skin. The slight wet sucking sound of Your finger delving into my core, into my heat, into my wetness. Then the gasp from my lips as Your touch draws lightning out of the heavens and into my belly. Into my core. Your touch, Logan, it is everything. I feel it with every atom of my being, the way You touch me. The way Your lips graze my throat, kissing each bruise. The way Your lips then descend to kiss the swelling slope of my breasts, swollen with pregnancy. You lap at my nipple with the flat of your tongue, flick it erect with the tip.

I spread my thighs wide, draw my heels up to my buttocks, let my knees drape aside, open myself for You. Clutch at the supple muscle of your back, the cool hard bubble of Your beautiful backside. Murmur in delight at the way the smattering of golden hair on Your chest rubs against my belly and then my thighs. Whimper in abandon as Your nimble tongue finds my folds and scours them for every drop of essence, every drop of pleasure. My hips roll and writhe as You tongue me to climax, and I give full voice to my orgasm, cry out loud. And then I tangle the fingers of both hands into Your hair and haul You roughly up to my mouth, and I lick at the corners of Your lips, lick away my own taste, and then kiss Your mouth with such fierce fervor that You moan, and I bite Your lip until You grunt in surprise and I taste blood.

Oh, Logan, my Logan, my love, I feel You now. Here, against me. One hand still tangled and knotted in the wild golden mane of your locks, I kiss You, and with my frantic other hand I seek Your hardness, and find it hard as steel yet soft as velvet and thick and springy and slick. Wetness beading at the tip. Heavy down under the root, tight to Your body with need. I grip You and stroke You and caress You until Your kiss falters, and then I bring You to me. Pull You away from the kiss by my grip on Your hair, and gaze into Your eye, my own filled with tears of love and passion and too many millions of other manic boiling potent emotions that all I can do is ride out the maelstrom of them and hope You'll be there to kiss me back to life, be there to hold me until I gentle from the hurricane.

For in this moment, I am a hurricane.

I guide You to my slit. Lift my hips and grip You at the root and spread myself open with the thick broad head and pant and moan as I slide You into me.

"*Logan . . .*" I whisper Your name. A benediction. A plea.

You move, root Yourself deep. Rut into me.

I retain my grip on Your hair, and now I jerk You down to my mouth, kiss You. Mouth to my mouth, hips to my hips, hearts beating in unison, in parallel, in syncopated rhythm.

I glut myself on You.

Beneath You.

You lift up, lean back, rise up to Your knees. Tuck my feet into the crooks of Your arms, and You begin.

Slowly at first. Never looking away from me.

Then harder, and faster.

I feel my breasts swaying and bouncing with the vigor of Your love. I cup one, pinch my own nipple. You watch, and move all the harder for it.

And then I touch myself. Fit the fingertips of my middle and ring finger to my core, to my clit, and I rub. I find that rhythm, that quick rough circling motion unique to the way I touch myself. You watch this too, my fingers at my core, fingers pinching my nipple, the other hand raised to brace back against the headboard, so I have leverage with which to push against You.

Because no matter how hard, no matter how deep, I always want You more, want You harder, want You deeper.

Frantic and furious, You fuck me with such wild love that I could cry with the beauty of it, the perfection of it. To love, to fuck, they are the same with us, in this moment. There is no definition in connotation or context or meaning.

"Isabel . . ." A breath, as You falter, gasp, and fuck harder, slower, deeper, as Your climax rises within You.

"Love me, Logan," I moan. "Oh God, Logan, I need you."

"You have me, Isabel. Forever. All of me."

My eyes fly open, and I feel myself losing all control, losing everything, losing my grip on sanity as we move together, as we find that space in the moment of oneness wherein my soul and Yours tangle and collide and mesh, when the fabric of me and the substance of You plash and twist and mate, as conjoined one to the other as my body is to Yours in this moment. I feel that unison, and I drown myself in it.

I orgasm, and feel myself tighten around You. Core gripping your slick length, clamping down with all the power I possess, I writhe against You and scream Your name. You come explosively, and I feel it unleash inside me, feel Your seed fill me and drip out down my thighs. And You are still coming, falling forward to press Your face into the hollow of my throat, kissing my jaw as You flutter

Your hips with quaking aftershock thrusts, each of which sends a flutter of ecstasy through me.

"I love you. God, I love you."

"How can it be that every time we make love it's better than the last time?" I ask.

"I don't know. But it's true. It should be impossible, but it's not." You lift up and off me, pull me back into the sheltering cradle of Your arms. "If it's that incredible now, how will it be after twenty years?"

I nip at Your chest. "I don't think it's possible to even fathom." I twist, crushing my breasts to Your chest, lift up to look at You. "And Logan, I don't believe you can fathom how much I love you."

"Oh, I can guess."

"Can you?"

"You chose me. That tells me everything."

I lie back down, my cheek to Your pec. "He told me everything."

"Caleb?"

"Yes."

"Everything?"

"It felt that way. And it felt like the truth." A beat of silence. "At least, as much of the unvarnished truth as he is capable of telling."

"Care to share?"

"I need time to process it, Logan. There was a lot."

"As long as you need, babe."

I am sleepy. I don't fight it. I give in, willingly.

As I fade, I glance at the digital clock on the bedside table: 12:41 pm. So much can change in such a short time.

# FIFTEEN

wake up, and Logan is gone. The bed beside me is still warm, though, so he hasn't been gone long. I get out of bed, dress quickly in yoga pants and a T-shirt, and go looking. The terrace is empty, so I descend to the main level. Kitchen, empty. Living room, same.

My heart rises in my throat. The clock on the microwave says it's 2:19, so I didn't even sleep two hours. Where could he have gone? There is a hammered copper bowl that Logan owns. It is the size of his two hands cupped together, tarnished, battered. It sits on a ledge near the front door, and it is where he puts his keys and wallet whenever he comes home. Without fail, he will walk in the door, close it behind himself with his heel, dig out his wallet and toss that and his keys into the bowl.

The bowl is empty.

I do not like this. Logan never just leaves. At the very least, he leaves a note, telling me where he'll be. Or he sends me a text to read. My phone is plugged in on the kitchen counter; there are no messages.

I take my phone off the charger, slip my feet into a pair of flats, and move in a near-run out the front door. To the elevator, down to the parking garage. Our reserved spot is empty, but I see Logan's G63 heading for the exit.

I run. Flat-out sprinting, even though I'm wearing neither bra nor underwear. I catch up as he stops at the exit, checking traffic. Smack my palm to the back window. He was just beginning to accelerate, slams on the brakes. I hear the locks disengage, a loud *chunk-chunk*. Open the door, slide in, close the door, buckle the seat belt.

A moment of silence, unmoving in the exit.

"Goddammit, Is, you're supposed to be sleeping," he breathes. "You need to go back home. Now."

"No." I glance at him.

He is dressed in the same jeans and T-shirt as earlier, but now has tied his hair back and put on a Blackwater ball cap. There is a pistol on his lap, huge and black.

"What are you doing, Logan?"

He pulls out into traffic. Doesn't answer for a long time, a couple of miles at least. "Ending this, once and for all."

"I walked away, Logan. He *let* me. He brought me back."

"Doesn't mean he's done with you."

"You weren't there, Logan." I touch his bicep; his gaze remains focused on the road. "That was the end of it. It's over."

"He put his hands on you." Logan reaches out, glances at me, touches the bruises on my throat. "He left marks on you. Your voice is hoarse."

"Yes, but he let go. He let go of me, and he *let me go*. It can be over."

Logan doesn't respond. He heard me, but he is determined to do this.

A mile. Two. Three. We're heading to midtown, to Caleb's high-rise.

"Logan, please."

"You're *pregnant*, Isabel." We're stopped at a red light; he turns, and venomous rage is written in every line of his expression. "He kidnapped you off my mother*fucking* roof in broad daylight. He shot my dog with a tranquilizer. He *choked* you. I have tried like fucking hell to let this be between you two, to let you handle it your way. I've tried to stay out of it. I haven't even tried to get even for the fact that he tried to kill me, and took my eye in the process. I can handle that shit. Revenge isn't my style, Isabel, but when you fuck with my home, my dog, and my woman in one move . . . you do *not* get to just walk away unscathed." He is quiet, his rage is a fierce, hot flame, all the more terrifying for the fact that he is utterly calm.

Back to silence, one hand on the wheel, knuckles tight, jaw flexing and tensing, the other hand on his pistol, thumb flipping the safety off and back on, over and over and over, finger lying along the outside of the trigger guard.

He brakes to a rough halt outside Caleb's building, tires barking as he parks in a clearly labeled no-parking zone. He doesn't seem to care.

"Stay here."

"Logan, I'm not going to let you—"

His expression silences me. This is a side of Logan Ryder I've never seen before, and it scares me. "Isabel, I will only say this one more time: stay . . . the *FUCK* . . . here."

I stay. But I can see the lobby of the building through the glass doors. I watch as Logan exits the SUV, gun held tight to his thigh. His stride as he shoves through the revolving door is liquid, smooth, determined. I watch as he stalks across the gaping lobby, and I watch as he spots Len leaving the private elevator. I watch as Logan levels the pistol at Len, from less than five feet away. The few people in the lobby scatter, fleeing out the doors. I can see both men, Logan and Len. Logan has the pistol against Len's forehead. I see Len's mouth move, answering whatever question Logan asked: *Where is he?*

Logan backs away, lowers the pistol.

I see it in slow motion.

Len reaches into his suit coat. Withdraws the most massive handgun I've ever seen, a long-barreled silver thing with a black handle, a handgun large enough to be a cannon. Logan is walking away, gun at his thigh once more. Not hidden, but not obvious unless you're looking.

I see Len's arm go up. The hand cannon is level with Logan's skull. I am screaming, I think. I don't know. Even from this distance I can see the moment when Len's finger slides inside the trigger guard, and the moment when a thick index finger squeezes the trigger.

Flames belch. The concussion is like thunder, even through the doors of the building and the insulated interior of the Mercedes.

But Logan isn't dead. At the last moment, he pivoted and sidestepped, pistol whipping up into a two-hand grip.

*BANGBANG!*

His pistol jumps twice; I see each buck of the barrel, tiny burst of flame.

Len flinches, staggers. Gun hand droops. The silver hand cannon hits the floor. Red florets bloom, become a rosette, and then a spreading crimson splotch, and then Len's once-white button-down shirt is painted red.

Logan shoves his pistol into the back of jeans, drapes his shirt over it. Bends over Len, withdraws something from an inside pocket of Len's coat, and then straightens. Turns away. Walks toward the exit. Emerges from the building. Gets in the car. The engine is still on; he never shut it off.

The whole scene lasted less than a minute, and now Len is dead.

Logan doesn't look at me. He is utterly calm. Too calm. He has a key card in his hand, uses one hand to drive, clutching the key card in his fingers. The card was once white, and now is spattered with red.

I am fighting hyperventilation.

"Keep it together, Is. Not done yet." He doesn't look at me as he speaks.

We don't go far, just around the block to the private underground garage entrance and exit. There is a yellow box with a card reader, and a red-and-white-striped barrier arm. A swipe of the card, and the arm rises, admitting us. Down, then, into the darkness. Into the belly of the beast. The Mercedes's bluish-white headlights turn on automatically, bathing the dimly lit garage.

There are several cars parked with plenty of space between them, all Caleb's, I assume. The Maybach, a low, sleek red sports car, a yellow one, a green one, a buglike silver one. I don't know the names or models of them, nor do I care. There, directly ahead of us, is the private elevator. To the left of it, a black SUV. *Range Rover*, the badge says. It is on, idling, rear passenger-side door ajar.

It is facing the exit. Thomas stands outside the driver's door, an earpiece in his left ear. He has two fingers pressed to the earpiece, receiving the news of Len, I presume.

The elevator door slides open as Logan brings the car to a halt. Shoves the shifter into park. Throws open his door.

Steps out, bringing his gun up as soon as his feet touch concrete.

"Hands up, Thomas," he orders. "On your head. Now."

Thomas complies slowly, placing his paws on his clean-shaven scalp. Calm, unafraid. Eyeing Logan as a lion might eye prey from behind a scrim of tall grass. Waiting for an opportunity to pounce.

Caleb is walking toward us, still, eyeing the scene, one hand in a trouser pocket, cell phone to one ear, suit coat draped over an arm. Hair slicked back, freshly showered.

I am outside the car, though I don't remember moving.

Logan has his gun up, still. Touches the barrel to Thomas's temple. "Weapon out, now. Slowly. Two fingers." Thomas complies. "Now. Get in the car."

Thomas folds his huge frame into the driver's seat, buckles his seat belt, closes the door, and places both hands on the steering wheel.

Only then does Logan turn his attention to Caleb. "You, motherfucker. Get on your knees." The pistol leveled at Caleb adds weight and immediacy to his command.

Caleb ends the call, slips the handset into a trouser pocket. Stares, unperturbed at Logan. "I think not. I have business to attend to. If you're going to shoot me, get on with it. I have no time for dramatics."

"You had time to kidnap Isabel from my roof. You shot my *dog*."

"No one suffered any harm."

"You *took* her from our *home*."

"And brought her back."

"You choked her. Left bruises on her throat. Cut her with a knife. You brought her back naked and sobbing."

"She had a robe on."

"You cut off her bathing suit, you sick fuck."

"She was mine first. I was her first everything, Ryder. First kiss, first fuck, first love."

"She never loved you. It was Stockholm syndrome."

Caleb's gaze goes to me. "If you think that, then you do not know her as well as you think."

I am frozen, pinned in place by Caleb's eyes. There is something

in them. That in itself is unusual. But what I see is . . . an apology?
Despair? Farewell? Something I cannot place. Something dark and
tragic and definitive.

Caleb moves toward Logan, who shifts his grip on the gun, jams
the barrel against Caleb's cheekbone.

"I'll repeat myself one last time, Ryder. Shoot me now, or leave
me alone."

"That's all you have to say for yourself?"

"You killed one of my most loyal employees, a man I've known
many, many years. I returned Isabel to you as I promised, unharmed.
And you barge into my place of business, into my *home*, kill my
friend, threaten me. What do you want, Ryder? Do you even know?"

"You, dead," Logan snarls.

"Then kill me. I am unarmed." Caleb speaks barely above a
murmur. I have to strain to hear him.

"Logan, don't." I take a step, reach out. For Logan? For Caleb? For
both? I don't know.

"Get in the car, Isabel."

"On this, your boyfriend and I agree. Get in the car, Isabel."

I ignore both of them.

Caleb turns his attention back to Logan. "You won't shoot me."

Logan pulls back the hammer. "Oh no?"

"Do you know what it would do to Isabel, if she watched you
murder me in cold blood?" Caleb is unmoving, allowing Logan to
keep the gun pressed barrel to cheekbone. "And ask yourself, Logan,
why you're here. Is it because I took her from your home? Is it really
about your dog? Or is it personal? This is about *you*, Logan. It's about
you and me. I got you put in jail. I set you up. I lured you in, waved a
few million in front of you, and you took the bait, hook, line, and
sinker. You spent five years in a white-bread federal pen and now you
want revenge. You probably won't even admit it to yourself, though,

which is why you're pinning this on me. Acting all outraged. But it's revenge, Logan, plain and simple."

"Shut up." Logan jabs with the barrel, cutting open Caleb's cheek. A rivulet of blood runs unchecked. "SHUT UP!"

"You're unhinged, Logan. You think you're in control? You think you'll get away free? You've already shot one person. I haven't reported it yet. I might not. Len is not a man anyone will mourn, save perhaps for me. And an investigation wouldn't do any good. Having you arrested wouldn't do me or Len any good, nor Isabel. But you still murdered him. I have reason to hold a grudge against you for that."

"He shot at me first."

"Because you threatened him. He is—*was*—not a man to take such a thing lying down." Caleb's chin lifts. "I'll ask you again: What . . . do . . . you . . . want?"

"Logan, let's go." I take a step toward the men.

"Get back, Is. Stay out of this." Logan lowers the gun, turns away, shoves it into his waistband.

Pauses for a moment, a thumb at the corner of his mouth. And then he pivots, swings his fist, and punches Caleb so hard I hear bone crack against bone.

Caleb flies backward, head rocking on shoulders. Logan follows, fist swinging again. But Caleb isn't down. A stagger, a stumble, and then a pivot, and Caleb plants a fist in Logan's belly, stopping his rush.

The fight is short and brutal. Both men are hard, powerful, and unafraid to bleed. I watch, cringing, as they batter each other with fists, knees, elbows. Both are bloody. I can only watch, weeping.

For Logan.

But . . . for Caleb, too.

Because despite it all, I cannot say with any certainty that I didn't love Caleb.

They are on the ground, rolling. Caleb's knee jerks up, buries in
Logan's gut. It's enough to buy Caleb time to roll away, and somehow,
when Caleb sways upright, Logan's pistol is leveled at its owner.

Logan is gasping, gagging, coughing. Bleeding from the nose, lips
split. Caleb isn't in any better shape, but Caleb is the one upright,
wielding the pistol.

Aiming it, in a moment of terrifying déjà vu, at a prone, vulnerable Logan.

"Caleb, no. Please, please don't. Not again."

"He came here, Isabel. He came to me."

Tears blur my vision.

I'm dizzy. Disoriented. Weeping, sobbing, gasping, unable to
breathe.

Staggering to Caleb.

To you.

To him.

I don't know anything.

"No, please, Caleb." I hear my voice. "Please. I love him."

"You loved *me* first!" You . . . he . . . Caleb . . . shouts. I don't think
I've ever heard a shout from those lips.

"Did I?" I'm in front of you. Gripping your arm, clutching your
bicep, pulling with all my strength, trying to pull the barrel away.
"Or did I just not know any better? I never knew anything but what
you allowed me to know! I never knew anything! I never knew you,
there was never anything to know. You were an enigma. You've
always been an enigma, Caleb! You are totally opaque. Nothing gets
in, nothing gets out. I never know what you're thinking, what you're
feeling. I never know what you want. You'd fuck me, but it meant
nothing. You never kissed me. You never touched me as if you cared.
You *possessed* me, and nothing else. Is that love?"

"Isabel—"

"NO! I heard you out, now you fucking listen to me! I don't remember much, but I remember going to see you at the café, once. How you turned me down, and how it hurt. But I was a stupid little girl obsessed with a good-looking older man. I didn't know what I wanted. And I don't even remember being her, anymore, that silly infatuated little immigrant girl. The problem is, I'm not her anymore, I haven't been for a long time. And you know what else I remember? All the times you dominated me, fucked me and fucked me and fucked me, toyed with me, played with me, got me right to the edge but wouldn't let me come, as punishment for some sin I never committed. I remember you fucking my mouth until it hurt, until I gagged and choked and couldn't breathe. I remember you pulling on my hair until I thought it was going to rip out by the roots. I remember you showing up in the middle of the night, fucking me, and leaving. I remember never seeing you face to face during sex. That's what I remember! Being a *thing* for you! Being your slave! Nothing but a . . . a *fuck-toy*! That's what I was, that's *all* I was. And then now that you start to finally show some semblance of humanity, of being a real person with real feelings, I'm supposed to go, 'Oh yeah, I guess I did love him after all'? What was I to you, Caleb? What did I mean? Why did you keep me all those years? If you really sat at my side while I was in a coma, not for six months like you always told me, but for four *years*, then *why*? Why? And why create this elaborate persona? Why keep it all secret? Why should I believe anything you told me? I want to, but I don't think I can. You've lied about too much, lied about you, about me, about everything. I don't think you even know the truth anymore yourself." I step over Logan, who has regained his breath, finally, and is working on finding his feet. I put myself between the gun and Logan. "Let it be over, Caleb."

"It *was* over, goddammit! I let you go. And *he* brought you back here. To me."

"Put the gun down, Caleb." I look into your eyes, Caleb, and I see a world of torment, I see hell, I see agony. Why now, Caleb? Why now?

Logan, You are behind me. Chest heaving. I can feel You, feel Your heat, feel Your chest against my spine as You breathe.

I am looking at you, though, Caleb. You stare me down. Stare *into* me. The pistol is held casually in your hand; you spin it and grip it by the barrel. Hand it to me.

Back up a step. A second. Your gaze never leaves mine, Caleb.

"You'll never know, Isabel."

"What won't I know?" I whisper the question.

"What you meant to me. I told you that, once. I told you that I'm not the kind of man who can . . . express such things." You swallow hard, Caleb. "I wish I were. I wish there were some way for me to make right all the ways I fucked up with you, for so many years."

"Caleb—"

Into the rear passenger-side seat, through the still-ajar door. A last glance at me. At my belly. Brownbrown eyes, normally so flat and cold and expressionless, blink. Hard. As if seeing the child within my womb, as if seeing in a single glance all that could have been.

And then you close the door, and Thomas puts the SUV into gear. Accelerates smoothly toward the exit.

I do not know why I follow. Why I jog through the cloud of exhaust, pistol still held in my hand, a heavy weight, heavy with the knowledge of Len's life cut short. Why I run out after you, Caleb, into the street. Cars honk, tires squeal. A voice shouts.

I feel You behind me, taking the weapon away, wrapping Your arms around me. Pulling me away.

I watch as you drive away, and I know it is the End. I know. I know.

Good-bye, Caleb.

A stoplight. A one-way street, three lanes abreast. In the right lane, a delivery van, white, featureless, old. In the left lane, a long black SUV. In the middle, an empty space. The Range Rover glides to a halt between the two vehicles. Idling at the light, waiting for the green.

I'm about to turn away, as red flashes into green.

I feel it first. In my bones, in my blood. A hum, a vibration. Followed half an eye blink later by a blinding white-yellow flash.

*WHUMP—*

*BOOOOM!*

I am thrown backward by an invisible wall, by a hand snatching me in hot unseen fingers and hurling me across the road, to slam back against the hood of a cab. The wind is knocked out of me; I'm gasping, panting, trying to cough, to sob.

You're there, You're hauling me into your arms, I hear nothing but a hum a buzz a ringing in my ears, see nothing but flames where the Range Rover used to be. The flames billow and ripple in slow motion. I see Your mouth moving, Your face obscuring my view of the burning wreckage. I see it behind You, though. Flames licking and flickering. Charred metal. Debris strewn across the road, chunks of burning cloth, twisted pieces, shattered plastic.

"—Bel . . . Isabel?" You are shaking me. "Isabel! Look at me, babe."

I slide my eyes to You, to Your one eye, Your indigo eye. Then past, to the flames, the wreckage. Beside, to the left, the Suburban is on its side, windows smashed, metal charred. Someone is crawling out of the broken passenger-side window, bleeding from cuts to face and body. Someone rushes to help, hauls the person out of the car, helps them stumble away from the wreckage. A crowd is gathered, staring, pointing, chattering. Taking photos with cell phones.

An oddity: The panel van is trundling around the corner. Vanishing. Unscathed. The white panels blackened a bit, but disappearing around the corner. I don't know why I notice this, but I do.

You lift me. Scoop me into Your arms, and I feel Your heartbeat. It is soothing, centering. I am dizzy. Disoriented. Ears ring. My face is hot, seared from the blast.

Sirens howl, somewhere in the distance and getting closer. A fire truck, huge and red, is first on the scene, firefighters in full gear jumping out and springing into action, putting out the fire. More sirens, police cars probably and ambulances.

I am settled into the passenger seat, buckled in. I feel the engine turn over. I am in shock, I think. Everything is slowed, my ears ring, my mind is blank, my heart numb.

Caleb is . . . dead?

The wrong way down the one-way street, far too fast.

Around a corner.

Another.

Out the window, all is normal. Crowds cross intersections, carrying shopping bags and purses and briefcases. Couples duck into restaurants, examine menus posted outside doors. Cabs, yellow and myriad, ply the avenues.

A woman, stopped at an intersection, waiting for the walk sign to light up. I play my old game, invent a life: She is still young, but older than me. Blond, beautiful. Wearing a skirt far too short, a blouse that hugs massive breasts. The blond hair is from a bottle, teased out, curled into ringlets. Wearing too much makeup. Wearing spiked heels too many inches high. A man approaches the woman from behind, waiting to cross the same as her.

I create a romance for the two, staring at them out the window, still shocked, reeling, unfeeling, as You wait for the light. She is a stripper, maybe. Or a call girl. But she has a secret, a son at home. A little towheaded, blue-eyed hellion who is her whole world. She hates stripping, but she does it for him, to provide for him with the one resource she has. And the man approaching the same intersection, stopping behind the blond woman, the stripper. He stopped far enough away that he can stare at her. He's a weightlifter, wearing track pants and running shoes and a tank top, despite the cool in the air. His arms are way too big, bigger than any man's arms need be. He's lonely. Spends his life at the gym, because despite his macho attitude, despite his massive physical presence, he's nervous around women, gets tongue-tied.

I imagine that the muscle-bound man finds the courage to say hello. And the stripper finds the courage to say hello back. She's afraid of being seen as easy, because of how she makes a living, even though she's not. She's anything but easy, in fact. So she comes across as aloof, arrogant even. But she's lonely, too. So she says hello. And they walk together. He asks if she wants to get a coffee or something. She discovers that beneath the rough, muscled, surly demeanor, he's actually a sweet, thoughtful person. A hard worker, and willing to see her for who she is. Willing to see past the teased-out hair and skimpy, slutty clothes and the nights dancing naked for strangers.

It's a diversion, this fiction.

Caleb is dead.

Caleb is dead.

I stare out the window and cry, silent tears sliding down my cheeks. I hide them, because I don't think You'll understand.

I don't think *I* understand.

Caleb is dead.

# SIXTEEN

relive that explosion in my nightmares.

Night after night, I feel the detonation. See the flames flickering hungrily.

*He had a lot of enemies*, You tell me, in an attempt to explain it.

It means nothing to me.

Caleb is dead. I do not weep, after that moment in the car. I don't know how. I think I have cried all the tears I possess. For you, Caleb, I do not mourn. I relive your death, over and over and over.

And I relive every moment we ever spent together. All the moments I spent naked, waiting, coming, being taken, being owned, being used. Every moment where you looked at me in that inscrutable way you had, giving nothing of your thoughts away. How you would fasten your pants: left leg first, always, then the right. A slight hop to tug them into place. Button-down next, fingers nimbly fitting each button into place. Tucking the tail of the shirt into the pants. Zip, fasten, buckle the belt. It took less than a minute, all total.

And then you'd be gone.

And I'd be alone.

Until the next time you showed up. At midnight, or between clients. Hands possessing me, as if my will had nothing to do with anything, as if my desires meant nothing. Stripping me, positioning me. On my hands and knees, or face to the window, as you were so fond of. On my knees, for a swift moment of oral pleasure, at the expense of my abused gag reflex.

Day after day, night after night. I was your sexual possession. You rarely spoke to me, except to order me to my knees, or to strip, or to go to my room and wait, or to tell me about the next client. We never just . . . talked. You appeared, commanded my body, and left.

And my body *obeyed*. That's what mystifies me, even still. That I always obeyed. That my body responded to your commands, that I seemed to have no will where you were concerned. As if you possessed some secret method to control me, to elicit responses from me.

Am I mourning?

Perhaps I am.

I don't know.

I know nothing.

Did you tell me the truth, that day in the empty building? Four years, three months, and nineteen days? Or six months? How old am I? Are the memories I've regained real? I remember sitting in the museum, in front of the *Madame X*, and then going with you to see *Starry Night*. I remember it. I feel it. The floor under the wheels of my wheelchair. The lights, dim, spotlights bathing each piece of art, islands of beauty in oceans of darkness. I remember you behind me, hands on the handles, pushing slowly. Pointing out pieces you know, telling me their names, carrying on a one-way conversation. Turning left, and then right, going down long hallways, and then finally coming to a stop at the *Starry Night*. I *remember* this. It is *real* to me.

But it isn't possible. The *Madame X* and *Starry Night* are at different museums.

My memory is a lie.

Humans can invent memories from whole cloth. We can convince ourselves a lie is truth, and truth is lie.

So then, in the absence of memory, what do I believe?

In the presence of contradiction, what is truth? You told me yourself, Caleb, that you lied. So then how do I know anything you told me, ever, is true?

Am I even Isabel de la Vega? If you can create Caleb Indigo from scratch, could you have created Isabel?

What if I am just some victim you saw, and wanted, and took? What if nothing I think I remember is true?

*Your name is Madame X. I'm Caleb. I saved you from a bad man.*

*I own your past. I own your soul.*

*You are mine.*

I am on the terrace. Hands on the grit of the ledge, staring out at the night, at the city as it breathes and lives and moves, reliving you, doubting you, doubting myself. Doubting everything. Doubting my name, my past, my memory.

Nothing is real.

Nothing is true.

Then, oh, then I feel You.

You lean on the ledge beside me, except You lean backward, ass to ledge. Cup Your hands around Your mouth, flick a flame into life. Smoke curls, billows. You inhale.

You've left me alone, for the most part. For days. I've been ruminating and stewing and floundering for days. Lost in memory, lost in thought.

"Enough, Is. He's not worth this." You speak the last sentence around a mouthful of smoke.

"I'm doubting everything, Logan."

You tuck the cigarette into the corner of Your mouth, pull me to You. Cheek to chest, heartbeat under my ear. "Hear that?"

"Yes."

"What is it?"

"Your heart."

"Exactly. My heart. And what is it doing?"

"Logan, I don't—"

"What is my heart doing, Is?"

"Beating."

"Why?"

"Why?" I wrinkle my nose in confusion, twist my head to look up at You. "What do you mean, why?"

"Why is my heart beating, Isabel?"

"Um, so you—"

"For you." An inhalation, cheeks hollowing, spewing a gray stream. "My heart beats for you."

"And mine for you, but—"

"What's your name? Your full name."

"Isabel Maria de la Vega Navarro." I let out a shaky breath. "But he lied about so much, Logan. I don't know what to believe anymore."

"Believe that I love you. Believe that I love this"—You put your hand under my shirt, to the little bump—"this life, growing inside you. I love you for everything that you are. I fell in love with Madame X. I fell even more in love with Isabel Maria de la Vega Navarro. I fall in love with you every single day. That week in Spain, do you remember it?"

"Of course! I'll never forget it as long as I live. It was the best week of my life."

"Did it matter what lies Caleb told you, while we were in Spain? Did it matter what the truth was or wasn't?"

"No." I whisper this, a tiny, heavy nugget of truth.

"No, it didn't." You toss Your cigarette out into the street. "And when you wake up next to me, do you think of him?"

"No."

"What do you think about?"

I blush. "You. Us. Making love to you."

"Does it matter, then, what the truth is or isn't?"

"No."

"No. It doesn't. You are Isabel. That's the truth. You *chose* to be Isabel, to *become* Isabel. You chose to love me. You chose to let me love you. Now you have to choose to let go of the past. The past doesn't define you. Our pasts shape us, Isabel. They influence us. Our pasts are part of us. Our pasts can inform our future. But our pasts are *not* who we are. You aren't Madame X anymore. Maybe Caleb lied about how you met, how old you were, how long you were in the coma, who he was, all of that. Maybe what he told you was the truth, maybe it wasn't. There's no way to know. He's dead, Isabel, and he was the only one who knew the truth. And you know something else? Even if he were still alive, I don't think we'd ever know the whole truth about you, and him, and whatever else."

You tip my chin up with a fingertip. "And here's the thing, Is: *It doesn't matter*. None of that matters. Not anymore. Because you and me, honey, what we have is a beautiful future together." You kiss my lips; I taste smoke, but it's You, and I don't mind. "It's unwritten. We can make our future whatever we want. But to do that, you have to let go of Caleb, let go of Jakob, let go of Madame X."

I just breathe. I breathe in Your scent. Press my palms to Your chest, flutter them up to Your throat, feel Your lips, the stubble on Your jaw, bury my fingers into Your hair. I breathe You.

Kiss You.

Taste You.

And in that kiss, in that taste of my lips on Yours,

I kiss,

I taste,

I breathe in the future.

With You.

# SEVENTEEN

Two months after the explosion, our doorbell rings.

I am reading; You are cooking.

You answer the door; I hear murmurs, an unfamiliar male voice.

"All right, come on in, I guess." I hear Your voice, wary and cautious. "What is this about?"

"I have to speak to Miss de la Vega, Mr. Ryder. I'm sorry, but I cannot divulge anything to anyone except her."

I am showing now. I have taken to wearing loose dresses and yoga pants with stretchy waistbands. I put my e-reader down, and wait. You appear first, casual and perfect in jeans and a tank top, barefoot. The visitor is tall and thin, slightly hunched, as if expecting a blow any moment. Balding, only a fringe of graying dark hair remaining. Dressed in an expensive three-piece suit, complete with a pocket handkerchief and a matching tie, and carrying a slim brown briefcase.

I stand up. "I'm Isabel de la Vega."

A hand, extended. "Good afternoon, Miss de la Vega. My name is Michael Yancey Bowen. I'm a senior partner at Bowen, Brown, and Callahan."

"How can I help you, Mr. Bowen?" I put on what I think of as my Madame X persona, cool, aloof, superior. I have almost forgotten her, I think, and it is a relief to know I can still summon her indifference when I must.

"My firm represents the interests of Caleb Indigo, and by proxy, the entire Indigo spread of companies."

"And again, how can I help you?"

Michael Yancey Bowen glances at a chair kitty-corner to the coffee table. "May I sit?"

I gesture, imperiously, to cover the nerves I feel. "Please. Would you care for coffee or tea?"

"No, thank you." Michael takes the chair, sets the briefcase on the coffee table, and opens it with a flick of thumbs against latches. Withdraws a manila folder, turns it to face me, and sets it down in front of me. "As you may be aware, Mr. Indigo was an extraordinary businessman. He was extremely wealthy, and conservative with his wealth, considering the scope of his assets. He owned the high-rise here in Manhattan, a few vehicles, a private jet, and a small estate in the Caribbean. Other than that, there wasn't much . . . except a startlingly massive amount of liquid assets in banks and tax shelters all over the world."

"What does this have to do with me, Mr. Bowen?"

Bowen gestures at the manila folder and the small stack of papers therein. "The tower, along with all of his other physical assets, businesses, and subsidiary corporations, have been sold. He had no outstanding debt, so everything sold was at a rather tidy profit, and added to the already significant sum of money he possessed in movable liquid assets."

"Again, Mr. Bowen, what does this have to do with me? Spit it out. I have no time for wading through legalese."

Bowen gestures insistently at the folder. Withdraws an expensive pen from an inside suit coat pocket, taps the topmost paper. "Mr. Indigo had a standing will, which I personally drew up for him several years ago, and which he had me update four months ago. The update was simple, but sweeping."

The line Bowen tapped, near the bottom of the paper, is a number. A large number. Three commas between dollar sign and period.

"One more time, Mr. Bowen; what does this have to do with *me?*"

"The update made four months ago was to make you the sole inheritor to all of his assets upon his death."

"What?"

"Once the tower, estate, and various businesses and enterprises were sold, the sum total to be distributed upon signature acknowledging receipt, is fourteen billion, eight hundred seventy-seven million, five hundred forty-three thousand, two hundred and thirty-one dollars and twenty-one cents."

My brain is spinning. "And twenty-one cents?"

Bowen checks the number. "Yes, twenty-one cents."

"You're serious?"

"About the twenty-one cents?"

"No, Mr. Bowen, not about the twenty-one cents. About—what did you say? Fourteen billion and what?"

"Fourteen billion, eight hundred seventy-seven million."

I am, yet again, having trouble breathing. "The fucking bastard left me fourteen billion dollars?"

"So it would appear, Miss de la Vega." Bowen flips the page over, starts rattling off the procedure for accepting the money.

It's more complicated than merely signing, apparently. I'm not listening.

I stand up, pace away from Bowen, the table, the will. Bowen keeps talking, and finally I pause, turn, hold up a hand. "Apologies, Mr. Bowen, but please . . . shut up for a moment."

I find myself going upstairs, out onto the roof terrace. Breathe in, breathe out. Find a seat, stare at the sky, the pale azure dotted with shreds of clouds.

I hear You, feel You sit on the lounge chair behind me, feel Your arms go around my shoulders. You pull me backward so my back is to Your chest. "I told Bowen we'd visit him at his office, that you'd need time to process this."

"Thank you, Logan."

"Fourteen billion dollars, Isabel. That's a fuckload of money. It'd make you one of the wealthiest people in the world."

"I can't believe he was worth fourteen billion dollars, Logan. I knew he was rich, but . . . *that* rich? Where did he get it all? Not from escorts and bride services. Not from Madame X."

"No, obviously not. He had fingers in everything. Real estate, stocks, technology. I think his real money came from the tech side of things, though. He owned a company that owned a patent on a medical device of some kind, something that every hospital, every doctor's office, every military base all over the world uses. He didn't invent it, but he bought the company that did, which was floundering in obscurity from lack of marketing and distribution resources. He recognized the value in the patent, and got it out there. Got the accounts one by one, until the owners of some truly sizable hospitals started catching on, and it took off like wildfire. This was while you were in the coma, I think. Before that it was all real estate, stocks, and a bunch of small companies all over the spectrum. After that medical device caught on, he was set."

"But . . . fourteen billion dollars?"

"It's a lot of money, Is."

My heart is twisting. "Too much. And it's . . . *his.*"

"Think about it, okay? Even coming from him, it's fourteen *billion* dollars, Isabel. You don't just turn that kind of money down."

"I . . . I can't, Logan. I just can't."

"No one could."

I shake my head. Stand up. Pace furiously. "No, Logan, you don't understand. I can't take it. Not a single dime. I can't. I *won't.* I can't take anything of his. He owns enough of me as it is. Even in death, he's trying to own me, control me. If I take that money, I'll still belong to Caleb Indigo."

"You're serious."

I turn and look at You. "Money has never really meant anything to me, Logan. Not in any real practical terms. It's just a number, objectively speaking. A large number, but just a number. I can't accept anything from Caleb. I can't have anything to do with him. I have to be done."

"I get that. I really do. But please, think about it. Just for a day or two, at least."

I shake my head. "No, Logan. I don't need to, and I don't want to. I'm not going to change my mind."

"You're absolutely sure that this is what you want to do? Just say, 'No thanks, keep your fourteen billion dollars'?"

"You make it sound foolish, Logan." I am irritated. A little mad at You, honestly. "I am taking ownership of myself in turning down this money, *Caleb's* money. I didn't win the lottery. I didn't earn it. It is Caleb trying to manipulate me from beyond the grave. Turning down Caleb's money is the only thing I *can* do. I cannot and will not be his creation, his creature, his slave, his *possession* any longer. If I accept the money, regardless of how much it is, I would be putting myself back under his thumb. Selling myself to him, yet again. It would be just the same as if I'd never walked away from him at all.

If I want to be free, truly free, of Caleb's domination of my life, then I have to be free of any and all ties to him. And that includes his fortune, vast as it may be."

You move to stand in front of me. Take my face in your hands. "I didn't mean to make it sound like you're stupid for not taking it. It's just . . . it's a fucking lot of money. I don't think there is another person in the world capable of saying no to fourteen billion dollars."

"Saying the number isn't going to make it any more real to me, Logan. I am incapable of comprehending the reality of that much money. I don't think anyone really is, but me least of all. My life thus far has not afforded me the kind of experience necessary to understand the value of money." I grasp Your wrists in my hands. "And what's more, I do not need to. You are not poor, by any measure. You will provide for my every need or want, and more besides. I have total faith in that, and in you. I do not *need* Caleb's money, because I have you. And hopefully, someday, I will earn money of my own."

"I'm with you, babe. I support you."

"But do you understand?"

"Yes, I do. I have a different view of money, because I've worked so hard for so long, because I came from nothing. I don't pursue wealth as a goal in and of itself; I pursue success. I enjoy what I do and want to be the best at it, and fortunately, being the best means I make a lot of money in the process. Having the money I do means I'm better able to fathom the reality of what fourteen billion dollars looks and feels like, what it can do for you. It means I can better understand what you're refusing. But it's not my choice."

"If it were your choice, if it were you making this decision, would you keep it?"

You take a moment, think about it. "I'd be a lot more tempted to rationalize why I should keep it, let's just say that."

"Let's go, then. I want to be done with this once and for all."

You are thinking again, and do not immediately respond. You look at me. "Can I make one small suggestion?"

"What?"

"Don't just refuse it outright. It'll get . . . I don't even know, really, parceled out. Wasted, gobbled up by whoever can get their hands on it."

"So what should I do with it?"

"Donate it. You know how many charities you could fund with that money? There's an endless amount you could do with it. With even the tiniest percentage, you could fund an entire school district for *years*. You could put an entire city full of kids through college. You could feed thousands of people. Put in wells in Africa. Build shelters for homeless people. My point is, don't just walk away from it. You don't have to keep it for yourself, but don't just . . . leave it sitting on the table. Take it, but use it for others. You could form a nonprofit, fund it with Caleb's money, and literally spend the rest of your life putting that money to use helping people. That's—fourteen billion dollars, Isabel?—that's world-changing money. Use it to change the world."

"You'll help me?"

"Of course."

"Then let's do it." I feel a fever coming over me, ideas spinning through my head one after another too fast to pluck any single one. "When you talked about the charities you donated to, I got this— rush, from hearing you talk about it. And just thinking about it now, I'm getting excited. What better way to use Caleb's money than to make the world a better place with it?"

"So you want to run a nonprofit? It's a lot of work, babe."

"But it's making a difference. Toward the end of things with Caleb, when the status quo started changing—because of you, you know—I was growing increasingly discontent with the fact of Madame X, of what I—what *she*—was doing. Questioning the value in it. We talked about it, I think. How I felt as if I were wasting my time, wasting my *self* trying to turn spoiled brats into half-decent men, especially as it became obvious I never really changed them, just showed them how to hide their inner bastards. This? You said it yourself, this is a chance to do something powerful and life-changing. I don't just want to distribute the money, though. I want to . . . *do* things. Dig the wells. See what the money does."

You are glowing. "This is going to be so cool, watching you do this."

"You're helping, Logan. *We* are going to do this."

"I'll help form the nonprofit, sort out the tax exemptions and all that, get you staffed and whatever else, the nuts and bolts of it, the mechanics of a corporation. That's what I do, after all. But this is you, Isabel. I'll support you, go anywhere with you. If you're digging wells in Africa, so am I. If you're rescuing girls out of prostitution in Thailand, so am I. But honey, this is going to be your project."

I do not argue. He's right.

For the first time in my life, I have a purpose, something I've chosen. And, oddly, I have you to thank, Caleb.

Again.

But this time it's a positive debt.

I wonder what you would think, if you could see what I'm going to do with your fortune?

# EIGHTEEN

am in the ultrasound room of my doctor's office, and You are in a chair to my left, hands both around one of mine. With my other I keep my shirt tucked up into my bra, so it doesn't get smeared with the ultrasound jelly.

The ultrasound technician, a woman named Lisa, has one hand on the wand, swiveling and sliding it all around my belly, angling it this way and that, tapping at the keyboard, sliding a ball that I think acts as a kind of computer mouse. Taking measurements, Lisa says—we'll get to the good stuff in a minute.

I peer at the TV screen opposite the bed/table I'm on, trying to decipher what I'm seeing. But it's all a mystery, nothing but blobs and shadows and black and white, and sometimes ribbons of pulsating, shifting color.

You glance at me, brows drawn down in a pinched expression of concentration. Maybe you see something I don't?

And then Lisa taps a key and the room is filled with a rushing, rhythmic sound. A heartbeat. But there's an echo to it, or an overlap—*thumpthump-THUMPTHUMP-thumpthump-THUMPTHUMP*, a sound too fast to even be a fetal heartbeat.

"Is that echoing sound normal?" I ask.

"Let me just . . ." Lisa doesn't finish the sentence, though, but rather shifts the wand around, does something to narrow and zoom the focus, and captures the heartbeat again.

Swivels, shifts, angles, utterly focused. But frowning, brow furrowed.

"Is there something wrong?" I ask.

"Not wrong, no. But I just want to verify what I think I'm seeing with another tech, okay? Just sit tight." And then Lisa leaves, comes back a moment later with another woman whom she introduces as Megan, an ultrasonographer.

Megan introduces me to the less-than-wonderful experience of a vaginal ultrasound, doing much the same as Lisa did, only inside me. What fun.

And I'm worried, because Lisa isn't telling me anything, and neither is Megan, and I'm starting to panic.

"Can you please tell me what's going on?" I ask, trying to keep the panic out of my voice.

You squeeze my hand, smile at me—*it's okay*, You're telling me, without needing words.

"Okay," Megan says, zooming the perspective in, bringing up the strange, overlapping heartbeat, then holding the wand steady at a specific angle, so that within the black oval of my uterus there are two small white blobs visible. Megan points at the screen with an index finger. "So what we have here, Mom and Dad, is two babies."

"What?" I sound as breathless as I truly am.

"You're having twins."

"Are you sure?" I ask.

Megan laughs, not unkindly. "Yes, I'm sure. There's no way to mistake it, not from this angle." An index finger, stabbing the screen. "One, two. And yes, there are *only* two."

Twins.

Not just one unexpected child, but *two*.

We go home, and I think we are both in a daze. Once through the front door, I slump, stunned, to the couch.

It is overwhelming. How does one prepare for motherhood? I don't remember my mother, aside from a few minor glimpses. I haven't remembered anything else, and I don't think I will. Nothing major, at least. I don't remember my mother. I don't remember my father. I don't remember my childhood aside from a couple of insignificant memories. With no examples, how will I know whether I'm doing it right or wrong?

I am not worried about loving them; I already do, fiercely, wildly. I think of them, whisper their names, and I feel this virulent, surging wash of throat-constricting emotion, a willingness to do whatever it takes. I have read so many books on parenting, read a thousand blogs on the subject, browsed through countless online chat forums. I go to the park and watch mothers with their children. Try to picture myself, a baby on each hip. Try to imagine waking up at midnight or three in the morning to feed them. Try to imagine buckling a little life into a car seat.

The visions are easy.

But I imagine the reality is always different. No one can ever be ready for parenthood, I think. You can't ever truly comprehend the truth of an entire life being solely dependent on you for survival, for guidance, for love.

Thinking about the lives inside me, more than anything, makes me miss my parents. Or, rather, the idea of knowing them. It is difficult to put into words, even for myself. I cannot miss them, because

I remember very little of them. I miss . . . the idea of them. I wish I remembered them. I wish I had them around to ask for guidance and advice. I wish . . .

So many things.

Too many things.

"Isabel?" You, on the floor in front of me, looking up at me. Searching me with Your one vivid blue eye.

"Twins, Logan." I speak the truth out loud, and I am no less afraid for saying it.

"Twins, Isabel." You seem calm. Too calm.

I look down at You. "You seem unaffected, Logan."

A shrug. "It's two babies rather than one. More diapers, more bottles, more everything. More love."

"I wasn't ready for *one* baby. Now we're having *two*?" I try not to cry, but it is futile. The tears leak.

You slide up onto the couch, shift me onto you, and now I am lying on top of you, hearing your heartbeat, slow, steady, reassuring. "It's going to be okay, babe. We've got this."

"We do?" I am not so sure, and I sound it.

"Of course we do. I've got love to spare, sweetness." You kiss me. Make me look at you so I understand, so I do not just listen, but truly *hear*. "If I have enough love for you and one baby, I've got enough for you and two babies. And Isabel? So do you."

"But I don't know how to have a baby. I don't know how to be a mother, Logan."

"Yes, you do."

I shake my head. "I barely remember my mother. All I have are a few random memories. How will I know what to do?"

"The memories you do have, what are they like?"

I breathe in, and then out, thinking. "I have the impression that she was a wonderful mother. She took care of me. She loved me. And she took care of and loved my father."

"That's all you need to know, Isabel. She loved you, she took care of you. And these babies inside you"—Your palm goes to my belly—"You will love them, *both* of them. You will take care of them. The how? The mechanics of being a parent? I don't think anyone is really ready for that, babe. But you do it. You learn, you figure it out. We'll figure it out together, okay? We'll love them, *together*. We'll take care of them, *together*."

I nod. I feel somewhat reassured, but still scared.

And it dawns on me that You found a way, once again, to tell me it would be okay without saying so.

The next several months are spent becoming increasingly big with pregnancy, and getting the nonprofit corporation set up.

I've decided on a name—for the corporation, not the babies: The Indigo Foundation. It's your money, Caleb. You earned it. You worked for it. It will be your legacy, carried out by Logan and me.

I couldn't begin to explain or understand the complexities of setting up something of this scale, so I am thankful every single day for You, Logan, for how easily You facilitate the process, creating accounts and interviewing staff and moving the money around and a thousand other things, on top of running Your own business. For my part, I have been researching charities, looking into the laws and regulations regarding donations and funding, deciding what I'm going to do once the whole thing is set up.

It is a lengthy process.

This will not be a small undertaking. It will be, as You said, a lifelong project. It is a gobsmacking amount of money, and there are an unlimited number of causes in need of funding and support. I am overwhelmed just thinking about it, compiling the lists. There is so much to know, so many causes that are worthy and in need. Which do I pick first?

You are in the chair beside me, working as well; You work from home almost exclusively now, having made some promotions in the office and rearranged things in order to be with me as much as possible. I am nearing my due date—*any day now*, our doctor tells us—and You don't want to be away from me for even a moment. You have attended every doctor visit. You personally painted the nursery—green, a neutral color, because, as we discovered at the gender-reveal ultrasound, we are having a girl and a boy.

Camila, for my mother, and Luis, for my father.

You put together bassinets and cribs and bouncers, picked out onesies and bibs—blue ones for Luis, and pink for Camila—stocked up on diapers and wipes and ointments from the Honest Company. If I feel them kicking, you put your palm to my belly. And what a belly it is. I feel mammoth, so enormous I can barely move. Everything hurts. Being pregnant is definitely real now. Too real. Camila and Luis are there, inside me, ready to come out. I need them out, I need to be done being pregnant. It is exhausting, taxing, draining. I am in a fog, and merely walking down the stairs from the bedroom to the kitchen takes an eternity, and I have to rest halfway down, and then again once I reach the bottom.

I try to picture doing this alone, being a mother, having an unexpected child. No Logan to comfort and provide for and protect and love. I try to picture a woman, large with child, making her way down the streets of New York, on aching feet, exhausted from working to keep the roof over her head, food in the kitchen.

And I know what The Indigo Foundation's first project will be: a resource center for single mothers, a chain of them across the country, even. Bills paid. Pantries stocked. Nurseries prepared. Childcare provided. Postpartum depression therapy. Regular get-togethers of other single moms in the area, for mutual support and willing ears who understand the hardship.

I draft an e-mail outlining my idea and send it to You. Within fifteen minutes, You have returned the email with practical next steps: find a location for the first center, begin interviewing staff, set up the charter and structure, find additional donors, locate resources to tie in, food pantries and daycares and patient advocates and babysitting services. The list is massive, and daunting. But it provides me with additional steps to begin working on.

I decide the first center will be in Queens, an area that seems, in my limited estimation, in need of such a service. I make a list of potential available locations based on a quick real estate search, send it to You, and You in turn send it to one of the assistants You hired for the foundation, who then immediately heads to Queens with an itinerary and a list of needs from a potential location.

The day is consumed with this work, and the hours fly by quickly. Karen, the assistant, reports three likely locations for me to choose from. Merely from a few e-mails You send to former clients, we secure several donors for the project, and I come up with a long list of resource providers that are interested in partnering with the center.

I need a name, though.

I decide, temporarily at least, on MiN: Mothers in Need.

Realizing I've been working for several hours without a break, and that my bladder is screaming at me, I decide to take a break. I've also been feeling occasional contractions for the last few hours, what I assume are Braxton-Hicks contractions, and usually getting and walking around helps them go away.

So I stand up, and I'm immediately gripped by a sharp, painful contraction.

*Pop*; warmth and wetness on my thighs, streaming down my legs.

"Logan?" I keep my voice quiet, calm.

You glance up. I'm wearing a loose, ankle-length dress, so there's no visible evidence of what's going on. "Yeah, babe."

"My water just broke."

You blink at me for the space of ten seconds, and then You're up, grabbing my laptop and Yours. You say nothing. We've discussed this. You take my arm, guide me inside. Grab the overnight bag You've had prepped for the last two months. I stop in the bathroom to put on a pad and grab a couple extra, and then we're in the car, and You're driving with barely restrained frustration through the typical Manhattan traffic. It's a Friday, six in the evening, which means traffic is a snarled nightmare.

You're holding my hand and driving with the other. Your jaw is tensing.

"Logan?" You shoot me a look. "Take a breath. It's okay. We'll get there."

"In this traffic, you could be having the babies in the car."

I gesture out the window. "Well, good thing there's an ambulance right there."

And there is, too, trundling along two lanes over, lights off, siren off, the driver's arm hanging out the open window.

You laugh, finally. "Why are you calmer than I am?"

I shrug. "Probably because the contractions haven't really started yet. Give me time, I'm sure I'll start panicking soon."

And, oh, how right I am. The contractions haven't even really begun in earnest yet, from what I've read. They're still several minutes apart, and yes, painful, but not as bad as what I've read has led me to expect. What has me panicking is the knowledge that—again, according to everything I've read—once my water has broken, the only options are to have the babies naturally or to have a C-section. What if I can't have them naturally? I don't want a C-section. I don't want to be cut open. But what if something is wrong that I don't know about? What if we take too long getting to the hospital and the babies go into distress? I *really* don't want to have the babies on the side of the road, for all that I joked about it with You. That was to calm You down; I need You calm, in control. Because I am panicking now.

And a contraction has me in its grip.

Sharp, fierce, aching, clamping, so sudden and crushing I can't breathe. So painful it makes me whimper.

"Breathe, honey, breathe through it. Remember? Like at the class." You went to the Lamaze classes with me.

I try to breathe. Just like a panic attack, I have to force the oxygen into my lungs, force them to expand and suck in air, and then I have to force them to contract, expel the air. And again. God, it hurts.

I'm starting to think the contractions I was feeling weren't Braxton-Hicks contractions—practice contractions—but real, actual labor. Which means I could be closer to having these babies than I thought. I glance at the clock as the contraction finally releases me: 7:32 P.M.

We inch through traffic, stuck between blocks, waiting through cycle after cycle of the traffic light. Inch by inch, forcing myself to think of nothing, to just breathe and just be. Fight the panic, fight the anticipation of when the next contraction will hit. Inch by inch, minute by minute. We make it through the intersection after five minutes. At the eight-minute mark almost exactly, another contraction strikes.

I try to remember what I've read about the stages of labor, but my brain will not supply the answers.

Two more sequences of contraction/rest, and we finally reach the block where we have to turn. And then, God, we're stuck on that block. And the next. Inch by inch, minute by minute. You aren't talking, which is fine, but You are still holding my hand, and You don't say a word when I bear down with each contraction, squeezing Your hand until I'm sure I'm close to breaking bones. You just tolerate it, and squeeze back.

By the time we reach the hospital, the contractions are six minutes apart.

You pull under the ER pavilion, and we're met by a large black male nurse with a wheelchair, who greets us by name; apparently You called ahead? I don't remember that. I remember hearing Your voice, but I was in the middle of a contraction at the moment and had no attention to spare.

I'm wheeled through the hospital—but You're not at my side. Where are You? Parking the car, I think. But I need You, Logan. I can't do this without You, not any of it.

I feel You first, as I always do. And then Your hand is in mine and You're beside me, kissing the back of my hand, telling me it's going to be okay. A contraction hits, and when it clears, we're in the maternity ward, and I'm being helped to my feet, out of my clothes, into a gown, into bed. Wires connected, monitors and leads. Another contraction, hard and painful. But still six minutes apart.

I need them closer together, not because I want the pain but because the closer they are together the sooner I'll have my babies in my arms. The sooner this will be over. The sooner I'll know my babies are safe, and healthy.

By the time a doctor shows up, I'm embroiled in the battle against panic. It's taking too long. The contractions are too far apart. It took over an hour before the OB showed up to check me.

The OB is an older man, medium height, thin, with small,

almost delicate hands. Bald, but with a short, trimmed beard going white.

I'm almost fully dilated, but not very far effaced. Which means more labor.

God, it hurts.

Another two hours of pain, and then another doctor shows up: the anesthesiologist. I'm turned to sit on the edge of the bed, legs dangling off the edge, my gown pushed forward, nearly off. A minute or two of preparation, packages being opened, sterile gloves tugged on.

"Dad, you may want to step out for this," the anesthesiologist says to You.

"I'm a combat veteran," You say. "Not gonna freak out over a needle. And there's no way in hell I'm leaving her."

"Well then, pull up a chair in front of her. Hold her hands and let her put her forehead on your shoulder." You do as he says, and there's a smear of cold on my back. "This is iodine, to clean the area. Now, hunch your back for me. Lean your forehead on Dad's shoulder and push your spine out toward me. Good. Yeah, now hold it like that—hold real still for me, okay? Deep breath in . . . and let it out all the way. . . . Now a quick pinch—"

Jesus, that's not a pinch, it feels like a fucking sword being shoved through my flesh. I breathe through it, teeth clamped, squeezing Your hands so hard I think I hear bones being ground together. You are stoic, letting me crush Your hands, watching the doctor insert the needle. I stare at Your feet, at the worn, beloved Adidas sneakers You've owned for so many years, the laces tied in a permanent double knot, tongue tugged to one side, heels scuffed and frayed from years of shoving Your feet into them. Breathe through the pain as the doctor fiddles with things at my back.

"Okay," the doctor says, "that's in, all connected. I'm gonna start you off kind of low, and they'll crank it up as you go. Good luck, Mom and Dad."

There's a rushing sense of numbness spreading through me, a sense of relief. Calm. I can see the contraction-measuring device's readout from my bed, and I watch with wonder as the readout shows a contraction, but I feel nothing. Blessed, peaceful nothing.

Another three long boring hours and the OB comes back, checks me again. "You're effacing nicely, Miss de la Vega, almost a hundred percent now, and fully dilated. That's good news. And your contractions are consistently a minute or two apart now, which means we're getting closer to baby time. You'll get there. Not long now." A pat to my hand, and then the OB is gone again, white coat billowing, bald head gleaming.

Despite the OB's promise of "not long now," it is still several more hours before anything changes. I'm dozing, rolling from one side to another. I start to feel an ache. Distant, but real. A sense of the contraction through the epidural, a clamping down of my womb. And a need to push.

You're sleeping, curled up awkwardly on the fold-out chair/bed, asleep instantly in that soldier's way You have.

I endure the ache and the need to push for a few minutes, but then it starts to become unbearable, pushing down on me, a kind of desperation infusing me.

I push the call button, and within seconds a nurse is bustling in, efficient, energetic, eyeing the monitor, casting a glance at You.

"Oops, looks like it's go time, Mama." A nudge to Your foot. "Wake up, Dad, you're about to have some babies."

You sit up immediately, rub Your eyes, blink a few times, and then the room is full of people. One person does something to the bed, removing part of it and unfolding stirrups, lifting my feet high and wide, spreading me open for the whole room to see. I'm beyond caring, though, because now even with the epidural the pain and need to push is all-consuming. Someone else has turned on blinding lights overhead. Another person is getting supplies ready, and yet another— or maybe it's the same few nurses moving in efficient harmony—is turning on a machine and shoving aside the chairs.

"Go stand by her head, Dad," the OB says, by way of entrance. "Hold her hand and when I tell her to push, you count to ten. She takes a breath, and then you count to ten again. Okay? Oh, yep, here we go. Moving right along, aren't we? Maria, can you cut the epidural off? She needs to feel the contractions now. It's gonna hurt a bit, but you have to feel them so you know when to push. Hold your man's hand and break his fingers if you have to, we'll fix them when you're done."

A nurse does something to the IV feed, and the epidural fades, a reversal of how it kicked in. Peace, calm, relief . . . it all fades away, replaced by crushing, all-consuming, fierce, fiery agony. All-pervading pressure centered on my womb and my bowels. There is no space between the contractions, it feels like, no chance to catch my breath, just wave after wave, one contraction on the heels of the last, and the need to push, push, push.

"Not yet, Mom, don't push yet." The OB is putting on a kind of gown covering the front, and then a kind of clear plastic face mask, and a pair of sterile gloves. "Okay, I think we're set. Here comes a contraction, Mom, get ready to push. Deep breath in . . . and PUSH! Count for her, Dad!"

I hear You, feel You. I bear down with every fiber of my being, teeth clenched. I don't scream, don't waste the effort on it. Just push, push, as hard as I can, while You count.

"... Seven ... eight ... nine ... ten!"

I let out the breath, gasping, whimpering, turn to look up at You, try to smile when You take a moment to brush my sweaty hair out of my face. And then I'm sucking in a breath and bearing down, pushing.

Again.

Again.

Again.

"Good, Mom! You're doing great, the first one is crowning! Keep pushing, keep pushing!" I take a quick breath and push even harder, and then there's a feeling of being emptied, something pulled out of me, and there's a moment of silence, a brief respite from the pain.

And then a sound fills the room, and I am irrevocably altered. A sound, and my heart now exists in the world outside of my body.

A cry.

Small, fragile, but strong and loud.

A wail, high and thin and quavering.

"You've got a girl, Mama!" The OB lays a wet, warm, wriggling, squalling body on my chest, still smeared with blood and effluvia. Light hair, blond, thick in a ruff over the top of her head in a mohawk. Little fists shaking, clenched. Little feet kicking.

"Hi, Camila," I whisper, clinging to her, cuddling her close. "Hi, baby girl."

But then another contraction rips through me, and I have to push again, because oh yeah, there's another baby inside me still, ready to come out.

A nurse takes Camila and then I can't think or breathe or feel anything but the ache, the grip, the pressure, and You're counting and I'm pushing.

It hurts.

I'm exhausted.

But I'm not done yet, so I push.

You count, and I push.

Is it hours, or minutes, that I push, crushing Your hands in a death grip? I don't know, cannot measure time, only the increments of one through ten and the brief respite between contractions and the push-pushpushpush*pushPUSH*, almost there, keeping pushing, Mama . . .

Another push, and then the same pulling emptying sensation, a sense of relief, and the silence . . . the cry.

Oh, that cry.

It pulls at my heart, slices me open, puts my world, my life, my being, my love into a little bundle, a wailing wriggling bundle of baby boy.

"Here he is, Mama, a boy! He and his sister have all their fingers and toes!" But there's an odd note in the OB's voice.

I see why, when my son is settled on my chest.

Camila is fair, and blond. I see her, being lifted, cleaned, diapered, swaddled, and her skin is fair, like Yours, only not tanned golden by the sun as Yours is. Hair is platinum, like yours. And I just know, when she opens her eyes and the irises have adjusted to their permanent shade, they'll be Yours, indigo, blazing blue.

But the boy on my chest . . .

He's dark. Thick black hair. Swarthy skin.

Utterly unlike You.

I sob.

Because I know.

I know.

He is yours, Caleb.

His name isn't Luis.

He is Jakob.

I look to You, and I see that You know as well. I don't know how it's possible, but one look tells me it's not just possible, it's undeniable.

You lean close to me. Kiss me. Brush hair from my face with a broad thumb, smile, that beautiful, sun-warm smile. "He's perfect, Isabel."

"But he's—"

"Mine, my love. He's mine. He's *ours*. Okay?" You lift him, slimy and afterbirth-gray, crying, shaking angry, indignant fists, and cradle him to your chest. "His name is Jakob."

Did I say that out loud? I don't think I did.

I know I did not.

So that is You, claiming the child as Your own, loving him as Your own, even though, somehow, genetically he is not. You claim him, but honor the genetic father.

Not Caleb, but Jakob.

Jakob, the man I could have fallen in love with, had I known him. Jakob, the man, I believe, who let me go.

I'm not quite done yet, though.

I have to push again, one more time, to deliver the afterbirth.

I push through it, but I'm focused on You, now holding Camila and Jakob both, one in each arm, and the pain is nothing to the fierce wild all-consuming ache of love.

Jakob is taken, cleaned, diapered, tested, swaddled, and I'm allowed to get up and shower and eat something—it's been hours, almost a whole day, and I'm starving.

And then I have my babies, my son and my daughter. Sleeping, nuzzling against me, mewling now, hunting. Latching on, fumbling at my nipples, and then latching on perfectly. Suckling, and the tug is sharp and beautiful as my milk flows.

And You're there, sitting beside me, watching me feed our babies.

"I love you so much, Logan." It's all I know how to say, right now. I don't even know how to verbalize or even understand myself the emotions regarding Jakob's genetic heritage. "I just—I love you."

You have tear tracks on Your face, and You are proud of them, I think. To weep at the birth of Your children is the mark of a man in touch with his emotions, I think; a sign of strength and confidence rather than a mark of weakness. You have brought a life into the world. A new life, and it is beautiful. It is enormous. Momentous, and life-changing.

You lean in, kiss me, kiss Jakob, kiss Camila—

So this is what completion feels like.

What we're looking at," the doctor says, a day after the birth, "is heteropaternal superfecundation."

The doctor pauses, taps the heel of a shoe with the tip of a pen. Glances at me, and I can feel the silent, unspoken, but very real judgment.

"In layman's terms, it's when a woman releases more than one egg in the same cycle, and those two eggs are both fertilized by sperm from separate acts of sexual intercourse with different males." Another pause, a glance to me, to You, back to the shoes. "It is extremely rare, but there have been a few other documented cases. I've been delivering babies for thirty-two years, and I've never seen it before. What it means, practically speaking, is that the two children are fraternal twins, genetic half siblings, despite being developed and carried in the same womb."

You speak up for me. "So how are they?"

"Camila and Jakob are doing beautifully. Healthy, scored high on all the postbirth tests, they're eating well from Mom, great lung development. Absolutely no issues whatsoever."

"So aside from genetics . . . ?"

"Genetics aside? They're beautiful, healthy twins. You can go home in the morning."

"Thank you, Doctor." You dismiss the doctor, standing up, extending your hand. Making it clear the time to exit is now. When the doctor is gone, You turn to me, take my hand. "What a dick."

"He didn't say anything unprofessional," I point out, even though I feel the same way.

"He didn't say anything, no, but the looks he was giving you, the way he explained it . . ." You shrug. "Whatever. He's gone. But I didn't like him."

"I felt it too. But it doesn't matter. He doesn't know me, or my life, or my situation. All I care about is you, and our babies."

"Me too."

And so we do.

We buckle the tiny little sleeping bundles into the car seats, murmuring at how tiny they look in the big seats. You carry them both, one seat in each hand, while a nurse pushes me in a wheelchair. You settle them on either side of me while You fetch the car, and then You click the seats into the bases, check that each one is secure, and then You help me into the SUV, practically lifting me up and in. I am weak, sore, tired, and exhilarated to be going home.

Emotionally, I haven't really sorted through the reality of Jakob, yet. Maybe I never will.

He's mine. He's Yours, Logan. But . . . he already looks so much like you, Caleb. When he blinks those big brown eyes, he's *you*. He cries when he's hungry, and there's a demanding note to his cry that, to me, sounds like you. It is eerie. His jawline is you, his nose is you. The bridge of his nose is you. God, he's *you*, Caleb.

I ruminate on it as You drive us home, Logan, driving slowly, carefully, defensively. Braking gently, accelerating gently. Music low, tuned to classical.

I am still deep in thought when we get home. You carry them in, instructing me to stay put, and then You come back for me. They are sleeping, so we leave them in their seats. We collapse together on the couch, and You pull me against Your chest, so I can hear Your heartbeat. I begin to doze. Sink, drift—*thumpthump, thumpthump, thumpthump*—sun warm from the windows soaking into my skin, bathing my closed eyes.

And then a cry. Small and quiet at first, a hesitant quavering. Just one.

You get up, unbuckle the crying child—Jakob. Hand him to me, and I cradle him against my chest. God, so tiny. So warm, so soft. So sweet. I lift up my shirt, expose my breast, and tickle his quivering lips with my nipple. He works his mouth, snuffles and snorts, shakes his head side to side, and then latches on with ferocious hunger and alert determination. He's so tiny still I can support him with one hand, and stroke his thick black hair with the other.

You watch, a little awed, a lot moved. "It's the most beautiful thing I've ever seen." Your voice is low, rough.

I keep stroking little Jakob's hair but my eyes are for You. "I have to say it, out loud, at least once." I glance down at Jakob, then back up. "Caleb is Jakob's biological father, and you are Camila's."

"But they're both mine."

"I know. And I—I don't doubt that for a moment," I say.

"It might be a little tricky to explain, if he ever starts asking questions when he's older."

"We'll figure that out when it happens." I smile. "I just had to say it, because . . . inside, it doesn't feel as if it matters."

"It doesn't. Not really." You offer me a smile, a quintessential Logan Ryder smile, the one that warms me from the inside out. "It's nature versus nurture, Isabel. If you were to separate identical twins, and one was raised in a hellhole of rage and violence, and the other in a loving home full of affection, you'd very likely have two wildly different people emerge as adults. Because the environment in which a person is raised makes all the difference. Caleb could have been . . . someone totally different had his parents lived. Had his cousin not turned him out on the street. Had any number of events in his life been different."

"You came out of some very difficult circumstances yourself, and look at the kind of man you are."

A shrug. "We each can only do the best with what we're given. That's all I've done. Yet, too, we each make our own choices in life. I chose to change. To try to improve myself. To be better. I think at some point, Caleb just . . . gave in to the kind of man his environment was conspiring to create, rather than trying to rise above it. It's not up to me to judge him, to either absolve him or vilify him. I didn't know him well enough, and it's not my place even if I did. I know how I feel about him, based on my interaction with him, and based on the way he treated you, but that's it."

"So what you're saying, then, is that despite being Caleb's, genetically, how we raise him will determine the kind of man he'll become."

"Right. He'll have the admittedly impressive genetic potential of Caleb, but you and I will raise him to not have the . . . questionable ethics Caleb showed as an adult."

"I like that idea," I say with a smile.

"So do I."

Camila starts crying just then, right as Jakob unlatches, a little milk dribbling down his chin. You unbuckle Camila, hand her to me and in exchange for Jakob, cradle him to Your chest, settle onto the couch beside me. You hold a sleepy, milk-drunk Jakob, I feed Camila, and we relax together.

A family.

That's when it dawns on me, hitting me like a ton of bricks, like a freight train:

I have a family.

The realization brings tears of happiness to my eyes. I let them roll, because it is a beautiful thing, this understanding. I was orphaned, not just of my parents, but of my entire self, of my life. I've come to find myself, but now, with You and Camila and Jakob, I have a family of my own.

And now, with these two little lives dependent on me, with Your love to sustain me, my past doesn't matter quite as much.

Perhaps not at all, honestly. Madame X is no more, except in being part of the formation of the woman I am now, Isabel de la Vega.

A wife, someday.

A mother now.

And, in time, a philanthropist.

# NINETEEN

Camila and Jakob are three months old now. Big, beautiful, healthy, perfect.

And we have not gotten one single moment alone. I don't mind. Not really. But I would like some time with You.

You, of course, recognize this. Beth is called in, because apparently babysitting *is* in the job description when one is Logan Ryder's assistant. Plus, Beth has experience, as an older sister had twins, and Beth often babysits them.

So, the twins in good hands, Logan tells me to put on a fancy gown, some killer heels, and a little makeup; time to go out.

Once again, he takes me to Gourmand, the restaurant in Hell's Kitchen he owns. We are regulars there now, a booth near the kitchen permanently reserved for Logan, Camila, Jakob, and me.

But this time, something is different.

The entire restaurant is empty, not a single soul in sight.

Odd indeed for a Thursday evening.

The lights are low, a single table near the center of the dining room lit with a candle, set for two.

My heart pitter-patters a little; You've shown me enough movies to know a setting like this indicates a proposal to follow.

I am ready.

More than ready, indeed.

A trio of musicians sets the mood: a guitar, a mandolin, and a violin, playing soft, beautiful music off to our right. We have wine, salads, soup, entrées, more wine, dessert. No ring, no proposal.

I am beginning to doubt my assumption, and to feel some level of disappointment now.

When we are done, you rise to your feet. Extend Your hand. "Did you know there's a little garden on the roof of this building?"

I didn't, and accompany You up an elevator and then a flight of stairs, out through a dented, rusted metal door and into a rooftop garden. It is tiny, intimate. Trellises form a maze, roses and lavender and wisteria and honeysuckle climbing and blooming, filling the air with a heavy, heady scent. Strings of soft white lights are woven through the trellises as well, shedding a golden glow on the magical scene. I hear the door open, but it is far away, somehow, and out of sight. I hear mandolin strings quaver, and then the violin joins in, and the guitar follows; the musicians have followed us.

You lead me through the maze of trellises to a hidden corner of the rooftop, where the trellises form an arch over a wrought-iron bench. Nearby is a little fountain, water spilling and chuckling over rocks, the pool lit from within.

The city seems an impossibility from here, sitting on the bench, in this garden, surrounded by flowers and lights and a fountain, music in the background.

"How have we never been up here, Logan?"

You grin at me. "Because it didn't exist a month ago." A modest shrug of a shoulder. "I had it built, just for us, for today."

"It is . . . a fantasy, Logan. Beyond beautiful."

You point at something on the other side of the little clearing in the garden, a small wrought-iron table, over which is draped a red velvet cloth. "Go look."

I rise, pull the cloth away.

Gasp, breath stolen, tears immediately stinging my eyes. "Oh, Logan."

"I'm not a master carver, but I'm pretty good with my hands."

"You made this yourself?"

A shrug. "Of course."

It is a wooden box. Two feet square, one foot deep. And despite his claim to the contrary, it clearly was carved by a master. It is . . . lovely isn't a good enough word. Breathtaking. The wood is a rich deep brown, polished to a shiny gleam, shot through with reddish streaks and whorls. The hinges are brass, as is the simple catch mechanism.

I tug on the lid; it is locked.

I laugh through my tears. "You're stealing from my father, Logan."

"Shamelessly. I figured if I couldn't improve upon perfection, why try? Why not just borrow?"

"So where is the key?"

A nonchalant shrug. "I've got it. You'll have to come find it, though."

I cross the garden, pull You close. Run my hands down your hips, feel in your hip pockets; You've left Your phone at home, as have I, since Beth knows to call Gourmand if she needs us. Nothing. I pat Your back pockets, and You use my proximity to steal a kiss. And then another. And then the kiss is spiraling out of control, and

I cannot help myself. I'm tugging at Your tie, at the coat, at the buttons of Your shirt.

But when I've got the shirt open, I see it:

A brass key on a red ribbon.

It isn't an exact match for the diamond-crusted one dangling between my breasts at this very moment, however. No, the bow of this key is shaped like a heart, forged out of a solid, flat, two-sided piece of brass. Three letters have been carved or punched out of the solid brass: LWR—Logan Wesley Ryder.

The key to Your heart.

I tug the ribbon off Your head, clutch the key in my fist. And I kiss You until neither of us can breathe, until my dress has found its way up around my hips and we're pressed up against each other, making love on the bench, right there on the rooftop, still partially clothed, desperate, wild.

"You have to open the box, babe," You tell me.

I disentangle myself from You, reluctantly, I must admit. Settle my dress back down where it belongs, cross once more to the table, to the box. Slide the brass key into the lock, twist the heart. The catch *snicks*, and I lift the lid.

Midnight-blue velvet lines the inside, and at the very center, a ring. Platinum, a huge, glinting, fiery diamond in the center, smaller ones on either side.

You are standing behind me; I feel You, as I can always feel You.

I turn, and You are reaching for me. Pulling me to You. Gazing down at me. Whispering against my lips. "Marry me, Isabel?"

I flatten my palm against Your chest; I've already put the ring on. "Yes, Logan."

"Have my babies?"

I laugh. "I already did."

"Oh yeah." You kiss me, softly, gently. "Them."

I pull out of your arms, remove my diamond Tiffany's key, place it in the box. Remove the plain brass key from the lock, and slide the red ribbon over my head, settle the cold brass between my breasts. "Now your heart will always be with mine."

"What was it your mother told you?" You gather me close, hold me tight. "Oh yeah. Your heart is what makes mine continue to beat every single day."

"Now you're stealing from my mother?" I tease him. "You need to get your own moves, Logan."

You pull back, just a little. "Was that a joke?"

"A little one."

"I must be rubbing off on you."

"Rubbing off *in* me, you mean."

"*Another* joke? And a dirty one?" An amazed laugh. "Could this get any more perfect?"

I reach down. "We could have sex again?"

"That would do it, I'd say."

# TWENTY

You have Jakob and Camila in your arms. It is sunny, bright and beautiful, a glorious Wednesday afternoon. The twins are eighteen months old. Camila is running around and shouting "NO!" to everything and about everyone, and Jakob is . . . chill. Quiet, content to sit and play, although he can and will get up and move if he wants something bad enough. He says a few words, and those clearly and distinctly, when he wants to be understood, whereas Camila is a wild bundle of nonstop energy and manic babbling, of which we only understand one or two words in ten.

Case in point: Jakob is utterly content to hang out in Daddy's arms and watch the proceedings. Camila, on the other hand, is squirming to get down, writhing and twisting in Logan's arms, wanting to run around and pull the plugs on the video cameras and steal the microphones and tug on dresses and cause a ruckus.

Mothers in Need is opening today.

It's been a year in the works, a lot of setbacks, a lot of negotiations, an absolute shitload of work. Donors backed out at the last minute and we had to scramble for more—donors we needed, because although Indigo is providing the start-up capital and some ongoing financial support, in order to run it day to day and eventually expand to other locations, in order to make this a nationwide chain, we'll need a lot more backing than just I can provide on my own. The location we originally chose turned out to be a poor choice, due to neighborhood concerns, architectural and structural problems, and a myriad of other issues. So we had to scrap all the prep we'd done and start over from scratch, hunting for a new physical home for MiN. We ended up in a trendy part of Brooklyn called DUMBO— Down Under the Manhattan Bridge Overpass—in a cute, quaint apartment building. The neighborhood welcomed us with open arms, as did the borough in general. Your marketing skills have proven invaluable, as has Your elaborate network of business connections throughout the city.

Through Your connections, we found a construction company willing to donate time and materials to the building of the center. We bought the entire building, a massive initial cost—well worth it—tore down walls on the main floor and created an office space for the day-to-day running of the center. We then turned the second floor into a medical clinic, the third floor into temporary living quarters for pregnant women with nowhere to go, or new mothers in the same straits, and the fourth and final floor into a supply warehouse and donation center for diapers, wipes, formula, baby clothes, maternity clothes, toys, books, and even a small selection of groceries on an as-available basis. We also have affiliations with several daycare centers and babysitting services. All the medical staff donates their time and expertise on a pro bono basis, and most of the medical supplies are donated as well. It was a colossal undertaking, and we packed a dizzying amount of work into a single year, but we got it all done.

Everyone is here, all the donors, the construction company builders and their families, the dozens of doctors and nurses and their families, the clerical staff, everyone. The whole street is shut down from intersection to intersection, the neighboring restaurants providing food and beverages, a live band playing music on a make-shift stage . . . all of it either donated or funded by Indigo.

Right now, however, I am on the stage, staring into a cluster of media microphones and video cameras, trying to fight down the panic. This is high profile. The whole city is watching. Much of the world, in fact. Something about it has caught the public's attention. Something about me, really. I've become sort of a media darling, the amnesiac who spent six years not knowing who she was, my former life and profession as Madame X—now that you have passed, Caleb, many of your secrets have come out—and my romance with Logan, my lovely heteropaternal twin babies, who are the sweetest of siblings under most circumstances, inseparable most of the time. And then my creation of The Indigo Foundation, using a colossal, exorbitant, unbelievable fortune for philanthropy, that really caught everyone's attention. I used it all, the attention, the media. Used it to leverage donations, to snag doctors willing to spend a day or two every week in the clinic, nurses willing to come in after their normal shifts and spend a few hours. The outpouring of support has been overwhelming, honestly, both for MiN and for The Indigo Foundation, and for me personally.

But right now, all I know is that I have to make a speech.

"I was lucky enough to have my husband with me," I start out, "when I had my babies. I didn't do it alone. Logan was there every single step of the way. Attending doctor's visits, helping me with the nursery—by helping, I guess I mean doing everything by himself because I was too pregnant to move. He was there for me. But not everyone is that fortunate. And that realization is what led to the creation of Mothers in Need. I thought one day about what it would be like to have to go through a pregnancy—an admittedly unexpected pregnancy, with *twins* no less—alone. How impossible that would have been. How impossible it would have been to juggle doctor visits with work. Assuming medical care was even a possibility, you know? I'd already found out about the money I was to receive, and I already knew I wanted to do *something* with it. I knew it wasn't money I could ever keep for myself. But I didn't know where to start. There's so much to do, so many causes in need. I've got pages full of ideas and projects and charities I intend to help. But where did I start? When I had that realization, about the impossibility of going it alone as a pregnant woman, I knew instantly where to start. So, after I had my babies, I got started. And now, a year and a half later, here we are, about to cut the ribbon. Although, I have to say, even though this is the official grand opening ceremony, we've already been hard at work. Drs. Minksy and Hartzell have both donated many hours of their time this past week in the clinic, over a hundred appointments taken between them just in the last seven days. I'm proud of Mothers in Need, proud of everyone who was part of making it a reality. Especially Mike, Jimmy, Abe, Luke, Danny, and the rest of the guys from McAskill Builders for working so hard over the past year to get the center built. Couldn't have done it with you, guys, so thanks. But most of all—Logan, my love . . . thank you. For supporting this crazy, over-the-top project of mine so fully, even when it seemed like it was overtaking your own work. To all of you who came out here today to support our opening, thank you."

Cameras flash, and the clamor begins.

I manage to avoid too much direct media attention after that, but near the end of the party, a reporter manages to corner me, camera pointed at me, light blinding, mic in my face.

"Isabel, can you tell us what's next, now that Minnie is off the ground?"

"Minnie?"

The reporter grins. "It's what everyone is calling it."

"Minnie. Huh. I like it. So . . . what's next?" I know the answer to this, because I've been working on it as the final details of MiN got ironed out. I smile, breathe, focus on projecting calm. "A project I'm calling A Temporary Home. Similar to what we've done with Mothers in Need, I'm planning to buy a building somewhere in the city— I haven't even really started looking yet, so don't ask where—and it's going to be a resource center for the homeless, for runaways, for victims of domestic abuse, for anyone who needs somewhere to sleep and the resources to improve their lives. There will be support staff, clinicians, a detox facility, a food pantry, therapists and psychologists and social workers, a warm bed to sleep in . . . whatever other resources I can wangle and cram into the space. Basically a safe, welcoming environment where you can get your life back on track."

The reporter, a beautiful young Asian American woman, pulls the attention of the camera back to herself. "I don't mind admitting, there was a time in my life when I could have used a place like that." A pause, and then a bright smile, focus turned back to the cameraman. "Well, there you have it, from Isabel Ryder herself. A Temporary Home, coming soon to New York. I can tell you I'll be making donations, and I hope everyone tuning in will too. Jake, Alessa, back to you in the studio."

The light turns off, the camera is lowered, and the reporter seems to wilt, the bright energy when faced with the camera dissipating. The young woman takes a seat on a nearby stoop, microphone still in hand.

"Are you okay?" I ask.

A shrug. "I was homeless for a few years, when I was a teenager. I was a runaway, bad home life, the usual. I got lucky, scored a job flipping burgers, just because the manager happened to be a decent dude. I worked my ass off, slept in an alley, and washed up in the bathroom before my shifts. I worked while being homeless for another year before I was able to score a little place of my own. And I worked my ass off to get where I am. But . . . I could have used a place like A Temporary Home back then. Would have been nice to have a bed to sleep in, somewhere safe to take a shower, you know?"

"That's why I'm doing it, and why it will work," I say. "Because people like you will step up and help out, because they've been there. And if you've been there, you want to help others who are going through it."

"Exactly." A bright, gorgeous smile. "So when you get that place going, let me know. I'll do a piece on it. And I'll probably volunteer, honestly. I remember being in that place. And almost as much as you need a bed and a roof and a meal, you need someone to talk to you like you're just a normal person, instead of seeing you as a damn charity case."

"See, I wouldn't have thought of that. That's why we need people like you." I hand the reporter a business card for MiN—Minnie, I guess. "You can volunteer now, if you want. The women going through there, they'll need someone to talk to as well, you know." I gesture at the center.

"Maybe I will." Another of those smiles, and then the reporter and camera are gone, on to the next story.

And You're behind me.

Handing me Camila, who immediately pats my face with both hands, hard, laughing. "Mama!"

"Hi, baby girl." I kiss her cheek, splutter, making her laugh.

And then she's babbling at me, pointing, wriggling to get down.

I set her on her feet, let her take my finger in her little hand, and let her pull me across the street, through the crowd, toward a stand set up by a nearby bakery. There are muffins, donuts, croissants, loaves of bread, other assorted goodies.

And my sweet little Camila, she's just like her mother. She has a bit of a sweet tooth. She's hopping up and down, a little unsteadily, jabbing her whole fist at a banana muffin behind the glass, shouting something that sounds not entirely like "banana muffin." There's both too many syllables and not quite enough, but when I ask the kid behind the counter for the muffin, Camila goes haywire, reaching for it, trying to climb up my leg for it, shouting and laughing.

While Jakob sits on his Daddy's hip, waiting. He doesn't say a word when I hand him a piece, just shoves it into his mouth. But his smile, the look of contentment, the joy, it's thanks enough.

And it's still all you, Caleb.

He looks so much like you, more so every day. It's an eerie resemblance, honestly. Anyone who knew you would instantly recognize you in Jakob.

But in his mannerisms, in the way he's so laid back, willing to go with the flow, easy to please, he's very much his daddy's little boy. So You were right, my love. He is all ours, Yours and mine. Completely, utterly, ours, even if I do see you, Caleb, in him, and even if it does cause the tiniest, vaguest, most distant little pang of something sharp, way down deep inside me. A little something, a pinch. A reminder, is how I think of it.

A reminder of where I've been, what I've gone through to reach this place. What has occurred to provide me with this happiness, the daily joy.

To be able to wake up next to You, every single morning. To lie down beside You every night, to feel You, to taste You, to have the privilege of loving you, it is a joy.

To kiss Camila and Jakob, to bathe them, change them, chase them, discipline them when they have tantrums, to love them, to be their mother, it is pure joy.

Even at three in the morning.

Even when You and I are in the middle of loving each other, and the monitor crackles with the howl of an unhappy baby.

It is still joy.

And that ache, down deep inside, it is a reminder that, perhaps if you hadn't taken the time to mold me, to feed me, even to lie to me about who I was, perhaps I wouldn't be here. You could have left me alone in the hospital. But you didn't. So for that, I am thankful.

For giving me a chance at life, even if it was, for a long time, on your terms, I am thankful.

For life,

for love,

for family,

I am thankful.

# INDIGO

watch you, Isabel.

You'll never see me.

You'll never even smell me; I am invisible. I am no one.

I am a ghost; I am the past.

I am not your future, not your present; I am nothing.

I am a shadow in the alley as you move from the now-darkened MiN center to your car—a gorgeous little Mercedes-AMG GLE63 S Coupe. I am the prickling on the back of your neck as you push the ignition. The shudder down your spine as you drive home, back to him, back to them.

Back to Jakob, my son that is not mine. My son that will never know my name, never know my face.

I watch him too. I watch him sleep. He sleeps soundly, without tossing and turning. Camila is the opposite, restless, frenetic, kicking blankets away, twisting in her crib like an alligator with jaws clamped around an antelope.

I am free, is what I am.

Death has freed me.

I am not really dead, of course; that was all an elaborate hoax to convince you and the world that I do not exist any longer. An elaborate and necessary hoax. I couldn't let you go. I couldn't.

I tried.

Again and again, I tried.

I fought it.

I would walk away from you, I would let you go, and I would find myself outside your door in the dim gray of not-quite-dawn, fingers curled into claws, a pistol in hand, lock pick in the other. Ready and able to jimmy those flimsy locks in no time flat, sneak into your home, and put a slug into Logan's head, end him for good, and take you away.

I had it all planned out.

A little needle in your neck, and you'd be out. When you came to, we'd be in Antigua, a little place I have there, bought off the books with a tidy sum of very well-laundered cash. You'd be naked on the beach, blindfolded, and I'd wake you up slowly.

With my tongue.

I dream of it, even still.

Ghosts can dream.

Especially since I am a ghost in spirit only, still a very real and alive creature of flesh and blood.

But I am a ghost, and so I dream of you.

Getting you alone.

Appearing in front of you, whispering your name, breathing in your scent.

I stood in an alley one night, slunk back in the shadows waiting for you to pass. And you glided right past me, flats patting softly on the sidewalk. You passed by me, and of course, of course you had no reason to even look up from your phone, no reason to look my way, to my little patch of darkness near the Dumpster, with its rotting garbage and scurrying rats and scuttling roaches.

But I caught your scent.

I caught a glimpse of you, a shred of you. You had on a dark coat, leather, slim, cut to fit you perfectly, and beneath that a knee-length skirt of white cotton. And Isabel, that skirt, it is gorgeous on you. Motherhood and happiness have made you more lush and lovely than ever. Your ass in that skirt was a delectable sight, a mouth-watering temptation. God, Isabel.

Isabel.

If only you knew.

If only you had any clue how much I love you.

How much I have always loved you.

If only you knew how I followed you, all those years ago, as you sneaked out of your parents' house to go get in trouble with that girl from your history class, to smoke cheap weed and watch movies too old for you. What would you say if you knew how many times you'd have been kidnapped and raped and killed, had I not been there, following you, a naïve, innocent, careless little girl. But I was there. And when you finally bumped into me in that fucking stupid café, it was my nightmare, my downfall, and my wildest dream come true, all at once.

If you only knew, Isabel.

How I held so much in check, to keep you innocent.

How I paid your father's gambling debt, and erased any evidence of it.

How I made sure the handsy and harassing manager at the hotel your mother worked at—*my* hotel, which I owned—was fired, and taken care of, so your mother wouldn't have to endure the embarrassing and fruitless and potentially job-hazardous process of reporting harassment in the workplace.

If you only knew about all the times I saved you, and you didn't even know.

You were nearly run over by a taxi, once. And I literally knocked you out of the way, made it look like an accident. Took the impact of the taxi's bumper to my own leg. Limped for a month. And you never even looked up at me, or if you did, you didn't really see me.

And when you did, finally, see me in that café, Isabel, you became obsessed. More so than I, I thought.

You would have run away with me, if I'd asked.

You would have let me fuck you in the alleyway.

You would have gone to your knees and choked on my cock, anywhere, anytime.

But I refused to speak, refused to lift a hand, because if I spoke too much, I would demand all of you. If I stood up, if I touched you, if I so much as caught a hint of your scent, I would have taken you for my own, sixteen or not, innocence be damned.

I hated myself for that, Isabel. Another truth you will never know. How I loathed and despised myself for being so addicted, so obsessed, so infatuated with a mere slip of a girl.

But, fortunately for you, I did possess enough control to keep you out of my clutches. Because you deserved better. I hated myself for wanting to sully you with my filth.

Do you know, Isabel, how I punished myself for that evil desire?

Hours upon hours spent alone, walking the sidewalks, hungry, tired, alone, so that I would not go home and into my bathroom to jerk myself off thinking about you. About your sweet, silky, dusky skin. About wrapping your long thick ink-black hair around my fist and fucking your mouth, over and over and over. About bending you over my bed and fucking you from behind.

About all the ways I could fuck you, own you.

Those hours on foot, I hated you for them. I hated you for making me want you so badly.

A mere slip of a girl.

An innocent little thing.

So unaware of the beast lurking just behind her.

And here I am, Isabel, become that monster in the shadows once more.

You know what I find surprising, Isabel?

How blind you are to my constant presence in your life. I am always there, somewhere. You could see me, if you were looking. But you think me dead, so you do not.

I follow you.

I watch you.

I am possessed of infinitely more power and control than when I was an ignorant twenty-five-year-old. So you'll never see me. Never smell me.

I've had a taste of you now. I've sampled you, licked you, devoured you . . . *owned* you. Now I *know* what it's like to have you, and I want you all the more for it.

I'll never emerge from the shadows to haunt you and taunt you.

But I'll dream of it.

I'll hide in the darkness and watch your perfect round ass sway and bounce in that fucking white skirt and dream of when I *owned* that ass, when I could hold it and slap it and spank it and fuck it to my heart's content.

And I'll dream of you having the slightest clue how much I love you.

How much I need you.

How I died to give you up.

How I gave you my fortune, the fruits of my blood and sweat, the product of twenty years of work. I gave it to you.

I died for you.

And still I cannot truly walk away.

You once said, Isabel, that I was a drug and you were an addict. But you had it backward. I am the addict.

I was a coke fiend, once. Back when I was a whore. I snorted coke and smoked meth and injected heroin, anything to numb the biting fangs of horror, anything to numb the slice of the claws of hell. I hinted at it, there at the end, and you shied away. Turned away.

I was screaming, Isabel, and you didn't see, didn't hear. I was begging. Pleading. I was mad with need for you, ripping myself apart for you. And you turned a blind eye.

Walked away.

Went back to Logan.

Left me to fall to pieces, alone.

You were my undoing, Isabel.

You could have saved me. Salvaged me, a piece of me, at least.

Your love could have patched the many holes in my soul. Perhaps your touch could have lit a candle to banish some of the darkness within me.

I hate you for that, Isabel. For walking away.

I know, I *know* you saw, Isabel. I was hiding nothing, there at the end.

But it was too late. You'd chosen your path.

And I, because I love you, truly love you, I knew I had to accept your choice.

I had to set you free.

But as long as I lived, you would never be free of me. I saw that too.

I had to set you free.

I *died* for you, Isabel. I am your Jesus, your Savior. Some would call that blasphemy, but it is true. I died so that you might live. So that you might be cleansed of your sins, absolved of your transgressions, washed clean of your iniquities, whose name is Caleb.

I hate you for walking away.

But I love you still, despite it.

I will always love you. Perhaps one day I will even love you enough to truly walk away, so the shadows trailing you will finally be empty.

I was a drug addict, but I got clean. I quit. I suffered through the withdrawals and I got clean, stayed clean.

But I cannot get clean of you.

I cannot quit you.

I have tried.

I cannot.


You are resplendent in white.

Draped from head to toe in virgin white, the slippery chiffon clinging to your hips and bust, cut deep to reveal an ache-inducing amount of cleavage, the train extending several feet behind you, the veil sheer enough that I can see the tears in your eyes as you waltz with slow grace down the aisle.

You are resplendent in white. The loveliest bride there will ever be.

But you are not walking down the aisle to me.

I am hidden, as ever, in the shadows. Up in a balcony, swathed in darkness, watching you glide away.

I lied; I cannot see your face. I can imagine, however. I can picture your eyes gleaming wet behind the sheer white lace. Picture your chest heaving as you work to fight down your emotions. You are always so emotional, all of your feelings worn on your sleeve. Oh, the time I had, teaching you to keep a blank face with clients. But even then, watching you through the cameras, I could see your thoughts on your face as clearly as if you'd said them aloud.

I've been here on this balcony for hours. I sneaked up here after everything was prepared, after the flowers were arranged by the pulpit, after the roses were tied to each pew endcap, after the red carpet was rolled down the aisle for you. When everyone was gone and there was nothing to do but wait, I sneaked up here. Stared down at the flowers and the pews and the pulpit, at the aisle. Imagining. Fantasizing.

Hating.

Raging.

Burning.

Envying.

They even sent someone up here to check, but the owner of the shoes didn't look under the pews.

So here I am.

Watching you take those slow, dancing steps, one by one by one, down the petal-strewn aisle. Camila prances before you, scattering white rose petals, taking a moment to throw a few handfuls at the crowd, getting petals in people's hair. So like you, Camila. You probably don't see it, but Camila is *you*, Isabel. Life has taught you to bury your mischief, to contain your wildness. But it is there. You are fearless. You panic and you forget to breathe and you freeze, but then you do what you must do. I tried to keep you contained, but I couldn't. Your zeal for life won through.

I kept you for myself, kept you locked up in my tower like fucking Rapunzel, a night-haired princess rather than golden. Not to keep you safe. Not to protect you, but because I feared if you tasted life beyond my walls, you'd leave me. You didn't love me, and didn't know yourself. But I feared if I let you free out into the world, you'd remember. You'd find life, find love, find your natural exuberance.

And even though I tried to keep you hidden away, a treat saved for myself, you still found a way.

You still found life.

You still found love.

You still left me.

I told so many lies, because I am weak, a pretender to strength. My body is powerful. My mind is sharp. But where you are concerned, I am weak.

"Dearly beloved, we are gathered here to witness the union of Isabel Maria de la Vega Navarro to Logan Wesley Ryder . . ." The minister begins his speech, rambles tiresomely.

You stare into Logan's eyes. I can see you in profile, standing there in the chancel. Your breast rises and falls deeply, and I picture your knuckles white as you clutch Logan's hands. I picture the bodice of your gown swelling with each breath.

I picture myself gazing into your eyes.

I clench my fists and close my eyes and breathe. Push away those images. I died for you, and I must keep my promise.

My death was a vow, you see:

*Touch no more; kiss no more; speak no more.*

I may watch only.

And if I picture myself there, with you, I will break my vow.

If I love you, I must let you love him.

If I love you, I must let you wed him.

I shouldn't be here, watching this. Torturing myself thus.

I'd very nearly rather enter that room with Caleb once more, endure his brutality once more, than endure this.

Watching you take his hand, his name, his ring.

Watching you weep for joy.

"Do you, Isabel, take this man to be your lawfully wedded husband, in sickness and in health, for richer or for poorer, for as long as you both shall live, so help you God?"

"I do." Your voice is clear and strong, steady.

"And do you, Logan, take this woman to be your lawfully wedded wife, in sickness and in health, for richer or for poorer, for as long as you both shall live, so help you God?"

"I do." His voice as well is strong, proud.

"Then by the power vested in me by the State of New York and by Our Lord Jesus Christ, I now pronounce you husband and wife. You may kiss the bride."

I watch him lift your veil. Your cheeks are wet, despite your clear voice. I watch his hands cup your face, watch his thumbs brush away your tears. I watch you bury your fingers in his long blond hair, watch you lift up on your toes.

You kiss, you and Logan.

Deeply.

Fiercely.

So passionately it becomes nearly unbearable, not for me but for the audience, composed of friends, donors to The Indigo Foundation, the many, many people you have touched and helped and moved and inspired. You have no family; neither does Logan. Except each other, and your children, of course.

As they do so frequently, my eyes go to Jakob. My doppelgänger, writ miniature. He is solemn and serious, holding the now-empty ring bearer's pillow. Watching you and Logan kiss. Unsure of what it all means, but knowing it is a serious occasion. Camila wriggles out of the grip of her minder, an assistant who has become like family. And once Camila is free, there is no catching her. She's like the wind, a zephyr run wild through the cathedral. Laughing, sprinting pell-mell up the aisle, throwing flower petals at everyone.

And Jakob, he watches her disapprovingly, brows lowered. "Mama, why is Camila so bad?" he asks you.

You only laugh, and watch Camila sprint through the narthex, stopping to splash in the holy water. "She isn't bad, my love. She's just . . . a little wild."

"I'm not wild, am I, Mama?"

I can hear all this, clear as day. His voice is small and soft and sweet, his eyes on you my eyes, deep brown, but so much more expressive, like yours in that way.

"No, Jakob. You are much more serious."

"Does that mean I'm gooder than her?"

"Does that mean you are *better* than she?" you correct him. "No, Jakob. It just means you are different from each other, that's all. No better, no worse. Only different."

"But sometimes she's bad."

Another laugh. "Yes, sometimes she is bad." A glance at the raven-headed boy. "And so are you, sometimes. You colored on the walls yesterday and then tried to let her take the blame, didn't you?"

"You knew?" He sounds amazed.

"Of course I knew, silly. Why do you think she didn't get in trouble?"

"Cuz you let her do whatever she wants?"

"No, because I knew it was you, not her."

"So why didn't *I* get in trouble?" Why indeed, I wonder.

You pick him up, rest him on your hip, brush his hair out of his eyes. Kiss his cheek, ever so sweetly. "Because it was a better punishment for you to see your plan go awry. You got very mad when I didn't punish her, didn't you?"

"Yes."

"And now you know you can't get away with things like that, and I didn't have to punish anyone."

"How did you know it was me, Mama?" Oh, that face, so confused.

"You had crayon under your fingernails. And the crayons used to color on the walls still had the papers on them."

"So?"

"So you're the only one who leaves the papers on. What does Camila do to all of *her* crayons?"

"Rips the papers off."

"The crayons were also intact, rather than broken. And what does Camila do to her crayons?"

"Breaks 'em."

"Correct. You failed to think of all the details, I'm afraid, my little mastermind."

"You're smarter than me, Mama."

"I'm not so sure about that, little one. You're awfully smart. I'm just older and wiser."

"Will I be old and wise too someday?"

"If you were to try to frame Camila again, and actually get away with it, she might try to kill you. She's got quite a temper, you know. If you can avoid that, you might just live to become wise, yes."

Jakob's silence is telling. He's thinking, hard. It's like you almost want him to be devious. "Coloring on the walls is babyish anyways."

You just laugh, and set him down. Logan has watched all this with a smile on his face, and now he leans down to ruffle Jakob's hair. Camila has realized everyone is watching her cause a ruckus, so she has quieted. She flips her curly blond princess locks out of her face dramatically, blinks her vivid blue eyes, and strides with demure elegance back to you, Jakob, and Logan. And together, you walk toward me, toward the narthex, the exit.

If you were to glance up, right now, you might see me.

But you don't.

You have a hold on Camila, and Logan has Jakob's hand, and you are all together, saying hello to friends in the pews.

Not looking up.

Not looking to the shadows.

It's better this way.

When everyone has left, I wait a while longer. Finally, I descend.

Fill my palm with white rose petals from the aisle. Stare at them, sniff them, but the scent on them has faded.

The reception is next. And I have a plan.

am unrecognizable. Not even you would know me, should you look directly at me. I have grown a beard since you last saw me, for one, and I have smeared food in it, back-brushed it to make it snarled and wild. I have temporary green tinted contact lenses in. An old beanie covering my head. I'm wearing clothes I bought new and aged by throwing them in the mud and having Thomas drive over them a few times, and then covered them in rotten garbage and actual shit.

Over that is an old, tattered, stained, foul-smelling blanket I bought from a real homeless man.

I walk hunched over, blanket up around my ears, hobbling as if my left knee is bad.

Instead of having a normal reception in a fancy hall or restaurant, you throw open the doors to A Temporary Home and invite everyone. There are no less than ten cakes in a variety of flavors, a buffet of free food ranging from standard fare such as chicken wings and tenders, mac and cheese, salad, and homemade soups, to real wedding reception dishes like chicken cordon bleu, a prime rib carving station, salmon. And when I say you invited everyone, I don't mean just your friends, but *everyone*. The mayor of New York has an apron on and is dishing out coleslaw to the homeless. There are celebrities, professional athletes, other politicians, even the vice president. It is one of the biggest nights of the year, and all the fancy, famous guests are behind the tables, dishing out food to the real guests, the homeless and hungry, who have shown up in droves.

I make my way in, and blend with the crowd perfectly.

There are party favors, voluminous waterproof backpacks for every guest filled with coats, wool socks, gloves, hats, scarves, blankets, and boxes of hand warmers, because you've opted for a winter wedding.

It is freezing outside, the mercury at −6 and still falling, less with the windchill.

I am legitimately stiff and numb with cold by the time I make it inside, and so my hunched posture isn't quite faked, and the way I smack my fingerless gloved hands together to beat some warmth back into them definitely isn't faked. The snow in my beard is real. The pink on my cheeks and ears is real. The growl in my stomach is real, too, because I've gone without eating for over forty-eight hours in preparation for this, so I would be genuinely ravenous when I receive my food.

You are at a cake station, cutting fat wedges of double fudge cake with vanilla cream frosting and serving them. I wait. I go through the line, let the mayor dish me coleslaw, let a famous New York Knicks player plop a pile of mac and cheese onto my plate next. A gorgeous A-list actress is at the salmon station, and a celebrity chef is at the prime rib station. It's genuinely staggering, the people you've brought in for this, the amount of money you've spent on food.

I am in awe of you.

The Indigo Foundation is incredible; the things you've accomplished through it in the last two and a half years are simply unbelievable. MiN is nationwide already; within two months of the first one opening, other cities were scrambling to get them built, so you did fund-raiser after fund-raiser, donated millions of my money, and built dozens of Minnie centers all over the nation. The first international one goes live next week, in South Africa, with more to follow in India, Indonesia, Thailand, and the U.K. A Temporary Home is also catching on, with locations popping up in L.A., Atlanta, Detroit, Dallas, and Chicago, and more to come as well, of course. You've not stopped there, my lovely, hardworking Isabel. You've donated money to dozens of existing charities. You've started a nationwide campaign to overhaul the foster care system, spurring sweeping investigations into current and prospective foster homes, establishing a more stringent psychological profile of each foster home in hopes of making sure the homes are safe and loving. You accomplish this by dangling the carrot of a five-million-dollar donation to any county that overhauls their foster care system, the think tank–designed profiling system being the key rider; thus far, you've donated over a hundred million dollars. That's not all. You've started a charity that raises money for adoptions, so that couples hoping to adopt have only to meet the home study requirements rather than raising the tens of thousands of dollars normally necessary. The charity also provides volunteer manpower to assist in sorting through the overflow of waiting cases, so that the children and parents don't have to wait as long.

I don't know where you find the time for it all, and this is coming from someone who routinely slept barely six hours a day in three-hour chunks.

I move through the buffet line, putting off dessert, putting off being face to face with you.

I eat with gusto, because the food is, indeed, spectacular. I even go up for seconds.

And then, finally, I can put it off no longer.

I wait my turn in the dessert line. Take a little plate and a scuffed, tarnished metal fork—yes, you are serving on real plates with real silverware, and I believe that is the lead guitarist to a rather well-known rock band collecting the dishes and carrying them to the kitchen. There are four people between you and me.

Three.

Two.

One.

And now, God—now I'm here. Inches from you. Breathing your scent, your perfume. I do not break character, dare not. Hunched, hobbling. I hold out my plate, the fork clutched underneath. My heart is hammering, galloping a million miles a second. I accept the slice of cake onto my plate, lift it and grunt in thanks. A wordless grunt, all I dare risk. You'd know my voice, were I to speak.

And, just like fifteen years ago, if I spoke, I would lose myself to you all over again.

But I do raise my eyes to yours. A moment, only, but in that moment . . . the earth ceases to spin. Hearts cease to beat. Time freezes. I see the joy in your eyes. The peace. Madame X is long gone; no trace of her remains. You smile at me, and the smile is bright and genuine and kind.

"Are you having a good time?" you ask.

I nod, grunt. Shovel a forkful of cake into my mouth, to gag myself.

"Is there anything you would like?"

You, alone.

For five seconds, your eyes on mine, your hands in mine, your lips on mine.

Your heart beating for me, as mine does for you.

Five seconds to know love returned.

Five seconds.

But I will never get those seconds, not with you.

All I get is half that time, perhaps, of your eyes on mine, not knowing me, seeing only a homeless man, as intended.

I shake my head to answer your question, and walk away. Sit at a table, shovel the cake into my mouth. Accept another foam cup of scalding, black coffee. Take it with me, leaving the backpack full of supplies for those who actually need it.

I did not give you all of my money, of course.

Most of it, but not all.

I kept something in the neighborhood of a hundred and twenty million, all carefully and thoroughly laundered, scattered in banks all over the world, untraceable. I need something to live on, of course.

And, while it's far less than I've been used to, a hundred and twenty million dollars is still a fucking lot of money. Enough to give me my freedom. It's more than most people can ever dream of, yet in comparison to what I left behind, what I gave to you, what you refused to accept for yourself, a hundred and twenty million is chump change. Pennies. In comparison, at least.

I'll make do.

I clutch the foam cup full of coffee and glide away into the snow and shadows. Reach the intersection, stop, stare up at the black sky, at the fat white flakes drifting lazily to the earth.

"I know it's you, Indigo." Logan.

I sip my coffee. Say nothing. Turn, standing straight now, pretense abandoned.

"Knew you weren't dead. That felt a little too neat."

"Let her continue to believe it." My voice is hoarse from disuse; I have little to say, lately.

"No shit." He has his own coffee, but his is in a mug. He's in the bitter cold in only his tuxedo jacket, seemingly oblivious. "She's come too far, Caleb. Don't fuck it up for her now."

"Caleb is dead." I swallow the last of the coffee, burning my tongue and throat. "He died in a car bomb."

"What do you want?"

"Nothing." I turn, look into Logan's one scorching blue eye. "There is nothing I want."

"Then why are you here?"

"Call it . . . a final farewell." I feel the truth of the statement even as I say it.

Logan stares me down, searches me. I let him.

There is a trash can nearby. I toss the cup in, shove my fists into my coat pocket—under the stink and the filth I smeared on it, the coat I'm wearing is a five-hundred-dollar mountain climber's insulated shell, with a thick wool sweater beneath it; I'm plenty warm.

I turn away from Logan. "Promise me one thing, Ryder. Make sure Jakob is . . . a better man than me."

He only nods, a single jerk of his head.

I walk away, then. I feel Logan's gaze on me until I turn the corner.

Thomas is waiting in a red Bentley Bentayga, three blocks north of the shelter. He pops the trunk when he sees me approaching. There are two bags waiting, one full, one empty. I quickly shuck the filthy disguise and re-dress in new, clean clothing—jeans, a sweater, boots. No more suits and ties for me. The disguise goes into the empty bag, zipped up against the stink. I keep it, though. It may come in handy again, someday. Thomas hands me a bottle of water and a towel. I rinse the stink out of my beard as best I can, pat it dry, finger-comb it straight. Slide a Rangers ball cap onto my head.

"I'll drive, Thomas." I stand beside the driver's door.

He looks confused; I never drive. "Sir?"

"I said I'll drive."

"As you wish, sir."

I take the driver's seat, adjust the steering wheel, the mirrors, turn on the seat warmer. Tune the radio to something hard and heavy as Thomas slides into the front seat beside me. He seems ill at ease, tapping the dashboard with a long finger, tracing the stitching on his seat, fiddling with the lumbar settings.

I input a destination into the navi: Miami, Florida; nineteen hours and twenty-one minutes, it tells me.

Thomas is alert as we leave Manhattan.

He's alert as we hit New Jersey.

He's alert, and confused now as we pass the hotel that marks the farthest I ever made it from you.

"Sir?"

"Yes, Thomas?"

"Where are we going, sir?"

I tap the navi screen. "Miami. White sand beaches and bitches in bikinis."

"And what about Miss Isab—"

"If you ever utter that name again, I will put a bullet between your eyes," I hiss.

Thomas is unperturbed by my threat. Merely eyes me curiously. "You are done, then?" He waves a hand behind us. "With . . . all of that?"

I drive a long, long time in silence, considering his question. Am I?

I have to be.

I must be.

I do not know how to be done, but I must be.

I do not know how to start over, yet again, but I must.

Finally, after thirty miles, I answer. "Yes, Thomas. It is done."

Thomas nods, tilts his seat back, crosses his massive arms over his broad chest, tugs his chauffeur cap down over his eyes. "Good. It is good." Lower, more to himself, he murmurs something else: "Took a very long time. Too long, I think."

"Fifteen years. That's how long it took."

But I don't think Thomas heard me; he's snoring already.

I put an entire tank of gas between us, three-hundred-some miles. Thomas sleeps while I refuel.

I put another tankful of gas between us.

Seven hundred miles.

You are seven hundred miles away, Isabel.

I stop somewhere in South Carolina. Pull off the road around dawn, nine hours after leaving Manhattan. I stand on the side of the road, heat on my back, joints stiff, eyes burning with exhaustion. I yawn, stretch.

Face north.

As if I could see you, even from here.

I can feel you, I think.

I can believe it is real now.

You are gone.

No, *I* am gone.

"Good-bye, Isabel."